To Keep the Sun Alive

TO KEEP THE SUN ALIVE

A Novel

RABEAH GHAFFARI

Catapult New York

Copyright © 2019 by Rabeah Ghaffari
First published in the United States in 2019 by Catapult (catapult.co)
All rights reserved

ISBN: 978-1-9482260-97

Jacket design by Donna Cheng
Book design by Wah-Ming Chang

Catapult titles are distributed to the trade by Publishers Group West
Phone: 866-400-5351

Library of Congress Control Number: 2018950158

Printed in the United States of America
10 9 8 7 6 5 4 3 2 1

For my father, Mohammad Bagher Ghaffari

Be the sun and all will see you.

—FYODOR DOSTOYEVSKY

Contents

CONTENTS

To Keep the Sun Alive

PARIS

March 20, 2012

The morning of the solar eclipse began like any other. Rue de Belleville was already littered with pedestrians. Car horns rang out. Metal grill gates thrashed upward. Children whined as mothers dragged them to school. Pensioners, in no particular hurry, made their way to the park, greeting one another in slow motion, while young professionals rushed by in a beeline to the metro station.

The faces on those streets were a strange mix: Jews, West Africans, Chinese, and Maghrébins among many others, thrown together as though in some urban refugee camp. Shazdehpoor was no different. He was as displaced as them, and as anonymous—a single unseen thread in a haphazardly woven carpet. Only older, frailer, wearing a seersucker suit with fraying cuffs and faint sweat stains on the crisply ironed fabric.

He struggled through the crowds, dragging his handcart down the subway steps, shooing away anyone who got too close with his walking stick. The Line 2 train was approaching and he barely made it onto the last car. A young man stood and offered Shazdehpoor his seat. Surprised, Shazdehpoor wanted to thank him, not for the seat, but for his kindness. As so often happened lately, he was too slow. The young man had already turned away.

At the Place du Tertre, tourists swarmed past the artists and artisans—most of them immigrants. Senegalese teenagers hawked woven baskets and tribal jewelry. Tunisian women, babies tucked into their skirts, sold richly painted ceramics with intricate Islamic designs. All for a few euros, a coffee or less. For more than three decades Shazdehpoor had made his livelihood spelling out the names of passing strangers in Persian calligraphy. Each year was harder and harder. He unlocked his handcart and opened the chair and table. He wiped the sweat on his brow with his hand-kerchief, then arranged the stack of rag paper, inkpot, calligraphy pen, and sander.

A young woman soon approached. American. He dipped his pen in the inkpot and, with the trembling hand of an old man, looked up. "What is your name?" he said.

She leaned over. "Mo-ni-ca," she said, slowly, as though he were deaf. He dipped his pen in the ink again and squeezed his arthritic fingers around it. Carefully, he began to write her name, from right to left, silently mouthing the equivalent letters in Persian. The roundness of *meem* flowing into the upward line of *alef*. Then the U-shaped *noon* straight into the half-moon *yeh*. Then he raised up the pen and began the triangular *kaf*, whose third point touched the last letter right before sweeping up into the final *alef*. The final touch of the dot over the *noon* and two dots beneath the *yeh* were done in calligraphic diamonds.

When he was finished, he shook sand over the paper and blew

off the dust. The ink was quick drying but the elegant flourish impressed buyers. He rolled the paper and tied it with a ribbon, shyly accepting the three euros from Monica's hand. Even now, taking money from people still shamed him.

The sound of shouting caught his attention. It was Madam Wu. A man was shaking the piece of paper she had handed him in her face. *"Mein name ist Adam not Yadang!"* he said.

She shook her head. *"C'est ton nom en chinois!"*

"Buchstabiere es wie A-D-A-M!" he said.

Madam Wu, a former Chinese literature teacher and professional calligraphist, purged from her homeland during the Cultural Revolution, had given up on explaining to customers the difference between logography and phonemic orthography. She stepped into the man, grabbed the paper from his hand, and ripped it into little pieces.

Shazdehpoor shook his head. He thought of his apartment. His radio. The cognac that awaited him at the end of the day, a cognac that he drank each night with great relief and ceremony.

A group of break-dancers with face paint and colorful clown wigs were setting up their boom box. Each week there were more and more street acts, all of them flashier, louder, and more youthful than his calligraphy. Gypsy children darted through the crowd today, selling plastic glasses for the eclipse this evening, long after Shazdehpoor would already be back in the cool, comforting isolation of his living room. For weeks, the eclipse was all anyone in Paris had spoken about, the first one visible in the city for thirty-three years.

"Three euros," said the Gypsy girl. Her face was golden brown, her mouth smeared with dark familiar juice. He leaned in, smelling the ripe sticky perfume of the cherries she had eaten. Handful by handful. Stolen, perhaps, from the Marché de Belleville. Or scavenged from the discarded bruised lots behind the stands.

"*Gilas*," he whispered with closed eyes.

She startled, and jumped back, alarmed by his foreign-sounding word, one she seemed to think was a curse. He was an old man to her, with a perfume of his own, that of brittle skin and sour breath and perhaps a little death. Off she fled. On the ground, the pair of glasses lay at his feet where she had dropped them. He had no need for glasses. Nor any need to join the crowds on the riverbank that evening. He had seen the sky go dark before, the shadows cast as the moon slowly swallowed the sun, until there was nothing left but a faint ring of fire in pitch black. He had stood in that darkness so total that nothing was visible outside his own mind. That was thirty years ago also, in another world, on the golden plains of Naishapur, in the orchard of his family. White snowy flowers clung to branches of the apple trees. Clusters of green cherries hung densely on the branches. In the breeze, there was the smell of pears and the droning of bees and the clean snap of cotton as the *sofreh* opened and his family gathered for lunch. It was spring, always spring, the sun ablaze overhead.

WINTER'S END 1978

The Mirdamad orchard was in the city of Naishapur, or "the new city of King Shapur," in the northeast region of Khorasan, known as "the land where the sun rises." The orchard had been in Bibi-Khanoom's family for generations, built by her great-great-grandfather. He had purchased four hectares of arid land from the local government and worked with engineers to build aqueducts that brought water onto the land from the Binalud Mountains in the north. The orchard was surrounded by one continuous adobe wall with massive wooden doors on the southwest corner. Upon entering, you followed a pebbled path that ran adjacent to the western wall. The path was lined on either side with trees and two narrow streams that led to the family living quarters. Most of the fruit trees were planted together in the southeast. There were various stone fruits such as plums, apricots, cherries, and sour cherries, and pome fruits such as apples and pears. The yearly harvest brought a steady income to the family coffers and supplied all the fruits for their own consumption, including preserves, jams, compotes, and dried fruit.

It was a good ten-minute walk to reach the end of the orchard, where you arrived at a fountain filled with red, gold, bronze, and black goldfish, and a large imposing black walnut tree. Up two steps lay the platform of the house. Along the northern wall was a small barn that housed a few goats and sheep along with a chicken coop. Next door was a storage room filled with grains, rice, spices, and all manner of staple foods. The northern wall, where the aqueducts entered the orchard underground, was covered in grapevines. On the south side of the house was a massive flower bed where rows of irises, tulips, and lilacs encircled a rosebush.

Bibi-Khanoom was the orchard's sole keeper and lived in it with her husband, a retired judge, and their adopted ten-year-old son, Jafar, who never spoke. Now, in the final weeks of winter, the orchard was coming back to life after its hibernation. That morning's light had melted the frost, and water dripped from the trees until there was nothing left but moist bark and branches. A slow-rising polyphony of birdsong and insect mating calls chirped and chirred through the greenery. Ants busily dug their subterranean dwellings. Birds gathered twigs for nests. Bees circled flower buds for nectar. And Bibi-Khanoom worked her way around the rooms, packing up the winter clothes and the blankets strewn over the southern wing of the house, where the family had spent the brutal cold months, as this wing had the most natural light. For the coming warm months, they needed the shade of the eastern wing, and it was Bibi-Khanoom who took charge of their relocation each year.

She made her way east through the vestibule and looked out

the French doors. Mirza, her Afghan helper, had hung all the carpets from the spring quarters of the house. Furiously he beat them with a stick, dust billowing up in the sunlit air. Bibi-Khanoom pulled her chador over her mouth, breathing through the long, white, gauze-thin fabric.

"Mirza-jan," she said—using the old familiar term of endearment. "Leave that for now. We have to start preparing lunch."

Bibi-Khanoom's husband had spent the morning sitting under his tree, which was the only tree that stood separate from the others in the orchard, the black walnut tree planted by Bibi-Khanoom's great-great-grandfather just in front of the platform by the northern entrance of the house. The long heavy branches hung low, creating a canopy around the thick trunk at the base of which the roots bulged like veins on a hand, spreading outward and disappearing beneath the soil. The judge, as everyone called Bibi-Khanoom's husband, had laid out his carpet at the base of the trunk, sitting in between two of these roots, as if they were the arms of a chair. He had discovered this spot on the day of his wedding. It shaded him in the summer and blanketed him in the winter. It was where he read his books, held his conversations, and contemplated his thoughts. It was also where he first kissed his wife.

Though ten years had passed since his retirement from his judicial post, colleagues and former pupils still stopped by the orchard to sit with him on his carpet under the tree and present the merits of their court cases over tea. Passing judgment on his fellow human beings had always weighed heavily on the judge. To spend the final chapters of his life leaning on a tree watching a bee pollinate a milk thistle filled him with a peace and stoicism that many mistook for coldness.

This particular day, a former colleague had sat with him

for more than an hour, when a scorpion that lived beneath the nearby rosebush scuttled out from its resting place. It did this every day, at exactly the same time, but today it happened on a wounded bee that had fallen from the hive above. Immediately the scorpion snapped its telson into the bee, paralyzing it before nibbling off a piece of insect. The judge's colleague continued to discuss his court case and how unsettled he was over its outcome. When the scorpion was finished with its meal, it turned and scampered back into its hole. The judge turned to his colleague, who had not noticed a thing, and said, "The laws of nature seem clear and without malice. Even in their arbitrary cruelty. While the laws of men seem vague and malicious. Even in their attempt at equity."

Mirza brought a crate filled with vegetables into the kitchen from the winter storage bin in the west end of the house along with some meat from the freezer box and frozen eggplant slices that had already been fried. Bibi-Khanoom took the tray of eggplant. She chopped onions and fried them in a pot while Mirza washed the meat under lukewarm water, cut it into small cubes, and added them to the pot. Bibi-Khanoom then added the eggplant. They continued their preparation for lunch in silence, moving around each other with the ease and coordination that comes with years of repetition.

Once the dish was done, Bibi-Khanoom evaluated the task ahead. Two pots with different stews simmered on the stove, a large bowl of uncooked rice soaked in water and salt, fresh tomatoes, onions, and cucumbers lay on a chopping block ready to be made into salad, and bunches of tarragon, basil, mint, and cilantro lay drying in a sieve. She wiped her wet hands on a dishrag and turned to Mirza.

"We'll need to have the fruit pickers start work sooner. It's an early spring."

"Yes, I will arrange it."

"I think I will do sour cherry jam and pear compote. The rest can go to market."

"And the grapes?"

Bibi-Khanoom knew exactly why he inquired about the fate of the grapes. They had the same delicate conversation every year.

"Will you be needing a crate or two for your medicinal juice?"

"Yes. It's very helpful with sleeping problems."

"Of course. For sleeping problems." Bibi-Khanoom shook her head in mock disappointment. Mirza tried to suppress a smile.

Bibi-Khanoom was a devout Muslim whose lips had never touched alcohol, but she never minded when others did. She peeked into the vestibule. "Where is Jafar?"

"With the chickens."

"Again?"

Inside the coop, Jafar circled around the dusty straw, following a particularly fluffy hen. He had a red ribbon in his hand and bent over, trying to catch her by the saddle. She picked up her pace and waddled faster in circles. He was a portly boy and breathed audibly from the exertion. The hen outmaneuvered him at every turn. He finally gave up and sat cross-legged in the center of the coop, his head in his hands. The chicken slowly waddled over. He smiled at her, reached into his pocket, and held out his hand full of seeds, dropping them on the ground. She hesitantly bobbed her head and pecked at the seeds. He wrapped the red ribbon around her neck and quickly tied it before she protested and flapped away. Off she waddled in circles, clucking protestations at the other hens like a brothel madam.

Bibi-Khanoom stood in the doorway of the coop holding her chador over her mouth and nose. She coughed and Jafar jumped to his feet, shame flushing through his face.

"Have you named her?" said Bibi-Khanoom.

Jafar nodded yes.

She looked at the hen and for a brief moment allowed herself to see it as Jafar saw it. The snow-white feathers, the sharp yellow beak, the satiny red ribbon. She almost resembled a wedding confection. Bibi-Khanoom looked at her little boy and put her hand on his head. "No harm will come to her. But you must stop naming them."

He nodded in reluctant agreement.

"Now come inside and change your clothes. Everyone is on their way. Including Madjid."

Jafar's face lit up at the mention of Madjid. He followed his mother back into the house as his beautiful chicken went back to her seeds.

The first lunch guests to arrive were Bibi-Khanoom's niece, Ghamar, her reluctant husband, Mohammad, and her willful daughter, Nasreen. Billows of dust rose as they hurried up the road—already arguing.

As they reached the orchard doors, Ghamar pushed her husband out of the way. The two doors had two separate knockers. The one on the left was an ornate pewter plate with an oblong handle hanging from a hinge. It was for male visitors. The shape of the knocker created a deeper sound. The one on the right, for female visitors, had a delicate round handle hanging from the hinge of the plate that made a high-pitched snap. Ghamar grabbed the male knocker and started banging. Her husband winced.

Mirza immediately recognized Ghamar's knock, not so much by its sound as by its ferociousness. He braced himself for her entrance by looking up to the sky and asking a god he did not believe in for his protection.

Ghamar burst through with Mohammad following behind, his eyes to the ground, and Nasreen already looking for her beloved Madjid.

"Keep up!" bellowed Ghamar.

A sparrow flitted off through a pear tree.

Ghamar was always the first one ready to go anywhere, as though she could never stand to be where she was.

Earlier that morning, she sat on the plastic-covered sofa, yelling until Mohammad finally took out worry beads, flicked through a few, then mustered the courage to leave his bedroom and face her.

Nasreen had remained at her vanity. She turned up the volume of her cassette player and continued to apply a mismatched array of makeup that she had collected from friends over the years. The dusty pink plastic Mary Kay lip palette case, a tube of Max Factor mascara with a comb wand, a pair of rusted tweezers, and an antique brass kohl holder. She sang along with the pop star Googoosh, "Help me, help me. Don't let me stay and fester here. Help me, help me. Don't let me kiss the lips of death here," as she inspected her face from every angle possible.

No matter where Madjid sat in relation to her in the orchard, she made sure she would be flawless. She spied a rogue hair in her perfectly groomed brows, plucked it without remorse, then continued to sing. "In my veins instead of blood is the red poem of leaving."

Her room was a shrine to cassettes, magazines, and books about theater. A large poster of a film, *Through the Night*, starring Googoosh, hung over her bed. The film, which had been released the year before, was the story of a famous singer-actress who falls in love with a young fan dying of leukemia. Halfway through, the actress showed her breasts on screen, a first for Iranian cinema. Traditionalists were outraged, furious. Boycotts and protests ensued.

For Nasreen, Googoosh was a proud, sensual woman she hoped she'd be one day. If her mother would only get out of her way.

She closed her eyes and hummed along to Googoosh's song about a fish imploring her lover to break them free into the ocean. She touched her lips and thought of Madjid—the green almond taste of his kiss, his soft, full lips.

Sweeping through the French doors of the kitchen, Ghamar made a beeline to Bibi-Khanoom. She let out a sigh and leaned against the wall. "Oh, Auntie," she moaned. "I'm boiling in this chador!"

"Water?" said Bibi-Khanoom.

"If it's not too much trouble." Ghamar coughed slightly and looked at Mirza, who handed her a glass of water.

Ghamar sniffed the water. She was suspicious of Mirza. She was suspicious of anyone who was an Afghan, Turk, Armenian, Arab, Mongol, Baluchi, Jew, or Kurd, which left no one in Iran for her to trust. On one occasion, Madjid—Bibi-Khanoom's grandnephew-in-law—made the mistake of pointing out to Ghamar that there was no such thing as a Persian and if she wished to meet one, she would have to go to India and find a Parsi. Ghamar had been leery of him ever since and often told her husband that there was something a little Indian about his olive complexion.

Mohammad had joined the judge in the living room. They sat on the floor pillows and flicked their worry beads and took tea.

"How is the tailoring business?" said the judge.

Mohammad shook his head. "The same. Mostly *abas* for the clerics. God never seems to run out of brand-new recruits and they all need brand-new robes. It should get busy with spring, though. Wedding dresses and suits."

"And the family?"

"Everyone is healthy and happy."

The judge studied Mohammad's face. There was something his nephew-in-law wasn't telling him. Over the past year, Mohammad seemed even more removed from his life, stopping by the orchard at odd times to say hello and stay for hours, as if he didn't want to go home. For her part, Ghamar had become even more confrontational and easily set off by the slightest offense. The judge could feel the tension between them, but it was not in his nature to pry. "And life goes on," he said with a smile.

The next to arrive was the judge's older brother, the mullah. He had just finished leading an especially successful prayer at the local mosque, wearing a white turban and khaki *aba* that Mohammad had made for him.

His following was growing. His Friday services were filled almost to capacity. That morning, he had begun with one word: "Dignity." Then he let the word ring out as he sat perched above the crowd. Men looked down at the ground, flicking worry beads and swatting away flies. Women covered their mouths with their chadors. The worshippers were a mix of bazaar merchants, farmers, shop owners, and workers from fields and offices as well as students and housewives. The men sat on one side and the women on the other. The older generation took in the words as a balm, the younger one as a call to arms.

"Money?" the mullah continued. "Power? Property? Status? Family? What do any of these things profit a man who has sold his dignity? A man can lose his fortune. He can fall from power. His home destroyed by natural disaster, his position ruined in the blink of an eye, and his family taken from him. But if he has his dignity, he loses nothing. If he has his dignity, he is in a state of grace. For dignity is given to us by God and can be taken from us only if we give it of our own free will."

The mullah opened his *aba*, put his hand in the chest pocket, and took out a document. "A man came to see me holding this piece of paper in his hand. He said to me, 'Haj-Agha, the authorities gave me this deed to land and said I could cultivate it and feed my family. But it's not enough land and I don't have the means to farm it.'"

He looked at the document with mock awe.

"It is an impressive piece of paper. It bears a very official stamp from a high office. But it is a piece of paper. Can this man live on it? Can he shelter his family with it? Can he eat it?"

The congregation let out a collective laugh.

"He asked me: 'Haj-Agha, what can I do? Where do I go? I am one man with no means. What can I do against such corruption?'" The mullah felt his eyes well up.

He began again. "Imam Hussein."

Sobbing broke out among the congregation.

"Imam Hussein stood on the plains of Karbala surrounded by an army ten thousand strong. He turned to his followers and covered his face and said, 'We are all going to die here. Those who want to leave, do it now.'"

The mullah sighed. "And all but seventy-two left. He stood with his family of seventy-two, mostly women and children, surrounded by an army, ten thousand strong. His family dying of thirst in the camps where they cowered, his own infant son, mouth bleeding from sores, his wife, weeping and begging for water. All he had to do to save them, his own flesh and blood, was to sell his dignity, his dignity for his life and theirs. But instead, my brothers and sisters—he chose to die."

The mullah's eyes were red, his throat dry. He began to weep and held the tail of his *aba* to his face as he wept and the believers all wept with him.

As he approached the house, his earlier triumph faded, replaced by the resentment he felt for his younger brother. The mullah had spent his whole life living under the judge's shadow. The mullah was as short and round as the judge was tall and slender. He wobbled when he walked, due to his bowed legs, while the judge strode effortlessly. His voice was loud and fiery compared to his brother's soft deep baritone, and he offended family members with his speeches. His brother seldom spoke, and when he did, it was to utter a few words of observation or ask a question. Everyone preferred the judge and the mullah knew it.

He entered the vestibule, taking off his sandals at the door. As soon as Ghamar and Bibi-Khanoom saw him in the kitchen doorway, they adjusted their chadors. Out of propriety, he looked away before greeting them. Bibi-Khanoom ushered him into the living room in the southern wing. "Haj-Agha," she said—using his honorific title, as she always did—"I am so sorry to have missed this morning. There was so much to do here. I couldn't get away."

Ghamar chimed in. "Haj-Agha, I would have come. I was dressed and ready to go, but I live with turtles so it is a miracle that we even made it here." She threw an accusatory glare at her husband and daughter. They both looked down at their hands.

The judge bent down and kissed the mullah on both cheeks and led him to where he was sitting. He poured him a glass of tea, which the mullah accepted, and offered him fruit, which he declined. The mullah took out his worry beads. Mohammad and the judge picked up their own. For a few minutes, the only sound in the room was that of beads flicking.

Nasreen felt uncomfortable in the mullah's presence. She was conscious of her uncovered hair and excused herself from the room, despite her mother's gaze. On the deck at the southern entrance of the house, she paced back and forth—pretending to sun herself while stealing a look down the orchard path.

Ghamar narrowed her eyes. Nasreen was looking for Madjid, she suspected. Over the past year, her daughter had become worried about her appearance, even with her family. There was also the eyebrow plucking, the makeup, and the floral dresses Nasreen had started to wear for the visits to the orchard.

Ghamar turned her attention back to her husband. "Mohammad-Agha, cut up some fruit for Haj-Agha."

"He doesn't want any."

"That's no reason to be rude." With some effort, she bent down and picked up an orange, two Persian cucumbers, and an apple from the bowl. She placed them on a plate and took it over to her husband with one of the paring knives. "Now cut those up nicely for Haj-Agha."

The mullah watched all of this devoid of any expression. "Thank you, Ghamar-jan. Some fruit would be nice."

Ghamar raised an eyebrow to her husband, who slumped over the fruit, peeling away. She dusted off her hands as she headed back into the kitchen.

The mullah shook his head and said, "You let a woman talk to you like that?"

Mohammad gave him a smile. "She's not a woman, Haj-Agha. She's a prison guard."

The mullah chuckled, then looked out the window at the orchard. "Spring has come early this year."

The judge nodded. "Yes, unseasonably early."

"Summer will be long and hot. You will have to keep the grounds hydrated and the fruit pickers will have to come before the summer solstice."

"Yes."

"I'm afraid it's not so easy for the peasants. They can't afford to irrigate, let alone hire pickers."

On his knees, Mohammad slid the plate of sectioned fruit in front of the two brothers. The mullah stared at the neatly laid out pieces. He did not take one. "This business of land appropriation is a great injustice. Not to mention the disrespect for our way of life. We are not godless Communists."

"The issue of land appropriation is a very legitimate concern."

"The people are angry at the preferential treatment for those close to government officials. The poor have gotten the worst of it. As usual."

"There are also those in the religious establishment who are not pleased that their family land has been taken from them."

The mullah stared at his brother with contempt. The most vocal opposition to land appropriation was the clerics whose family lands the government had seized. But that was a side issue to the mullah. His concern was for the poor who were affected, and therefore this concern was righteous and indisputable. "This is a matter of government corruption."

"I think it is a complicated matter," said the judge. "There are many factors that—"

"Indecision complicates matters that injustice clarifies."

The judge flicked his worry beads in silence. He was fully aware of the unethical practices of government officials but he was equally weary of activist clergy who usurped real issues to further their personal crusades.

For months he had struggled to formulate some deeper understanding of the land issue. Whenever he thought he had come to a conclusion, he found a counterargument. And these arguments and counterarguments raced through his mind, leading him to believe that there was no right side when it came to an individual's struggle for power.

His brother cut short all discussion with a proclamation of faith.

Faith, to the judge, was a surrender of control, not an exercise of it. What he saw in his brother was not faith but certitude, the same certitude he had witnessed at the bench, year after year— men and women, rich and poor driven to acts of cruelty by their convictions.

What if certainty was madness? Would it not follow that doubt was reason? In the beginning of his career, the judge had been seduced by the satisfaction of placing blame: punishment to those who had wronged, justice served to those who had been wronged. But over the years, he had watched as cases involving political dissidents were summarily removed and taken to military tribunals where they vanished. So-called threats to national security and accusations of treason poisoned the halls of his court. How could there be justice if even a single person was above the law? He became unsure of his own ability to see clearly. He looked deeply at each case that came before him, trying to alleviate his sense of guilt for working in such an autocratic system. And much to his surprise, he began to see the fractured humanity of every person whose life and future he determined, and this paralyzed him. Eventually he could no longer perform his duties.

The mullah saw doubt as weakness. He could hardly contain the disdain he felt toward his brother, a man who had been given every advantage in life, a man who had married into wealth and comfort, never knowing the horror of poverty, degradation, or abandonment, a man who had reached the pinnacle of power only to abandon it, a man of no conviction.

This chasm between them always left their conversations unfinished.

In the kitchen, Bibi-Khanoom and Ghamar stood at the kitchen counter over a pot full of triangular blocks of Lighvan cheese from East Azerbaijan, which Bibi-Khanoom had brined during her winter seclusion. Ghamar put a piece in her mouth. "This is perfection. The Bulgarians use too much salt, the Greeks too little. Those Turks finally got something right."

Bibi-Khanoom shook her head. "Ghamar, don't discriminate. It's shameful."

"I don't discriminate, Auntie. I hate everybody." Ghamar peered out the kitchen window at her daughter. Nasreen had picked up a broom and was aimlessly sweeping the deck.

She sucked her teeth but Bibi-Khanoom grabbed her by the arm. "Let her be. Don't you remember what it was like?"

"Yes, I do. That's why I'm going out there."

"Madjid is a fine young man," said Bibi-Khanoom, still holding on.

"How fine can the seed of a *fokoli* be?"

Bibi-Khanoom looked at her—shocked. "That is enough! So Shazdehpoor likes sitting on chairs and *chocolat*. This is not a crime."

"He is an insufferable snob!" Ghamar pulled her arm back and left the kitchen. Through the window, Bibi-Khanoom watched her niece argue with her daughter, but it was for Ghamar that her heart ached. How unbearable must her misery be that she had no choice but to spit it on anyone who came too close: Shazdehpoor, Madjid, her daughter, her husband, Turks, Armenians, Jews, France, Europe.

A brisk wind moved through the trees, drowning out the voices on the deck and the clattering of Mirza as he beat the bedroom rugs. Bibi-Khanoom closed her eyes, listened to the sparrows and nightingales rustling through the trees, and thanked God for another spring.

Shazdehpoor rapped sharply on his son's door with his walking stick. "Come, Madjid!" he said. "We are late already." Shazdehpoor was the nephew of the judge and the mullah and the only child of their sister who had died giving birth. He was also the family's *fokoli*. Today, like most every day, he wore a three-piece seersucker suit with a rose tucked carefully in his lapel. He took great pride in telling anyone who would listen that seersucker came from the Persian *shir o shakar* or "milk and sugar." He was so thin the suit looked almost the same on him as it did on the hanger. His slim build made his nose and bushy eyebrows even more prominent.

He held up his walking stick and tapped on the door again. The stick was mahogany and had a silver lion's head handle. He had purchased it from an English gentlemen's catalog. It was his prized possession. He took it everywhere, using it to bat stones out of his path on the unpaved, provincial streets of Naishapur, while muttering "barbarism" under his breath.

"Coming, Father," Madjid said as he closed his book. Madjid's bedroom was the product of vigorous thought and raging hormones. Stacks of books lined an entire wall, some of them so dog-eared that they resembled the bellows of an accordion. A shrine of photographs was taped onto his mirror: the iconic "Guerrillero Heroico" (Che Guevara's steadfast gaze during a memorial for those killed in a CIA explosion on *La Coubre* off Havana); the impassioned Mohammad Mossadegh (defending the nationalization of Iranian oil against Britain's Anglo-Iranian Oil Company at the International Court of Justice); and a defiant Muhammad Ali (surrounded by fellow black athletes at a meeting of the Negro Industrial and Economic Union explaining why he refused to be drafted into the Vietnam War). This disparate trinity—an Argentine Marxist revolutionary, a nationalist Iranian prime minister, and a black American Muslim athlete—were united by one thing: they were all men of conscience. Madjid longed to be such a man in this world but he had not quite figured out how to do this. He slept on a small cot and thought of only two things, the part he would play in the future of his country and being with Nasreen. Both of which he knew were intrinsically and irrevocably tied to the other.

His father had no place in his future. Shazdehpoor longed for a world of order and civility, filled with cobblestone streets and dining halls with gilded chairs. He had fashioned his room after a European salon and often sat up at night in his leather club chair, sipping cognac and listening to the Adagio from Schubert's String Quintet in C major, remembering the contours of his dead wife's face. A face that bore a striking resemblance to that of their son, Madjid.

Madjid's father held up his walking stick as they proceeded through the orchard, Shazdehpoor swatting pebbles and muttering furiously under his breath, Madjid ignoring his father's futile battle with the stones. The scent of plums and cherries mixed with the dust in the air. Madjid had grown up in the orchard. As a boy, it was the only place where he was free to roam without supervision or restriction. Half-naked, alone, his face stained with the juice of fruits he had shaken from the trees, he escaped bee stings and ran with a child's ferocity, unaware of his scrapes and cuts. He stood over anthills and watched their efforts with total admiration. Then, just as easily, wiped them off the face of the earth with a kick of his foot.

The guilt helped him instinctively understand what he would consciously later learn, that a man's character is determined by how he chooses to wield the power he has over others.

As Shazdehpoor and Madjid entered the house, Nasreen laid eyes on her beloved and felt her heartbeat quicken. Their first few minutes together always filled her with anxiety. She leaned against the kitchen doorway as he and Shazdehpoor greeted the family, waiting for his eyes to meet hers. Madjid had brown eyes.

But not just any brown eyes. If you looked into them long enough, you saw the dark embers of his mind at work. Framed by long, almost girlish lashes.

Nasreen felt a sudden pinch and jumped.

"Stop standing around like a sheep," said her mother. "Go bring more tea."

Nasreen scurried to the kitchen, not looking back to see if Madjid had noticed her embarrassment. The samovar was percolating. She stood, fuming: Why was her mother so brutal and intrusive? Why did she try to control every waking moment of her life, crushing something as delicate as the anticipation of meeting her lover's eyes? She did not hear Madjid's soft steps as he came into the kitchen with the empty teapot. He stood beside her, leaning into her to reach the spigot of the samovar. As soon as his arm touched hers, all of the tension in her body dissipated. Knowing he could affect her so made Madjid feel protective of her, especially near his family, who he believed had no idea what was happening. As he finished filling the teapot, he whispered, "Hello, friend."

Nasreen smiled. This was his new greeting for her, one he had given her after their first kiss. The kiss had happened at a Friday lunch the previous summer. They had stolen away during the afternoon siesta and walked side by side through the trees, as they often did, to talk. He spoke at length about theories, and she listened. But on that particular day they had been speaking about love. Madjid had been thinking aloud about the ephemeral nature of romantic love. How once the veil between two people dropped, the passion dissipated and all that was left was a circadian bind that was either too complicated or too comfortable to break. He spoke of how delusive it was for all the great poets to speak of *eshgh*, or "love," when it was not possible to sustain such a feeling. And therefore, he concluded, it was infinitely better to remain alone. Nasreen was quiet for a few moments, then said, "Perhaps you are right. But I suppose that is why *asheghetam* is a literary term. Mostly used in books. In life, people say *doostet daram* to each other, which literally means 'I have you as a friend.'"

Up to that point, she had simply been someone to talk to, someone who was always laughing and verbally sparring with him, someone who provoked a tenderness he had experienced only in the presence of his mother. Among the many sensations he felt as he kissed her, what came rising to the surface was a sense of loss.

The creak of the swinging kitchen door broke the silence as Mirza came in. Madjid took the filled teapot and whispered to Nasreen. "Until siesta."

Nasreen looked around, trying to find something to get busy with. "I'll start on the salad," she said, then stood at the cutting board and began to dice the cucumbers, closing her eyes as she imagined the meeting to come. Mirza grabbed her hand and shook her out of her stupor. She was about to slice her own finger with the knife. She smiled, embarrassed, and went back to cutting the vegetables with her eyes open this time. He stood beside her, at the sink, washing herbs. "It's always best to keep one's mind present," he said. "One step ahead or one step behind and the world will slip from your grasp."

LUNCH

Preparations for lunch were in full swing. Mirza had spread the *sofreh* on the deck just outside the house. He squatted on the thick cloth and set plates on the edges with a spoon and fork for each. He then brought out a tray with two pitchers of *doogh* and glasses. He placed each pitcher of the yogurt drink at opposite ends of the *sofreh* and added a glass for each plate. He stood back and looked, satisfied everything was in its right place.

Bibi-Khanoom and Nasreen were in the kitchen negotiating a giant pot of rice while Jafar hovered in the doorway. The scent of saffron and butter wafted through the air. Bibi-Khanoom filled the sink one inch deep with cold water. She and Nasreen placed the pot of rice in the sink and Bibi-Khanoom dished the rice onto a silver platter. When she got to the bottom, she held a round silver platter over the pot and together they flipped it over and set it down on the counter. Bibi-Khanoom slowly pulled the pot up and revealed a perfectly round crust, the *tahdig*, slightly burned to a golden brown. The *tahdig* was the delicacy of the meal. There was never enough and it was always a tense experience for all involved as it was broken down and dished out.

After Nasreen's first kiss with Madjid, she had placed her *tahdig* on his plate. During the siesta that immediately followed that meal, Madjid chastised her for her carelessness as they kissed. "Do you want them to know what is going on?"

"Of course not."

"Then stop giving me your *tahdig*."

During the lunch preparation Bibi-Khanoom philosophized about food to Nasreen. You can tell a lot about a person, she said, by how much and what parts of the *tahdig* they take.

"Those with quiet personalities with a slimmer build always take pieces of the light golden edges. And those with rousing personalities and gluttonous tendencies take pieces of the burned, browned center."

Next they dished out the *khoresht*. One was *khoreshteh ghormeh sabzi*, a lamb-and-kidney-bean stew made with finely chopped parsley, chives, and fenugreek, and dried whole lemons. Turmeric softened the bitter scent of the lemon and the lamb and kidney beans gave the stew its earthy color and depth of flavor. The second *khoresht* was *khoreshteh bademjan*, made with eggplant and lamb in a tomato base with sour grapes and rich, aromatic cinnamon.

Bibi-Khanoom loved to talk to Nasreen during their preparations. She explained how some foods, such as cucumbers, watermelon, mint in hot water, eggplant, and radishes, had a cooling effect on the body, slowing down its functions, while others, such as garlic, onions, walnuts, lamb, and cinnamon, warmed the body and stimulated its functions. To know these qualities, she told her, was to know your own body.

Persian cuisine, according to Bibi-Khanoom, was a study in equilibrium, an intense negotiation of opposing flavors that somehow found a way to coexist without being overpowered by each other. The tartness of fruits was tempered by the delicate fragrance of saffron, turmeric, and cinnamon—a perfect union of masculine and feminine, of prose and poetry, of earthly and mystical.

She let out a sigh and wiped her hands on a dishrag. The food lecture had tired her out more than the preparation. Talking demanded the vitality that doing created. She reached out and stroked the young woman's cheek. Nasreen turned and looked at her shyly—the gesture a tonic to her mother's criticism.

Jafar slipped into the kitchen unseen. His favorite part of lunch, the *loghmeh*, happened before the meal. He stood in the doorway staring at his mother until she noticed. Bibi-Khanoom took a spoonful of the *ghormeh sabzi* and used her hand to mix it with leftover crumbs of *tahdig* in the bottom of the pot. Jafar hummed as he waited, rubbing his stomach in anticipation of the *loghmeh*. Bibi-Khanoom bent down and pushed a large, savory dollop into his mouth with her fingers. Then she prepared a plate with rice, stew, a piece of *tahdig*, and pickled eggplants, which she covered with a cloth and handed to Jafar. "Take this to the midwife and come straight back for your lunch."

The family gathered around the *sofreh* and waited in silence for the judge. As soon as he sat down, silverware clanked against plates, dishes were passed. The mullah couldn't keep the frustration off his face. Only moments earlier, when he had sat down, no one made a move to begin the meal. His presence was barely acknowledged. And he was the elder.

Ghamar sank into her chador with a pouty look on her face as her husband piled the rice onto her plate. She then chastised him for overserving her, even though she had asked for it. "You are always trying to fatten me up."

Nasreen served herself only the tiniest of portions, which didn't get past her mother. "Why don't you eat something? You eat like a cow at home."

Nasreen shot a look at her mother that would make a bull wither and drifted away into the recesses of her mind. She had spent a great deal of time there. She played out scenarios of ways to kill her mother at the hammam. She could hold her mother's head in the basin of water and drown her; during the afternoon siesta, she could swat the beehive in the tree and let the bees devour her. At last, Nasreen would be liberated. She would stay up past midnight and blast her music and sleep in her own bed with Madjid. This final thought brought a smile to her face as she served herself another portion of rice.

Shazdehpoor fidgeted, trying to find a comfortable position. He hated sitting on the ground. He selected one piece of meat from the stew at a time, then added a few vegetables, then rounded out the plate with a scoop of rice and some herbs he diced on the corner of it. Ghamar whispered to her husband, "*Fokoli* is dining on *bifteck* with the queen of England."

Madjid always sat next to the judge and used it as an opportunity to speak about his newest books, but today he was unusually quiet. The judge studied his face. "What have you been reading?"

"We just read Chekhov's *Cherry Orchard* in our literature class."

"What did you think of it?"

"The discussion we had about it in Mr. Moeni's class was very intense. So much of what is happening around us here is in that play." Madjid looked down at his food and pushed it around with his fork.

"What is troubling you?"

Madjid leaned into the judge and whispered, "Yesterday when we got to class Mr. Moeni wasn't there. He had been taken away by the secret police. They said he was spreading Communist propaganda. What does Chekhov have to do with Soviet Communists?"

"He was Russian. And that's about as much thought as they've given the matter."

"What are they afraid of?"

"People in power are always afraid of losing it, Madjid. But the play is a revelation. I saw it performed in the capital many years ago."

"Yes. I was very surprised by it. People can be so frustrating. The choices they make. The things they don't do. As if their privilege breeds inertia."

A smile of pure delight crossed the judge's face as he listened to him. For a man of barely eighteen years of age Madjid thought with gravity and nuance. It gave his presence a melancholic quality that was strangely comforting.

Madjid stopped speaking and half-closed his eyes. He could hear the clanking of silverware and the voices around him and the wind moving through the trees. He thought of the play, in which an orchard is chopped up into little pieces for maximum profit. He turned to the judge. "I can't imagine this place not being here."

The only person missing from lunch was Madjid's brother, Jamsheed, who was older than him by two years. Like Madjid, he was tall, but with a stocky quality to his frame and an outsized personality. He was charming and witty, with a loud voice always on the verge of laughter. But he had been banished from family gatherings due to his addiction to opium. The addiction had caused a rift in the family, which everyone felt and no one mentioned. On many occasions the judge attempted to intervene on Jamsheed's behalf. He tried to help him overcome his dependency, but it was to no avail. For Shazdehpoor, his son's very public demise, coupled with what he saw as a crass personality, left him unable to feel anything but shame and contempt for Jamsheed. Pretending that he did not exist seemed like the most civilized solution.

As the meal was coming to an end Shazdehpoor watched the judge motion Mirza over and whisper to him. He knew exactly what was happening, because it happened every Friday. The judge quietly instructed Mirza to prepare a dish of food for Jamsheed, which Madjid would take to him.

Jamsheed was sitting against the wall outside the orchard. He had nodded off, waiting for his brother. He had no desire for food, or family for that matter. In fact, he couldn't remember the last time he had wanted anything. He simply showed up out of habit. "That is the beauty of opium," he once told his brother, "it takes away everything."

Madjid had learned many things from Jamsheed. Jamsheed was the one who had taught him how to read. In fact, all of the books in Madjid's bedroom once belonged to his brother. But Jamsheed was able to let himself go in a way that Madjid wasn't. He had spent his entire youth in trouble with his father, his elders, the authorities, and women. Madjid admired this ability to be reckless and wished to emulate it, but he was plagued by thought and consequence.

Jamsheed drove fast, drank hard, and had a charisma that drew people in. Before their mother's death, his boisterous demeanor would make the most mundane activities seem exciting. He could dissipate any tense situation with a wry remark and distill any argument to its most ridiculous ingredient, thereby ending it. Nothing was sacred to him. He took nothing seriously and therefore he couldn't be touched.

His descent into an opium haze was the final disconnect. He began to disappear for days. When he returned, he brought armloads of gifts for the family, draping beautiful fabrics over his mother and holding up shiny gold earrings to her ears. He tossed contraband books into Madjid's lap, whispering to him, "This one will really give you a few sleepless nights," and handed his father fine cognacs, which Shazdehpoor accepted but never drank. He told bawdy jokes and outlandish stories of his adventures, one more unbelievable than the next.

One night, during the month of Muharram, on his way to a friend's home for a gathering, he had been caught in an Ashura eve procession, commemorating the death of Imam Hussein in the desert plains of Karbala. He couldn't get across the street so he began to march with people, beating his chest and chanting with them, even though he had a bottle of vodka hidden inside his coat. The fear of being caught with alcohol drove him to chant and march more fervently than the most devout believer. The moment he saw a chance to slip out of the procession he swiftly stepped into an alley and made his way to his friend's house, rejuvenated by the unexpected trancelike experience. His mother was always taken in by his stories. Shazdehpoor was embarrassed by them. Madjid was delighted by them.

One evening, Jamsheed came barreling into the house, out

of breath, a wild look in his eyes. By that point, his mother's illness had broken her spirits and she was lying on the sofa, frail and despondent. Shazdehpoor and Madjid sat next to her in silence. Jamsheed walked straight over to her and swept her up into his arms. Much to his father's protests, he took her outside. "You see that, Maman? It's a motorbike."

It was a Suzuki GT750 with royal-blue paneling and a black leather seat dusty from the road. She leaned against him and mustered a faint smile. He propped her up in front, then took off before his father could stop them. They rode through dirt roads and across the town square. People stopped and stared at his sickly, chadored mother. He cut over toward the sand dunes of Old Naishapur, abandoned since the time of Genghis Khan's invasion. They sped along the stretch of the old city as the sun set. His mother pulled her chador down off her head, leaned back into Jamsheed, and let the wind blow through her hair.

She died two days later, cradled in her husband's arms, her two boys holding on to her hands. As the water filled her lungs, forcing her to expel one final breath, the three men knew that whatever had held them together was broken. Nothing would ever be the same again.

Madjid sat against the wall next to his brother. He laid the plate of food in front of him and Jamsheed pushed the food around on the plate with a fork but did not take a bite. "How's Monsieur Shazdehpoor?"

"He changed his cologne from Ravel to Aramis."

"Is he still bathing in it?"

"I can smell him from my room."

The two brothers laughed together, their shoulders bumping. Then the moment tapered off. They fell silent again. Madjid watched Jamsheed push his food around some more. Whenever he saw his brother he felt rejuvenated and restless. As though there was something he was missing out on. The idyllic torpor of his life at home kept him from things that were of real importance. He nudged Jamsheed. "Have you been to the capital?"

"Yes."

"And?"

"It's coming to a head. You can feel it in the streets. In the dormitories. You should see the students huddled around in earnestness." Jamsheed spent several weeks out of the month in the capital selling opium to the students. It was his way of keeping his own habit afloat. Once the money and drugs were quietly exchanged, he was invited to take tea, and as he faded into the background, the boys forgot him and resumed their discussions about the coming unrest. He found their passions quaint and utterly futile. He smiled as they spoke about injustice, poverty, political repression, and forced progress. He nodded as they spoke about illiteracy, lost lands, rampant corruption, and a government that had dragged its bewildered children into the Western century, a country that stood with a dead empire on its back.

"They are fools," he said, shaking his head. "None of the factions are strong enough to replace the monarchy. They are at one another's throats. Do you not see the futility?"

"The unrest is not about factions, Jamsheed. It is about social justice and economic equity."

"Don't be so sentimental, Madjid. There are only two established power structures in this country: the monarchy and the religious authority. And even those are pawns."

"My God, Jamsheed. You are such a cynic."

"No, brother. I'm a realist. We are nothing more than a nation held together by dead poets and living despots."

The brothers fell silent. Jamsheed picked up a piece of *tahdig* and bit into it. The butter covered his tongue like film. He dropped the rest of it on his plate and pushed it away, taking his cigarettes out of his jean-jacket pocket. He offered one to Madjid and took one himself, lighting his brother's first.

Madjid wasn't a smoker but he always took a cigarette from Jamsheed. He liked to make rings by tapping his cheek, and like all nonsmokers, held the cigarette with his fingertips. Jamsheed held his between his index and middle fingers by the knuckles. Together, they leaned against the wall. Jamsheed's smoke drifted into Madjid's rings, then floated away into nothing. Madjid leaned toward his brother. "Do you remember that carpet in the living room, the one from our great-uncle?"

"Yes. Father is so proud of it. Always telling everyone that it's hand-stitched silk."

"When you started school, I used to sit on that thing and stare at the motifs for hours. The medallion at the center is a square buttressed by a paisley, topped by two circles. If you sit in the center on the medallion and work your way outward, you see that all of the geometric shapes correspond to these three motifs. Even as they get smaller and smaller. Each cycle flips directions but still correlates to the central square, paisley and circles. Only once you reach the edge does the pattern fall apart."

"And I'm the one smoking opium."

Jamsheed held his cigarette with his teeth and slid his arm around his brother's neck.

"Madjid, real life is neither elegant nor balanced. There are no patterns. You can think about our national character all you want but until you see the world as it is, you will have no place in it."

"Is that what opium is? A place in the world?"

"No, brother. It's a way out of it."

SIESTA

After lunch, Mirza unfurled a massive *gelim* on the deck where the family had just finished lunch. Unlike the house rugs, the *gelim* did not have a pile weave or intricate designs, but rather bold and blocky tribal patterns. He laid down a pillow and folded sheet for each siesta taker. Inside, the men were changing into *shalvar kordi*. Even though Shazdehpoor relished the comfort of the pantaloons, their casualness unnerved him. Mohammad slipped into his with an air of relief, and Madjid poked fun at Jafar for pulling his up to his chest.

The mullah's preparation for siesta was far more formal. He disrobed in a separate room in order to maintain the privacy and sense of decorum appropriate to his status. First, he took off his *aba*, which he carefully folded and set down on the carpet. Then he took off his *ghaba*, which he also folded. He then took off his turban and set it down on his clothes, leaving the skullcap on top of his head. He made his way to the platform in his pantaloons and white knee-length shift like those martyrs wear.

The judge always disappeared during siesta. No one knew where he went except Bibi-Khanoom. As soon as lunch ended, he washed up and took a long solitary walk on the dirt road that led to the sand dunes. He found a rock to rest on, closed his eyes, and stared at the sun. It was, in its own way, a kind of sleep.

The family gathered on the platform, waiting for the siesta to begin. Mohammad took his place on the edge of the *gelim* so that he could turn his head away from everyone, especially his wife. He had lived a measured life, meted out in one small increment at a time by another human being. To everyone around him, it seemed like a life of serfdom, a life in captivity under a domineering woman who controlled every moment of his existence, save his sleep. But he had only ever known such a life. Before Ghamar, he had lived with a mother who ran her household like a military prison—every day scheduled, duties allocated according to age and gender of each child, deviances dealt with harshly and quickly. For him, life with Ghamar was a continuation of the familiar, and gave him a sense of permanence that all beings crave, sometimes at the cost of their own happiness.

His fantasy life was an entirely different matter. Siesta time allowed him to lay his head on a pillow and slip away into his dreams, all of which were about one woman. A woman he had seen once as a young boy, the day his mother had taken him to the public hammam. He sat there, next to his mother, and watched this woman wash her hair. Wrapped in a linen cloth, she knelt next to the pool and poured bowlfuls of water over her head. She gently squeezed the excess water out, then threw her head back and looked up at the skylight. He saw her face at last—and the light and the warmth that emanated from it.

Over the years, he had built an imaginary life with this woman. He courted her, married her, and she bore him children. They quarreled and laughed together, made love and broke bread. He knew the contours of every inch of her face and body. She aged with him, always becoming more beautiful. He set up a home and she decorated all the rooms with fine silk-woven carpets and heavily embroidered floor pillows strewn about for guests. He had given himself a noble profession like that of a judge or a doctor, and this gave him a proper place in society. He was able to provide her with the most exquisite clothes for which she kept her figure trim. Their children were always clean and well behaved, and his wife doted on him and fulfilled his every wish. When Mohammad put his head on a pillow, a smile crossed his face and a calm swept over him, for he was about to see his beautiful, gentle, warmhearted wife.

Mohammad's real wife spent the first few minutes of siesta staking her claim to space on the *gelim*. For Ghamar, napping was a full-contact sport. Once situated, she focused on falling asleep as quickly as possible by repeating observational phrases in her head, such as "that cheese was delicious" or "Jafar is a strange boy" or "Madjid is getting browner." If there was one thing that she feared, it was to be alone in self-reflection.

Nasreen lay next to her mother, unbothered by her constant kicking and pushing. She closed her eyes and focused on the very particular scent of Madjid's skin. It was elemental and organic like the smell of hard rain on dry rocks.

A safe, modest distance away was Shazdehpoor. He lay on his back staring up at the sky. For him, napping was yet another third-world humiliation he had to suffer. He went over future purchases he planned to make from the English gentlemen's catalog. He had his eye on an amber glass ashtray, even though he didn't smoke. And next to him was Madjid, who forced Jafar to lie down next to the mullah. It was always the same. Jafar would stare at Madjid with rounded maudlin eyes, worried already about the mullah's propensity to release gas as he slept, gas potent enough to choke the life out of the hardiest of men, let alone a small boy.

The mullah's gastrointestinal issue was a result of dairy intolerance, which would not have been an issue if he practiced moderation. And yet at every lunch he devoured an entire bowl of yogurt with sautéed spinach, browned onion, and turmeric. Poor Jafar was laid to waste in the aftermath.

Madjid looked at the dejected boy and whispered, "Just remember that someday you'll be able to fart on someone else."

The food induced sleep in everyone immediately, except for Madjid and Nasreen. They slipped out of the pile of bodies and tiptoed their way into the thick cherry trees. The whole affair felt exhilarating and dangerous; each time they met seemed wildly urgent.

It had been almost a year since their relations had become sexual. Their first innocent kiss that took them from friendship into courtship, followed by an afternoon where they devoured each other's neck, Nasreen later concealing Madjid's love marks with a chiffon scarf. Next, Madjid had explored her bosom. After that, it was not long before they were naked and entwined, fumbling their way through an act that was at once innate and acquired, at times even comical and inept.

And now, finally liberating.

After their tryst today, Madjid burrowed his head between

Nasreen's breasts. Then fell asleep, while she stroked his hair and looked up at the black cherry tree, its branches hidden by a thicket of oval leaves enveloping clusters of dark fruit. The wind let shards of warm sunlight intermittently cut through.

The sun was at its highest point and its strength washed over the sky. Crickets, wasps, and bees sang all around them, with a constant "zhhhh" that vacillated between a soft tone and a deafening, monastic drone. With eyes half-closed, Nasreen let herself fall into its trance, always aware that she could not let herself fall asleep.

She woke him with a gentle kiss to his forehead. He rolled onto his back and stared up at the canopy of trees with her. She squeezed his hand and turned to him. "Let's get out of here."

"Already? We have more time."

"No. I mean out of this place. Let's go to the capital. Anywhere but here."

He turned to look at her. Their faces almost touched. He saw the desperation in her eyes. "Nasreen, if your mother can get to you here, she can get to you everywhere."

Nasreen sat up and started buttoning her dress. "So that's it? We're just going to stay here and wither away like our parents?" She caught herself and turned to him. "I'm sorry. I didn't mean your mother—"

"It's all right. But if we leave, it should be for something better. Not just to get away from something unbearable."

"My mother is relentless. Every day it gets worse. The only time that I have any peace is when I'm in my room or with you. I want to go to the capital and try out for the theater troupe. Maybe work at the box office and work my way onto the stage. Take classes. Get an apartment. Meet up with friends at the coffeehouse. Talk about things that matter to me. Laugh as loudly as I want. Lie in a real bed with you—"

He was sitting up now, no longer listening to the litany of her desires, but watching the tears pour down her face.

"I don't have a life, Madjid. And I want one. With you."

He pulled her up, cupping her face in his hands as he spoke. "I know what you are up against. I see how hard it is on you. But you are more alive than anyone I know, and if we have to go somewhere else just so that you can see what I already see in you, then I promise you, we will do it."

Nasreen brushed away her tears and smiled.

They began their walk back toward the house side by side. Right as they were about to step out from the row of trees, he turned to face her. They stood there in silence looking at each other. He kissed her on the forehead, and watched her walk back to the siesta, then made his way to Mirza.

Mirza lived in a small shack in the orchard that he had built himself near the entrance. It was one room with one door and one window. The décor was Spartan. The most prominent item was a carpet given to him by Bibi-Khanoom as a housewarming present. He took his meals on that carpet and he slept on it as well.

As Madjid reached the shack, he saw the door was open. Mirza was busy in the corner fiddling with the spigot of an oak barrel. He whipped around with a cup in his hand as he heard Madjid approach. "Some medicinal juice?"

Madjid let out a hardy laugh. "Of course."

He took the cup and sat on the carpet as Mirza filled his own and took his place beside him. Mirza studied Madjid's face. The flushed skin and tousled hair of a young man in love and full of lust gave him pleasure. He lifted his cup to Madjid and toasted him as he always did, with a quatrain from Omar Khayyam's *Ru'baiyat*. "Come, fill the Cup, and in the fire of Spring your Winter-garment of Repentance fling: the Bird of Time has but a little way to flutter—and the Bird is on the Wing."

They both threw back the wine and rolled their tongues around their mouths, tasting resin residue. Mirza bounced to his feet to refill their cups with an almost childlike enthusiasm. He tilted and shook the barrel to get the wine to flow. "It's getting to the bottom. Time for a new batch at Chateau Mirza."

Madjid remembered the first time Mirza had invited him to his room. He had sat on the carpet and, as he looked about, he had realized that other than the carpet and the oak barrel, the only things there were a wooden backgammon board, a small pile of clothes, and some toiletries. Not one book or photograph. Not one trace of a past life. "Who are you?" he had asked.

"I am no one," said Mirza. "More juice?"

Today, Mirza spoke of mulching plants and pruning trees. He spoke of the turning of leaves and the migrations of the birds and insects. He spoke of the movement of the sun and the motion of the wind in spring, summer, autumn, and winter. He spoke of the moodiness of the hens and the stubborn old goat that would latch on to his pant leg during the morning feeding. An animated glee had swept over him as he went on about these things, and Madjid realized that Mirza had become the orchard itself. And he wondered how unbearable some lives must be that they have to be abandoned to go on living.

Mirza brought out the backgammon board. It was made of heavy walnut wood with intricate geometrical engravings. "Black or white?" he said.

"Black."

They each took their checkers and set up at a rapid pace. Mirza tossed one of the rounded ivory dice to Madjid. "Less or more?"

"Less."

They simultaneously threw them. Madjid's landed on six while Mirza's continued to spin. It landed finally on three and Mirza immediately grabbed the dice and started the game. They played fast, tearing through two games in under five minutes, with Mirza winning both. On the third game he was so far ahead of Madjid that it was likely he would beat him before Madjid was able to get all his pieces home. Mirza shook the dice in his hand, mocking the young man. "I smell the stench of *marse.*"

A double loss. But Madjid was not ready to admit defeat. Not yet.

Mirza blew on the dice and threw them. They both watched the dice spin and slow to a halt, landing on a double six.

"My God," said Madjid. "What luck you have!"

Mirza looked up at him and smiled a smile that barely masked a sadness he would never explain. "My luck begins and ends with dice."

Bibi-Khanoom stood at her kitchen counter with her *ghelyan* and a tobacco box. She refilled the base with fresh water and packed the bowl with tobacco and covered it with a screen. She placed a small square of coal on the screen and lit the coal. She gently blew on the coal and carried the *ghelyan* back to her bedroom to wait for the arrival of the midwife.

The midwife was Bibi-Khanoom's oldest, dearest friend. She lived in a one-room shack just a few minutes' walk from the orchard, on the outskirts of town. It was surrounded by sand dunes, desolate and barren.

The midwife had delivered Naishapur's newborns for more than fifty years, but had been forced into retirement after a difficult birth that almost killed the child and mother. Though it was through no fault of her own, the townspeople no longer trusted her.

The midwife rarely came to the Friday lunches. She preferred spending time with Bibi-Khanoom alone during the siesta that followed. She would always show up to return the plate that Jafar had delivered, and they spent the afternoon together in Bibi-Khanoom's room, smoking. Each would recline on a floor pillow, holding her own *amjid*, an ornate mouthpiece they put on the hose as they passed it back and forth. Sometimes they would play a few rounds of backgammon or a card game such as *hokm* or *pasur*. Other times they would sit silently inhaling and enjoy the lightheadedness of the nicotine, speaking in turn in a call-and-response. The midwife always went first. Lately, her subjects were morose. "I am afraid of death," she said.

"How can you be afraid of what you do not know?"

"It is exactly why I am afraid."

The midwife had spent her whole life in the service of creation, losing count of how many births she had facilitated. And yet the mystery and wonder of the act had never ceased to move her. That very moment when she would yank a blood-covered infant from the birth canal, holding it up and slapping a first cry from the child—a sound so primal, so primordial that she believed it was the voice of God, if ever there was such a thing.

But death was silent and this frightened her. "There is no wisdom that comes with age, Bibi-jan, only acceptance."

"But that is wisdom, my dear."

"Each night I go to bed fearing I won't wake up. I am waiting to die."

"We all are, my dear. It is just that those of us closer to it are waiting with greater anticipation."

"I am tired of waiting with anticipation."

"Some tea will make you feel better."

"Yes, that would be nice."

Bibi-Khanoom looked out her window now and saw the midwife coming down the path toward the house. She was a whisper of an old woman, gangly, hunched, and bowlegged, but she moved with the spirit of a young girl. When she reached the house she went straight to the kitchen and set down her plate, then headed to Bibi-Khanoom's room and gently knocked on the door.

"Come in."

She took her place on the pillow and let out a sigh. "Thank you for sending Jafar. You didn't have to do that. You are too kind to me."

"It was my pleasure. Besides, that boy can use some exercise."

They looked at each other and laughed, each of them cupping her chador over her mouth. As soon as the laughter subsided, they let go. Bibi-Khanoom shook her head as she took her *amjid* off the hose and handed it to the midwife. "I worry for him so."

"It's just baby fat. He'll grow out of it."

"No, not for that."

"He still hasn't spoken?"

"Not a word."

"And at school?"

"Just reading and writing."

"And what does your husband have to say about it?"

"He said, 'Let the boy be. He'll come to things in his own way. Everybody talks but how many people can listen?' I should never have let him tell Jafar he was adopted. I think it frightened him. He insisted that the truth would make Jafar strong, but I think it made him sad."

"The only truth that matters is that he is your son and you have raised him."

The midwife slid her *amjid* out of her bra and put it on the hose. She kept everything she owned pinned to her bra. Whenever someone needed something, she would reach in and pull it out: tissues, pins, stockings, lip stain, and even a small container of rubbing alcohol. She also kept her jewelry in there. And if anyone looked at her strangely, as she dug around, trying to find something, she would say "keep what you need close to your heart and let the rest fall away."

The midwife had delivered Jafar. She was the only one who knew the identity of Jafar's mother and he was the only child that she had ever delivered who had been born in the caul. The moment she split open that amniotic sac, she knew she was exposing him to a world of fiction, because she would never tell a soul that his birth mother was a prostitute who lived in a shack across the road.

Jafar's mother had refused to look at the child and put her hands over her ears so that she would not hear him and finally screamed to have him taken away. The midwife pumped the mother's breasts and fed the boy herself. His mother lay in bed, despondent and stoic like a factory cow. Even after the midwife had taken the boy to Bibi-Khanoom's, she returned to the mother to collect the milk and bring it to the orchard, only once speaking of the boy—to falsely declare that a family had been secured for him in Mash'had.

The midwife pulled deeply on the *ghelyan* and let out a gust of smoke.

"The pickled eggplants were delicious," she said.

"I made them for you."

"They are my favorite."

"And the *tahdig*? I think it turned out perfectly this time."

"What *tahdig*?"

Bibi-Khanoom stood up, muttering to herself, "That boy!" She pushed the window ajar and whisper-yelled, "Jafar." Half asleep on the platform, he opened his eyes in terror. He knew why his mother was calling him and he began to hiccup-sob, just as the mullah let rip another clarion call of gas.

TEA AND SUNSET

The post-siesta tea always began as a nebulous affair with everyone still groggy with sleep. The men gathered outside the house by the tea service and fruit, which Mirza had set up for them.

The women gathered in Bibi-Khanoom's room to take their tea, oohing and aahing over her winter sewing projects. This time, she brought out a stack of mittens she had crocheted for skin exfoliation called *leafs*. Most of the *leafs* were natural white, save for the baby blue with red flowers. That, Bibi-Khanoom handed to the midwife. Ghamar and Nasreen tried on the others for size.

Next she spread out the brightly colored chadors she had sewn. Ghamar and the midwife inspected the various flower-print fabrics in blue, pink, and white, while Nasreen looked on with disinterest. Ghamar held one out to her daughter as she spoke. "You don't want one?"

"I don't need one."

"But you used to love mine. I always had to go get them from your room."

"It was fun for playtime. I wore them as floor-length dresses. Not draped over my head."

"Nasreen, watch your mouth. This is not a joke."

Bibi-Khanoom jumped in. "Now, come. It's just a piece of cloth. How you wear it is how it's defined. For Nasreen it's a dress and for us it's a tradition. To each her own."

Ghamar stared at Nasreen as if to say, "Wait until we get home."

To change the mood, Bibi-Khanoom brought out her jewelry box. She opened it for the ladies. Whichever piece a woman seemed to notice with intensity, she offered as a gift. At first, the woman modestly refused, then, at Bibi-Khanoom's insistence, she gleefully accepted. Much to everyone's surprise, the midwife took a jewel-encrusted bobby pin. She pulled her chador off her head, revealing a shock of bright orange hennaed hair with inch-long brighter white roots. She looked like a sunflower. She swept her hair to one side of her brown face and stuck the pin in. Then admired herself in the handheld mirror. Ghamar took a gold chain from which hung a teardrop-shaped piece of turquoise. She opened the clasp and tried to close it around her neck but the necklace was too short. She huffed and pouted until Bibi-Khanoom dug out a longer gold chain from the box and transferred the turquoise teardrop to it.

Nasreen sat back and watched. Only she had noticed that each spring Bibi-Khanoom gave away another piece of her material life. Her gold bangles she had given to Nasreen, one by one. Today, Bibi-Khanoom pulled off the last three remaining and pushed them onto the young woman's arm. Nasreen looked up at her in disbelief, but Bibi-Khanoom smiled at her and quietly said, "It's all right. They're all yours now. I am far too old to make so much noise. It is your time now."

On the deck, the men took their customary positions on the floor pillows. Each poured his tea into the saucer to cool it. The mullah motioned to Mirza to bring some dates. When Mirza returned, bending down to set them in front of the mullah, the cleric caught a whiff of his breath and his face reddened. "Go wash out your mouth."

Mirza put his hand over his mouth and hurried into the kitchen unaware that the scent of wine lingered on his breath. He stood at the sink and took handfuls of water into his mouth and gargled.

Outside, the mullah launched into the morality tale of why alcohol was forbidden to Muslims. How drunkenness made one forgetful of God and prayer. He cursed the bars and liquor stores that had opened for business over the past several years, selling the forbidden liquids with impunity. He went on and on about the evils of intoxicants, eventually moving on to the perils of games of chance. "If a man does not stand by his principles," he said, "he cannot call himself a man." From there, he somehow found a way to work Imam Hussein into the speech, which was a gift that all clerics seemed to possess. There was not a subject in the world that did not somehow relate to Imam Hussein.

Madjid was not surprised by the mullah's reaction. He knew the Islamic stricture on drinking. Even though under the present regime there was no law against alcohol, it was still frowned upon. What did strike him was that the mullah chose to make his point by humiliating a man who was clearly his subordinate. He leaned into the judge, who sat motionless, listening to his brother go on, almost longing for a cold shot of vodka as a reprieve from all the righteousness. "If a man degrades his fellow man," he whispered, "he cannot call himself principled."

This drew a smile from the judge's face. But the mullah kept going. His eyes were half closed and he was completely unaware that all three men in front of him were drinkers. None suffered more from the mullah's sermon than Shazdehpoor. Shazdehpoor despised his uncle's faith as much as he loved cognac.

Madjid noticed him looking his way and slightly raised his hand as if to say, "to your health." Shazdehpoor was so tickled to be included in the conspiracy that he giggled aloud. The cleric fell silent and looked right at him. "You think a child dying of thirst in the desert is funny?"

Shazdehpoor froze. He had laughed exactly at the moment in the mullah's story where Imam Hussein's baby boy was dying of thirst. Madjid leapt to his father's defense. "Haj-Agha, this story is so terribly sad. Father was stifling a sob. Not laughing."

Shazdehpoor put his hand to his forehead for good dramatic measure. The mullah eyed him and, once satisfied, went back to his sermon.

Madjid now listened to the cleric in earnest. Shazdehpoor watched the sweet expression on his boy's face—an expression that so resembled that of his mother's that Shazdehpoor was overwhelmed, once again, by the loss of his wife. No one had been beneath his wife's sympathy. She used to gather leftover food from their meals to give to the prostitute who, years ago, had been forced out of business by the mullah. The prostitute lived out by the sand dunes in a one-room shack. Every so often she would get some business from an out-of-towner but those occasions were few and far between and she had been left destitute.

Each week, Shazdehpoor's wife arranged the leftovers into a proper serving and left the food at her door so as not to shame her by making her acknowledge the handout. She mended her old chadors for the woman and made sure she had toiletries. All these she also left at the door. They never once spoke.

Shazdehpoor would have never known of this if the prostitute had not come to his wife's funeral. She was too afraid to walk among the mourners and waited for him by the backyard entrance. Once everyone had left, she knocked on the door and told him everything. She never once looked into his face, nor did she ask for his help. She only asked if she could see a photograph of his wife. The prostitute had never seen her face before. She had once followed her home and that was how she knew where she lived.

Shazdehpoor went into the living room where all the family photographs had been displayed for the mourners. He picked out a small black-and-white photograph of his wife, holding Madjid, which had been taken in the orchard many years ago. He handed it to the prostitute. For a few minutes, she looked at it and smiled. Then she asked, "What was her name?"

"Saba."

"And the boy is your son?"

"Yes. Madjid."

She thanked him and began to walk away, then turned back and said, "I had a son once too."

The sun was growing dim. The final chapter of Friday lunch. The women came out of Bibi-Khanoom's room, breaking up the mullah's sermon. One by one the guests expressed their gratitude to their hostess, said their farewell, and started up the path to home. The mullah led the way, then Ghamar, grumbling under her breath about an upset stomach brought on by too much food. Her husband followed a half step behind and then Nasreen, holding the midwife's arm. Madjid walked at the end of this line, admiring Nasreen's effortless gait while feigning interest in conversation with his father. Shazdehpoor had suspected that there was something between the two young people and now he was certain. He looked at the space between the young lovers and could almost feel the love between them and he thought, in that moment, that if they were to metamorphose into musical tempos, she would be *allegro ma non troppo* to his *grave con brio*. Shazdehpoor hummed along, batting stones out of his way with his mahogany walking stick.

The mullah beckoned him to the head of the line. Shazdehpoor picked up his pace. "Did you know that every thirty-three years the lunar and solar calendars overlap?" said the mullah.

"The mysteries of the cosmos! There will be a full solar eclipse as well, I have heard."

The mullah looked sternly at his nephew. "It's not a mystery. It's a war. Chaharshambeh Suri falls on the same day as Ashura. If I catch one person celebrating that pagan ritual when they should be mourning, they will have to answer for it."

Shazdehpoor did not believe that the Zoroastrian fire-jumping ritual was an affront to the day that Imam Hussein was killed in the Battle of Karbala. Zoroastrian rituals from Chaharshambeh Suri to Nowruz were so much a part of the culture that they were celebrated by all Iranians regardless of their religion. Shazdehpoor hated Ashura, though. He hated anything related to

Shi'ite Islam. Every year during Ashura he would hide in his salon and drink his cognac, while the weeping processions of people
beating themselves passed by outside his door.

For him, the great tragedy of Iran had been the arrival of Islam. For him, its infiltration into the everyday life of the people
was a descent into the dark ages. The public demonstrations of
grief for, as he once put it after one too many cognacs, "an Arab
who died in the middle of the desert thirteen hundred years ago
on his way to seize power" was the lowest a nation could stoop,
and to add insult to this injury was to be told to submit, three
times a day, to this contrived narrative in Arabic, a foreign tongue
which was, for him, the end of Persian civilization. He turned to
the mullah and said, "I am sure people will be respectful of the
serious and unique nature of the overlapping of the calendars."

"Things are changing and people will have to start answering
for their indiscretions."

Shazdehpoor knew full well what the mullah was alluding to.
He spent every evening in his salon listening to the BBC. The rum-
blings of unrest in the cities were growing stronger and stronger.
It was just a matter of time before it ruptured the ground beneath
his feet. No matter how quietly and elegantly he sat in his club
chair trying to drown it out with adagios, andantes, and allegros.

Golden hour descended upon the orchard and the sun bowed
in long shadows cuing the moon. The insect chorus raised their
evensong to praise her ascent then sank into soft vespers under
her gaze.

Bismillah-e Rahmani Rahim. Bibi-Khanoom whispered with
her eyes closed, standing on a small carpet with nothing but a

prayer stone from Karbala. She knelt and bent to this stone and touched it with her forehead where a small mark had formed from years of prostration.

After a few lines of prayer, she raised her palms to the sky, then knelt again and put her head to the stone.

The words she whispered were spoken by rote in Arabic, a language foreign to her but whose strictures allowed her to enter a space where she was alone in the presence of God. *Al-hamdu lillahi rabbil'alamin.* Words as a means for invocation. She repeated the same gestures several times, and when she was done she folded her prayer rug and put it away.

Mirza had finished his work in the kitchen and walked back to his shack with his kerosene lamp, the sound of the gravel beneath his feet. Marsh frogs rhythmically croaked and chirped their mating calls along the streams. Eagle owls hooted in the trees before taking off on their silent hunt. Mirza sat down on his carpet, the glow of the kerosene lamp enlivening the room. He flipped back the edge of the carpet and took out a photograph hidden beneath it. It was of a smiling woman and a small boy no more than ten years of age. His wife and son. The two were killed in a market square bombing one sunny afternoon during the family's shopping excursion in his Afghan hometown. He had just called out to his wife to come smell the cherries he had purchased for her to make jam with, when a car rammed into the kiosk where she was standing with their son—and exploded.

Stunned into silence, a piece of shrapnel lodged just under his left eye, he began to walk, with only the bag of cherries in his hand, until he reached home. There he collected a small satchel and kept walking until he crossed the border, resting in the by-roads and on highways along the route. By the time he reached the town square in Naishapur, the cherries had rotted and the shrapnel had formed a bluish cataract in his left eye. Before, he had been a Farsiwan medical doctor from Herat who went by his given name, Mohammad Ali Khan. Now he was Mirza, who cooked and cleaned in the orchard.

He had come to his work only by walking through the open doors. There, under his tree, sat the judge. He sat next to him. They did not speak for an hour except for the offering of tea. After taking tea, he had turned to the judge and asked if there was work to be done and he had remained there ever since.

He now lay on his carpet staring at the photograph. He leaned it against the lamp and spoke to it in hushed tones about his day. He told his son how perfect the *tahdig* had turned out and the scolding Jafar had gotten for stealing the midwife's portion. He told his wife about the mullah and the wine and how ashamed he was to have been caught with it on his breath. Lowering his voice, he whispered to her about Nasreen and Madjid's tryst among the trees and how it made him ache for her—as he always ached for her. After he was done, he kissed them both good night and put them back under the carpet. He blew out his lamp and lay down to sleep.

In the moonlight, the judge sat under his tree. Bibi-Khanoom sat with her back to him. She pulled down her chador and handed him her hairbrush. He began to brush her hair, sometimes sweeping it off her neck and caressing her skin there, which still made her quiver. "You did so much today," he said. "You must be exhausted."

"I'm fine. Mirza bears the brunt of the work."

"My brother embarrassed him about the wine."

"We call it medicinal juice."

The judge laughed. "That's what you call the alcohol?"

Bibi-Khanoom giggled and asked God for forgiveness by blurting out an *astagfurallah* before saying, "Yes!"

She leaned into him and he put his arms around her, and as she sank into his embrace you could not tell where one began and the other ended. Their laughter had died down and they sat together, in this stillness and silence. They sat together in each other's presence, in solitude. Sometimes passion is so quiet, you have to close your eyes to hear it.

PARIS | II

Shazdehpoor looked up from his calligraphy. The cafés surrounding the square had already started filling up with the lunch crowd. It was Friday and Shazdehpoor was due for his weekly meal with his friend Monsieur Trianant. He touched his face and felt the stubble. In the daze of the morning rush he had forgotten to shave. Such an oversight worried him.

He had shaved, every day, for the past sixty years. Even the morning after his wife's death, he shaved. He had taught both his boys, as well.

First Jamsheed, then Madjid. He had taught them how to properly hold the razor, how to pull in the direction of the hair, how to use the heat and pressure of the brush instead of the blade, to raise the hairs away from the face. He had ordered each of them his own shaving kit from the English gentlemen's catalog.

After his lesson, Jamsheed had sat in his father's study, devouring sweets and washing them down with tea. He had a nick on his neck that Shazdehpoor had blotted with paper. He kept touching it. "Stop!" said Shazdehpoor. "You'll infect it."

The boy continued to eat like an animal, barely chewing. "Can't I get an electric shaver?"

"We'll see," he said, disappointed that his eldest son did not appreciate the ritual he had been made privy to. It was one of many disappointments that would eventually gather into full-blown contempt.

Madjid, on the other hand, had taken his father's initiation very seriously. He had sat in the study after his first shave and discussed the origin of shaving. He had spent some time in the library studying it. He had noticed how his father was able to shave in ten strokes or fewer. "In the ancient times," said Madjid, "people used two shells to shave with. They dragged them across their face."

"Yes," said Shazdehpoor.

"Men going into battle used to shave to keep their beards from being grabbed during combat."

It had given him great pleasure to see his son's enthusiasm. But his wife implored him on Jamsheed's behalf. Each time she saw her husband take a step away from her eldest son toward her younger one, she said, "You must show him kindness. It is cruel how you favor Madjid."

"Madjid deserves my kindness."

"The one who you say least deserves your kindness is the one who needs it most."

Those words haunted him now. What had seemed impossible at the time was now so simple.

Shazdehpoor packed up his handcart and headed away from the square. He stopped off at a small pharmacy and purchased a single plastic razor, then headed toward Rue Marcadet. La Divette was a small, old dilapidated bar with a *tabac* in the front. The display windows were jam-packed with old radios. In the evenings, musicians, dancers, and singers crammed into the back and, after a few glasses of wine, performed for one another.

Shazdehpoor stopped in from time to time for a quick demitasse at the bar. The owner nodded to him as he walked in with his handcart and headed straight back, past the *tabac*, past the bar, the table football, and the vintage pinball machines to the *pissoire*. He stepped into the stall to relieve himself, then stood before the small sink wedged into the nook beside the door. He took off his jacket and laid it over his handcart. Though the water in the spigot was hot, he had no foam for the usual ritual. He took the piece of old soap on the sink ledge and lathered it up between his hands.

Looking up at himself in the scratched shard of a mirror, he was momentarily taken aback by his own reflection. The face looked unfamiliar, somehow strange. He looked down at his hand, focusing on the thin blue veins that jutted through the translucent skin.

With several quick strokes of the razor, he shaved his stubble and splashed hot water over his face, then ran his wet hands through what remained of his hair. He patted himself dry, rolled down his sleeves, and slipped on his jacket, straightening out the wrinkles. He stood back and looked at himself. He looked crisp and clean, elegant, even.

The wheel of his handcart banged against a chair as he left the café. He hated dragging this cart back and forth from his studio apartment to the Place du Tertre. It was heavy and awkward, a clanking reminder of what he had to do to survive in his new life. The idea of Monsieur Trianant having to sit beside it at their lunch was too much to bear. As he did each Friday, Shazdehpoor left it behind the bar of the café with a promise to return later and fetch it. Then he took up his walking stick and strode out of La Divette a freed man.

Delivery trucks jammed the streets outside. Shazdehpoor dodged and weaved through the foot traffic. At the intersection of Rue de la Fontaine du But and Rue Caulaincourt he waited for the light to change as he headed to the metro station. As he stepped into the street he felt something soft and slick under his shoe— dog excrement. He stood there for a few seconds in disbelief, then stepped back onto the sidewalk, discreetly dragging his foot to remove the smear from his sole. The litter, the stench, the flashing lights, the car horns followed by the screeching brakes and human profanity, the bodies bumping up against him, pushing against him, was more than he could stand. "Barbarism," he muttered.

He caught the next light and descended into the metro, taking the 12 train two stops to Pigalle and switching to the 2 train to Père Lachaise.

When he came up the steps at Père Lachaise, he was only a few blocks away from La Mère Lachaise. Monsieur Trianant was waiting for him at an outdoor table. Trianant was a Frenchman, both brusque and sophisticated, a friend who spoke mostly about ideas and never pried into Shazdehpoor's history nor shared any of his own. On any other day, this comforted Shazdehpoor. As did the fact that Frenchmen in Paris were always stepping in dog shit. Trianant would think nothing of the smell. Shazdehpoor could not bear to face him. Not soiled and half-shaved. Not today. He felt the droves of people pushing past him, but it was as if he were invisible, a piece of litter blown backward in time.

THE TOWN SQUARE

Madjid stood in front of the bathroom mirror, shaving. He had been doing so for four years and it had become more habit than ritual. He had exchanged his father's leather shaving kit for a plastic razor and a can of pressurized foam cream. As soon as he was done, he splashed some hot water on his face, wiped with a towel, and headed for the door.

His father was in his salon listening to the BBC. Almost a week had passed since the inaugural spring lunch at the orchard and the mullah's warning about liquor, principles, the unwillingness of the masses to tolerate blatant hypocrisy and injustice. He ran to the doorway as Madjid began to leave. "You should stay home, son," he said.

"Don't worry, Father. I'm just going to the square. I'll be back in a few hours."

"Madjid, I have been listening to the news. Things are getting very heated. It's not safe."

"Father, you are listening to the *British* Broadcasting Corporation about what is happening in our own backyard."

"They have accurate reporting."

"They have their own agenda."

"Madjid, please."

"Father, I will be fine. I promise that if there is any sign of trouble I will walk away."

Entering the *maydan* could stimulate the dead back to life. The collection of storefronts connected by four open archways functioned as a marketplace during the day, with shops for cheese, meat, tea, fabric, and lace; *ghelyans* and tobacco; a *tanoor* for bread making; a cobbler, a gold souk, a dressmaker. Here and there throughout the square stood farmers who had traveled into town to sell their fruits and vegetables. Everywhere you could hear a babel of voices buying and selling and haggling or calling out after the occasional thief, as smoke rose from snack stands that sold grilled beets and roasted nuts to noshing shoppers.

The square was also the town meeting spot. Old men gathered on a carpet in front of the *ghelyan* shop where they puffed away and took tea, while arguing politics in circles, falling silent at the mention of the recent passing of a friend or neighbor. Young seminary students stood around their teacher, flicking through their worry beads as they listened earnestly to the cleric speak about a hadith or sura from their daily lessons, most of them admiring their teacher's beard, hoping their smooth, young chins would yield such bounty some day. Young girls huddled in front of the dress shop, giggling coyly at the group of hooligan boys who moved through the crowds like a school of angry fish, swindling trinkets they took to the prettiest girls in the group.

On his way through the square, Madjid stopped to say hello to those he knew and smiled and nodded at those he knew of. He loved the garish excitement of the square. As much as he loved the green isolation of the orchard.

In the orchard, it was easy to forget all other humans existed. He liked to stand at the threshold of the wooden doors before entering. The air inside was denser, the light more distilled. With his eyes closed, he listened to the throbbing of the insects, the breeze, so like an orchestra tuning its instruments before playing a movement of music. Just as the symphony was about to begin, he took a few short breaths and ran through the fruit trees. The path Madjid ran was never straight as no natural path ever can be. He cut right without any forewarning and wove through the trees with his arms stretched out, tapping them as he sped by. He then cut left and did the same. Symmetry was his only criterion. He darted out of the cluster of trees and leapt over the stream onto the path and ran as fast as he could toward the house. His lungs burned from the gulps of air he inhaled.

As the house came into view, he slowed to a trot, sticking his hands in the reflecting pool and frightening the fish and then running into the henhouse and chasing the chickens around, pelting them with water. He then entered the barn and greeted the goats and sheep. They looked at him with blank stares. The same look they had when led to slaughter.

The first slaughter he had witnessed was a fainting goat that had been brought to Naishapur from abroad. No one knew where she came from and no one wanted her due to this condition, but Bibi-Khanoom purchased her and brought her to the orchard. The sight of human beings moving toward her hastily made the goat stiffen and fall over. It gave her deeply human characteristics. The goat even learned to spread her limbs or lean against a wall at the start of a fainting spell. But after a few years, she became weary and there was something in her eyes, a knowing look uncommon in an animal. The human beings who goaded her to faint for their own amusement had diminished her somehow.

When Madjid visited her, he moved slowly and softly. He spoke to her in hushed tones and petted her gently. His own stillness was alien to him and he did not understand, at the time, that it was sadness, and a sadness that once felt always lingered.

The goat fell ill one spring day not too long after Mirza had begun work there, and he took her to the back of the barn. Madjid followed and watched as Mirza laid her down gently and held her limbs under his legs. He told Madjid to look away as he turned on the hose and poured water over her mouth. Madjid asked him why he was giving her water and he said it was a kindness. He took out his knife from the scabbard in his belt buckle, held her head back, and slit her throat. The only sound was the swishing from her severed windpipe. Madjid stared into her eyes and watched her blink several times and then she was not there.

What stayed with him from that day was not the look in the goat's eyes but the look in Mirza's eyes. As he picked up her limp body, he looked at the boy for a brief moment and Madjid saw in them something that he would later come to know as grief.

If the orchard was a symphony, the town square was a brass band—in perpetual motion. A group of young men had gathered in the center, along with a few of Madjid's friends from school.

He walked over to see what was happening. As he got closer he saw it was an argument. Two young men were shouting at each other, their respective factions standing behind them. One was clean-shaven. The other's face was covered in thick stubble. Madjid knew the unshaven one from the mosque.

"What are they going on about?" he asked a boy from his literature class.

"The usual," said his friend.

"Any news about Professor Moeni?"

"I heard they let him go."

"Do you know what happened?"

"All I know is we won't be reading any Russian novels anytime soon."

Madjid was familiar with all the factions working against the government. He had explored them, in an effort to find out what he believed. He sat in with the religious faction whose contempt was directed at Western decadence and the royal capitulation to it. He sat in with Communists, a group of intellectuals who disdained religiosity and superstition. He sat in with the nationalists, who were now a shell of their former strength—their once powerful leader dead for a decade. There were other groups, including a strange combination of communism and Islam led by a cultish figure. What made them all a threat was that, despite their differences, they were united against the establishment itself, which was supported by the well-off, well-heeled, well-to-do, well-traveled, well-connected, well-cared-for, who were left alone by the government. As long as they did not cross any lines. But, as Madjid saw with Professor Moeni, it had become increasingly difficult to know where that line had been drawn.

All of these groups had their own particular ideas of how the world should be. He found kernels of validity in all of them, some more than others. In his mind, they should all have the right to advocate and govern.

Jamsheed laughed about his idealism and his various excursions to meet in these groups—where the fear of a raid by the secret police was growing more real with each passing day. Street protests were summarily crushed and protesters were arrested. It seemed that the only places immune to the authorities' reach were the mosques. "Find something to believe in and ask yourself, are you willing to die for this belief?" said Jamsheed. "And more important, are you willing to kill for it?"

The crowd began to push toward the argument, which was escalating. The two young men stopped fighting over political beliefs and were now hurling epithets. Accusations of Westoxification, zealotry, Arabization, communism, and elitism flew between them. The clean-shaven young man stepped into the other one's face, jabbing his finger into his chest as he yelled. Shoved off balance, the stubble-faced young man took a swing. Both young men started throwing punches, their factions jumping into the row.

Madjid and his friend from school pulled themselves away from the fray. As they stood to the side, his friend looked around nervously. "I'm out of here," he said. "I can't afford to get into trouble. I've reached my quota this month."

Madjid kept watching. "Sure," he said. "See you in class."

Several policemen swept into the square. The crowd dispersed as swiftly as a flock of feeding birds at the sight of a fox. Only the clean-shaven young man did not run away. He stood there, frozen, looking off to nowhere. The policemen walked past him, as though he were an apparition. They swept through the square looking for his adversary.

Madjid realized that all his friends were gone. He walked over to the fountain and sat on the ledge. The boys who had argued were his age, eighteen, and already so convinced of their beliefs they were willing to hate each other. Whatever the cruelty of nature, animals, fish and birds never sought revenge or redress. So why did all human cruelties and injustices have to be accounted for? Carried from generation to generation until someone was called upon to pay the note, setting the cycle in motion again?

He looked up and saw that the clean-shaven young man was now sitting on the ground with his legs sprawled out, as he held his left side with his hand. His hand was filled with blood. The ground around him was dark with it and he looked down in disbelief.

Madjid walked toward him but was pushed aside by the crowd. Various men tried to help him up but he screamed in agony. The disbelief in his eyes had given way to fear and helplessness. He looked about him at the strange faces, his mouth moving, no words coming out. Madjid pushed forward. The young man was now only staring and blinking.

By the time the police brought a stretcher to the scene, he had bled out and lay dead on the ground. They lifted him and took him away as the crowd dispersed. Madjid stood by the pool of blood left behind. He tried to imagine the mother of the young man as she was told her son was dead. He heard her scream out, "My child, my child, my child," as she beat her own head.

He imagined the young man who had committed the murder and was now hiding in the mosque surrounded by fellow believers. The young man who would not sleep that night and would, the following morning, be praised for his courage and willingness to defend the faith.

THE MULLAH AND
THE MURDERER

The mullah rose before the sun and went to the bathroom to do his ablutions. He studied his beard in the mirror, pleased with the abundance of white hairs. He then did his morning prayers before taking tea and breakfast. He lived in the house in which he was born, several streets away from the town square. Much to his humiliation, his father had left the house to his younger brother, but since the judge moved into his wife's home in the orchard, it had passed to him.

The mullah, whose given name was Habib'ollah—his family called him Habib—was the oldest son in his family. The judge, whose given name was Akbar, was the youngest son. They had one sister between them, named Zahra, who was, for the most part, ignored because of her gender. Zahra was Shazdehpoor's mother and had died giving birth to him. The mullah had once overheard

Ghamar tell her aunt Bibi-Khanoom that the only thing remaining of Zahra's miserable short life was a *fokoli*. As cruel as the comment was, the mullah was impressed by its accuracy.

When Habib was a boy, he did not have his own room and slept in his father's study. Each night, he spread out blankets on the carpet in front of his father's reading chair and gathered them up right after he awoke so as not to disturb his father's morning tea and newspaper reading. He kept a small satchel by the study's door. It held all his belongings, which he carried to school every day.

Even though the mullah had plenty of bedrooms, he still chose to sleep in the study. Only there was he comfortable and slept soundly.

In his youth he had loved a girl. She passed by his home every morning on her way to school, and when she did, he grabbed his satchel and hurtled out the front door without breakfast to walk beside her. At first, she did not acknowledge his presence. Then one morning, he overslept. She turned and waited for him in front of his house. He ran out, disheveled. She giggled as he clumsily tried to straighten out his clothes. This went on for months. They never spoke, not once. The girl came from a good family, and to engage in conversation with a boy unsupervised was unseemly.

One day his father instructed him to wash up and dress in his best clothes. The family had an important matter to attend. He was told to make sure he did not speak unless directly addressed and to be mindful of his pitch if he did speak, as his voice was nasal-sounding, shrill and unpleasant.

The family had walked together in silence, his younger brother, Akbar, walking ahead with his father and Habib relegated to walk behind with his sister, Zahra, despite his position

in the family as the eldest son. The death of their mother had occurred years before but the event still caused Habib much loneliness and grief. His father didn't allow him to speak of it.

As they walked down the path toward a house, he saw a girl
in her living room window, sitting quietly in a jewel-colored dress
with a lace scarf draped on her head. Her hands were clasped on
her knees. It was the girl he walked to school with. His heart began to pound against his breastbone and beads of sweat trickled
down his face. He thought perhaps the girl had mentioned something to her parents about him and they must have approved. He
felt a smile cross his face and fought to control it from turning into
a full grin as they neared the house.

The girl's family all stood and greeted them as they entered.
He sat next to his sister in the corner of the room and stared at
the girl. She did not look at him but kept her eyes on her lap. He
planned what he would say to her once they were told to go to the
other room to sit and speak to each other in private. It would be
the first time they had spoken, and he wanted to make sure he
spoke well. He wondered if it would be too forward of him to tell
her that he thought she was beautiful.

His father, who usually spoke directly and confidently,
seemed to be acting strangely. The heavy silk carpets, gold embroidered ottomans and floor pillows, the intricately engraved
silver trays overflowing with sweets, and a formidable tea service
had turned him into an overeager child. He spoke quickly in fragmented thoughts, waving his hands around.

The girl's family sat as still as stones yet humored him. Despite their lineage and show of wealth, they had no money. But he
did. After a few minutes of tea service and light conversation, his
father turned to the girl's father and said, "We have come to ask

for your daughter's hand in marriage to our son Akbar. That is, if Bibi-Khanoom will have him."

At that very moment, a door within Habib closed and bolted shut from the inside. From that day forth, he would never open that door and no person would ever cross its threshold again.

The next morning, he gathered his blankets and pillow and waited in the study. His father walked into the room with his tea and newspaper and took a seat on his reading chair. He opened the paper, blocking his son from view. Habib stepped forward. He cleared his throat and said that he wished to go to the Naishapur Seminary.

He was nervous and his voice came out shrilly. His father folded down the top of the newspaper to get a good look at his son. He was not impressed by his son's aspiration to become a cleric and was irritated by his voice. He immediately agreed and the boy set off. He was eighteen years old.

When the bus pulled up in front of the seminary, Habib stumbled out in his only suit. The suit was navy, worn out by use, the pants covered in grime, his shirt frayed from repeated hand washes. He looked at the other young men who disembarked with him. They were all dressed in fresh clean clothes with proper luggage. He dusted himself off and slung his satchel over his shoulder and crossed the street.

The seminary was a massive two-story concrete building. The wrought-iron entrance gate was decorated with turquoise tiles that vibrated with cool color against the drab gray walls. Students passed through the central courtyard, dressed in *abas* and turbans. In one hand, they held their books, in the other, their worry beads. Their voices echoed through the enclosure.

The young men from the bus started laughing. He looked

around. He had not realized that he was holding on to the gate bars with both hands and with his head wedged in between. A young seminary student strode toward him with a welcoming smile. "Brothers! Welcome. Welcome."

The student threw open the gates and led the young men across the courtyard to the main hall. Habib looked up at the second-floor landing that encircled the courtyard. The scent of rosewater and prayer stones drifted through the air. Young seminary students wove in and out of rooms, some leaning on the railing, flicking worry beads, engaged in light banter, others engaged in serious debate. He caught a glimpse of an older man, a high-ranking cleric, probably a teacher, standing in the doorway of a classroom. Unlike the young men, his gaze was stern and heavy. His dark deep-set eyes followed Habib into the main hall.

The student host walked the young men through registration and took them on a tour of the building; the mess hall, the classrooms, the prayer hall, the library and study hall, finally leading them upstairs and showing them to their rooms, two in each. Habib was the odd man out and given his own room. He stepped in and closed the door. The room was small and windowless with a vent over the door. He dropped his satchel on the ground and looked at the two beds, one on either side with a seminary student uniform laid out on each. He had never had a room to himself let alone two beds to choose from. This sudden largesse filled him with a feeling of overwhelming shame.

He walked into his first class dressed in his seminary uniform. It was slightly large on him. The other boys were seated on the carpeted floor, in small groups of what appeared to be the start of friendships, engaged in conversation while wrapping their turbans. There was no opening for him to sit, so he found a seat in the corner of the room by himself and copied them. He propped up his knee and used it as a mock head, carefully wrapping the fabric around it and tucking the end underneath. He lifted it off his knee and placed it on his head just the way the other young men had done.

The cleric with dark deep-set eyes walked into the room. The young men scrambled into rows facing the front. The cleric took his seat on a slightly raised platform in front of the class and looked at the assembly before him. He unfolded a bookstand and put his Koran on it. He opened the book and began to page through it, not looking up as he said, "One of the most important skills you must master is public oration. It is a fundamental part of the propagation and renewal of our faith. And if you fail in this endeavor, you will have failed God and His Holy Prophet, may peace be upon Him."

The class mumbled the "peace be upon Him" refrain. Habib was terrified. His voice had been nothing more than a source of nuisance and shame in his household. In school, he had always skirted the obligation to speak before the class by diligent study and high marks on written examination. But here, there was no escape. He looked at the door and for a brief moment entertained the thought of running out. But where would he run to? He heard the cleric say "you" and turned to see who he meant. The whole class had turned to face him as the cleric held out his finger pointed at Habib. "Read the first sura."

Habib froze. He just stared at the cleric with a pained expression.

"What is it, young man? Are you mute?"

Habib shook his head.

"Then why don't you read?"

Habib looked at the others. They all stared at him. Some were embarrassed for him, some were enjoying his humiliation. His neighbor handed his Koran to him. Habib opened it and looked at the first sura. He knew it by heart. He took in a deep breath, closed his eyes, and recited the first verse. The high-pitched screech of his voice rang out through the room. His classmates suppressed their laughter but he could hear the breathy convulsions. He stopped reciting and opened his eyes. The cleric shushed the room and addressed Habib. "I can see why you hesitated. Come forward."

Habib closed the book and pushed himself to his feet. His legs were still slightly numb from fear. He slowly walked to the front of the class and stood at the foot of the platform where the cleric was seated. The cleric got up and ushered Habib onto the platform with him. They faced each other before the class. Habib turned his head to look at the boys staring at him.

"Eyes on me, young man," the cleric said.

Habib looked back at the cleric. At close range, his gaze was not so much stern as certain. It felt comforting to be looked upon with purpose. The cleric pressed his hand against Habib's larynx and said, "Now speak the first line."

"In the name of God," said Habib, in a high-pitched screech. The cleric smacked his larynx with such force that Habib stepped back to regain his balance. The cleric ushered him forward, put his hand back on the spot, and said, "Again."

Habib braced himself for another hit as he let out a high-pitched "In the name of God." It came with even greater force as the cleric said, "Again."

Habib's throat was on fire. He opened his mouth and, just as he was about to say it again, the cleric smacked his larynx once more. The force of his hand sent Habib's voice down to the floor of his diaphragm and a deep, honeyed sound came rising out of his throat as he proclaimed, "In the name of God."

Habib looked out at the boys. The room was silent, stunned. The cleric stepped back and said, "Continue."

From that day on, Habib's voice remained where the cleric had trained it. The boys in the class clamored to befriend the cleric's star student, this firebrand orator. Habib spent the next four years cloistered in the seminary studying everything from Islamic philosophy to jurisprudence to theology, interpretation of the Holy Book, history, and logic, arguing through many nights with fellow students and teachers, honing his oratory skills and his political leanings. It became clear that within the seminary there were two schools of thought: the quietists, who believed that it was not possible to create Paradise on earth and therefore refused to be involved in politics; and the activists, who believed that it was their responsibility to fight in this world for divine justice. His teacher was in the latter school and Habib followed his teachings.

Habib did not leave his teacher's side until news of his father's passing. Dressed in full clerical garb with a lush black beard, he returned to oversee his father's burial and move back into his childhood home.

Reading the newspaper as his father once did, the mullah now sat in his living room staring at the photograph of a son of a wealthy local merchant. The young man who had been killed in the square. He had seen him around town, always dressed in the latest European fashions, leaning on his shiny red Citroën, winking at girls passing by. The young man was a scoundrel, born into privilege. After one year, he had dropped out of the university to live at home. He worked in his father's business after squandering a small fortune on pleasure, and his father, the mullah knew, had to pay off a young girl his son had impregnated. The girl was from a religious family and he had sent her off in the middle of the night to Mash'had for a back-alley abortion. The mullah looked at the young man's clean, fresh face in the newspaper. The obituary read like a canon to a saint. It made his blood thicken.

He was pulled out of his seething by a knock on the door. When he opened it, the other young man, the one who had done the killing, was standing on his step. He took off his shoes at the door and bent down to kiss the mullah's hands before entering the house. He followed the cleric into the living room and stood to the side with his hands clasped in front of him, eyes to the ground until the mullah bade him to sit at the tea service. The mullah poured him tea and sat back, flicking his worry beads, and said, "Have you recently come home?"

"Yes. I was at the university in Mash'had."

"What brought you home?"

"My family needed me."

"I see."

They continued drinking their tea in silence. The young man had a pained look on his face. "Haj-Agha," he burst out. "I did not mean to hurt him. I swear to you. I was arguing with him about the state of affairs for the poor of our country and the responsibility he and those of his privilege bear. I did not mean to hurt him."

"Then why did you?"

The young man looked down at his hands and fell silent for a few moments, then said, "A blackness covered my eyes and I felt a hate so powerful that it forced my hand. I watched the rage lift my hand and push the knife into his side. I stuck him like the animal he was. I wanted to tear him to pieces. I was prepared to stand there and stab him repeatedly but the others pulled me away when the police came."

"What did he say?"

"It's not something he said."

The young man kept rocking back and forth. He looked at the door as though he were planning an escape route.

"What did he say?"

"It's not what he said. It was what he did."

"What did he do?"

The young man stared at the wall behind the mullah and began to speak in a monotone voice, as though he were describing a film he was watching. "She came to my room at the university. My sister. I hadn't expected to see her. She looked so frightened. She tried to tell me what had happened, but the moment she mentioned being with a man, I started to beat her. I screamed at her for shaming our family and I kept beating her. She just cowered in the corner of the room, apologizing. She ran out and I went after her but she disappeared into the streets. I went to bed and I was woken up by one of my roommates. I went into the hall and picked up the phone. It was my father. I could hear my mother wailing in the background and I knew something terrible had happened."

He turned his eyes to the mullah and continued, "She'd hanged herself that morning in the backyard. She had hanged herself from a tree that we used to play under. The baby was still in her womb. She never went through with the abortion."

The anguished tension on the young man's face slowly disappeared and it almost seemed as though he turned to stone as he said, "He took my sister's life, so I took his. And I will face whatever the consequences."

"I will go with you to the police station."

"Yes."

"You realize that once we go, there is no turning back."

"Yes."

"They will hang you."

"Yes."

"Are you prepared for what this will do to your mother?"

"Yes."

"Perhaps you should go home and spend some time with your family. I will come by in a few days and we will walk over together."

"Yes."

The mullah was overcome with love and pride. This young man who sat before him for a mere few minutes was like a son to him now. And yet it was the mullah who had instructed one of his followers to seek out this young man and to tell him the name of the wastrel who had impregnated his sister.

The martyrdom of this young man would lay the foundation for a great uprising. He was a soldier in a war for the soul of a nation. The mullah vowed to use every ounce of his oratorical skill to make sure this death would mark the beginning of the end for the monarchy and save thousands of innocent young women from the predatory elite. He put his hand on the young man's shoulder and led him to the door and said, "I will be by in a few days."

The young man smiled at the mullah as he put on his shoes and headed out into the street. He felt a lightness wash over him that he had not felt since his sister had come to visit him—asking for his help.

A SYMPHONY IN RUINS

The annual Festival of Arts in Shiraz and Persepolis had taken place for the last decade to great acclaim. Every year, Nasreen glued herself to the television and radio, watching and listening to performers of music, theater, dance, and film from home and abroad. The festival had shaped her desire to perform onstage and led to fantasies in which she raced to rehearsals and cafés, ran off on global tours, free from tradition. This last notion appealed to her above all else. She wanted to express herself. She wanted to be herself. The only place in her life where she had found this freedom was in the moments she shared with Madjid.

Madjid knew of the depth of her ambitions. Her eyes lit up every time she spoke about a performance. His own passions were about the world, how it should be but was not. At times, Nasreen's singular focus on the arts seemed frivolous to him. "How can you not care about politics?" he finally said. "To ignore injustice is a crime."

She gave thought to her answer before she spoke. She wanted to be honest with him, something she had never considered in her relationship with her mother and father. She wanted him to see her. "Madjid," she said, "I want my own life to be worth living. And if I can do something that moves you, maybe makes you feel less alone in the world, how is that a crime?"

At first, Madjid brushed off her confession as nothing more than childish sentiment. He had spent so much time in the company of idealistic young men who spoke of "we" and "them" that to be confronted by a young woman who spoke of "me" and "you" seemed trifling. But a few days later, he was handed a pamphlet at a political meeting. It was a Persian translation of Tolstoy's "On Anarchy."

The last line was: "And yet in our world everybody thinks of changing humanity, and nobody thinks of changing himself."

Straight after the meeting, he rushed to her house and apologized for not listening to her. He told her that he would support her in her pursuit. "How you choose to live your own life does matter," he said. "I will follow you anywhere."

At the weekly family lunch, Bibi-Khanoom and Akbar-Agha announced that they would be attending the festival. Did anyone care to join them? Shazdehpoor almost squealed with delight. He was particularly interested in a Polish chamber orchestra that was scheduled to perform Samuel Barber's String Quartet in B Minor. But if his uncle and aunt hadn't gone, he wouldn't have gone alone. Only in his salon was Shazdehpoor a man of the world. He had many brochures and itineraries and dreams of traveling Europe's great cities to see museums and symphonies. But he approached the planning stage with such fervor and imagination that when the time came to act, his enthusiasm had already waned. And his fears took over.

For the festival this year, he was careful to keep his feelings in check and only see to the necessities: he briefly glanced at the brochure for performance times, called a hotel to make reservations, and checked train schedules to Tehran. He did not hold grand imaginary concerts in his salon or buy a leather valise or linen traveling trousers.

Ghamar was absolutely against going. She couldn't understand the point of traveling all the way across the country to see strange performances by foreigners. Mohammad simply shrugged in agreement.

Only Bibi-Khanoom noticed the dejected look on Nasreen's face, despite her smile.

That evening Nasreen slipped into her father's tailor shop at the back of their house. The shop had a telephone on which she could speak with Madjid without her mother hovering over her. She sat at her father's worktable, slumped over and stifling tears. "She will never let me come."

"Just tell her that you will be with Akbar-Agha and Bibi-Khanoom," said Madjid. "It's the truth anyway."

"She doesn't care. She knows you're going and she thinks we'll . . . you know."

"No. Tell me."

"Come on, Madjid."

"Say it."

"Stop it!"

"San Francisco."

"Madjid! Stop it!"

Madjid heard Nasreen's muffled laughter through the receiver. "San Francisco" was the code word for sexual relations used by a character on the television series *My Uncle Napoleon*. Neither of them had ever gotten over the joke.

"Have Bibi-Khanoom speak to your mother. You have to come," he said. "You love this festival more than any of us."

Days passed. Nasreen moped around the house like a woman in mourning, torturing herself by listening to radio programs about the festival and watching snippets of news footage about the preparations in Shiraz and Persepolis. She even watched a documentary program on the history of the ancient citadel, which had been designed in such a way that horses could easily ascend the many steps that led inside. Her heart ached with longing to be there, to be free, to be away from her mother.

The day before leaving for the festival, Bibi-Khanoom paid a visit. Nasreen didn't dare come out of her room for fear of upsetting her chances. She was even afraid to hope too loudly. She could hear the women arguing in the living room and hurriedly packed a bag for the trip, just in case it tipped the decision in her favor.

When the voices fell quiet, she stuck her head out and saw her mother on the sofa admiring a silver platter—a bribe from Bibi-Khanoom. From her mother's sighs, Nasreen could tell their agreement was tenuous at best. She grabbed her bag and repeatedly thanked and kissed her mother, insisting on leaving with Bibi-Khanoom right then and there. "You will stay by Bibi-Khanoom's side at all times," said Ghamar.

"Yes, Mother."

"No funny business."

"Yes, Mother."

"You will do exactly as Bibi-Khanoom tells you."

"Of course, Mother."

Bibi-Khanoom started for the door. "Don't worry, my dear," she said. "I'll look after her. Akbar-Agha is sharing a suite with Shazdehpoor and Madjid, and I will be in a room with Nasreen. Everything will be fine."

Nasreen could hardly contain her euphoria. There would be no sleep for her that night. She would bathe and fix her hair and nails. She would pick out all the shows to see.

"Bibi-Khanoom, do you have the festival brochure?"

"Yes, we can look at it. There's a very nice restaurant at the festival, right in the hotel lobby. All the performers go there. You will like it very much."

Nasreen was so excited that she started skipping as they approached the orchard door. Bibi-Khanoom knocked and they waited for Mirza to open it. Nasreen turned to her and said, "Did my mother just trade me for a silver platter?"

"My darling," said her great aunt, "we have often been traded for less."

The trip to Shiraz was nearly thirty hours, but flew by. For the first leg of the trip, Bibi-Khanoom, Akbar-Agha, Shazdehpoor, Madjid, and Nasreen shared a train car to Tehran and spent the whole time talking, laughing, eating, joking, and napping. Nasreen was especially animated. Without Ghamar there, she sang songs made famous by cabaret singers, joked about her mother's demanding ways, and acted out scenes from movies and television shows, especially the variety television series *The Kaaf Show*.

Her audience was entranced, no one more so than Madjid. During the lulls in the journey, when the car fell quiet, Nasreen stared out at the passing world, the rhythmic heaving of the train wheels sinking her into the melancholic state that often follows the euphoria of performing for an audience. She wondered if it was possible to live life as it were theater—with the same excitement and freedom. She felt Madjid's hand taking hold of hers. Everyone had fallen asleep except for him. She looked into his warm, admiring eyes and thought that perhaps it was.

By the time they reached the train station in Tehran, it was night. They slept at a hotel and the next morning they rented a car for the fifteen-hour drive, stopping for lunch in Isfahan. They arrived in Shiraz in the middle of the night. Nasreen walked into the opulent lobby of the Kourosh Hotel, staring at the domed atrium with its intricate carvings and massive chandelier with the awestruck expression of a child. Guests meandered into the hotel lobby bar, women and men commingling, smoking, laughing, and clinking glasses of wine. It was hard for her to even distinguish the foreigners from the city residents. One particular woman dressed in the latest urban fashion, coiffed and manicured, might have been an Iranian who lived somewhere in Europe or might have been a European on an adventure to Iran.

Bibi-Khanoom perched on the lobby sofa in a maroon skirt suit and tan monteau with a silk scarf draped over her head and loosely tied around her neck, waiting for her husband to check them in. In this place, her colorful chadors would read as downright provincial and she did not want to be a spectacle for city sophisticates or foreigners.

The following day, they all headed to Takyeh Mosheer to see a Ta'ziyeh performance. Inside the traditional open-air congregation hall there was a raised stage encircled by bleachers. The chadored and head-scarfed women sat on one side and the men with worry beads in hand on the other. A few foreigners, scholars, and handfuls of students were strewn among them.

Ta'ziyeh theater was difficult for Shazdehpoor. The passion plays enacted the Battle of Karbala and the death of Imam Hussein and were usually performed on Ashura, the day that Imam Hussein was killed. He was impressed by the horseback riding and sword-fighting skills of the performers, their singing and acting abilities. He was aware of the centuries of sophistry practiced by the performers who preserved Persian classical music in the face of intense periods of religious oppression when music and human representation were forbidden. It was the story lines of the plays that he objected to. They were the stories of a religion that he did not believe in.

Madjid sat between Shazdehpoor and Akbar-Agha, looking across the stage at Nasreen, who sat with Bibi-Khanoom and the other women. He caught her eye and winked, mouthing the words "San Francisco."

"Stop it!" she mouthed back and giggled. He smiled at her then turned his attention to the program. Madjid had always loved the Ta'ziyeh. As a child, he was mesmerized by the horseback riding and sword fighting, and as he grew older, he found himself moved by the music and the tragic nature of the stories. "The actors were handpicked from troupes from all over the country," he said as he read the program. "Many different fighting styles. They are doing the Ta'ziyeh of Imam Hussein."

Shazdehpoor sighed. He had not traveled all this way to see religious folk theater. It was bad enough that he had to endure it in his hometown. He complained of an upset stomach and left the hall. His beloved orchestra was not performing until that evening in Persepolis, so he had a few hours to kill. He walked leisurely along the strip. The street was crowded with people from all over the world—a sight he had never seen. Two tall blond women strode along arm in arm, disappearing into the bazaar that veered off into the alley. Street performers worked the sidewalk, each with a cluster of spectators. Food sellers called out next to their snack stands. Packs of students rushed by. He looked up at an apartment building and saw an old woman sitting in the window with her chador over her face. She stared with a furrowed brow at something across the street. Shazdehpoor followed her gaze. Multiple television monitors had been set up in a storefront. On the screens there was a naked man with his back turned. The man suddenly brandished a gun in his hand and pushed its muzzle up his behind. The few people who had gathered around gasped in horror. Shazdehpoor immediately looked up at the window but the old woman had slammed it shut. He continued his walk back to the hotel. He vaguely recalled reading about this performance group from somewhere in Eastern Europe. It was some kind of avant-garde theater, which in his mind was nonsensical.

Near the hotel, Shazdehpoor took the bus to Persepolis. He climbed the double stairs toward the 125,000-square-meter terrace, passing by homes, hammams, military quarters, and reception halls from the Achaemenid Empire, running his hands over the bas-reliefs of royal subjects, trees, lotus flowers, and animals. A few remaining marble columns stretched up to the blue sky, one topped by a double-sided griffin. Inside the Persepolis Museum, he studied what had once been the royal harem and perused the artifacts inside: fragments of vessels, wood remnants, and burned pieces of fabric that had survived the fire set by Iskandar in 330 B.C. It made him angry. As angry as he felt about the Muslim conquest of his country nine centuries later. As though both were attempts to erase him personally.

Akbar-Agha had once told him that his anger was misplaced.

"Any country that has survived as long as ours will inevitably measure its history in loss," he said. "The only thing to blame is time."

The evening's chamber orchestra performance took place in front of the wall of the double stairs. The orchestra was situated against a backdrop of a massive bas-relief of a lion hunting a bull as it sinks its teeth into the prey's rump. Rows of chairs were lined up before them for the audience members. The sun was beginning to set as people arrived, casting the ruins in an amber glow.

To the applause of the audience, the musicians entered the stage single file and seated themselves next to their instruments and immediately started tuning. A distinguished conductor in tails walked across the stage to more applause and situated himself before his musicians. Music sheets were shuffled. Shazdehpoor could hardly contain himself. He had heard this piece on the radio and seen it on a television screen, but to experience it firsthand was an entirely different experience, especially in such a place of pride.

The sound of the opening strings of the Adagio started quietly, weaving the melody through the ruins, the yearning in the music so expressive. Then the resignation. The yearning again. Back and forth it went, on and on, until without warning it arrived at the crescendo—a loud, primal sound that echoed through the vast wreckage of an ancient empire. Shazdehpoor closed his eyes. A tear ran down his cheek. If only he could stay forever in this moment of musical grace.

After the Ta'ziyeh performance, Nasreen wanted to go see an American troupe that was staging *Alice in Wonderland* in a fruit warehouse. Bibi-Khanoom and the judge decided to return to the hotel for an early dinner and bed. Bibi-Khanoom discreetly slipped money into Madjid's hand. "Madjid, why don't you both go together?" she said. "You can have something to eat afterward. That way we won't worry."

To be cut loose in the heart of a city in the throes of a celebration was almost overwhelming to the two young lovers. Without a word they ran together down the street as though they were physically testing the boundaries of their new freedom. As the crowds swelled Madjid slowed his pace and took Nasreen's hand. They walked side by side. The sounds of actors and singers wove through the murmur of conversation, the calling of vendors.

They sat together on a crate inside the fruit warehouse watching the barefoot American troupe create a magical world of rabbits and mushrooms and disappearing cats. Drinks that made Alice shrink and cakes that made her grow. Alice was dressed in nothing more than patchwork rags—and yet she was fussy, spoiled, lost, the real Alice. They were mesmerized. Was it the play alone? Or their being together in public?

Perhaps both. They held hands for every minute of the show.

After the curtain call, they erupted into applause, clapping until their hands stung, Madjid blowing whistles between claps. It was a cool night and the scent of coals and kebab wafted through the air on the street. They sat at a plastic table outside a shack and ordered a platter to share, then washed it down with Coca-Colas. Nasreen was still electrified by the play they had seen. "Have you ever seen such a thing?" she said. "They were all so good. It was just, so, oh, Madjid, wasn't it magic? Didn't you see the place, the animals, really see it?"

"I did. I really did."

"They did it with nothing more than their bodies and voices. Pure magic."

"I liked how they stepped into each role then stepped out."

"Yes! And how they didn't use lighting tricks or costumes to transform themselves. This is what I long to do, Madjid."

Madjid watched her face so full of passion. He thought of the train ride and the way in which she was able to sing a song, tell a story, or act out a scene, moving effortlessly from one character to the next with her whole body and voice. "You will do it. You already do."

They finished their meal and headed back onto the main street, walking slowly now with Madjid's arm around her shoulder. Nobody paid them any mind. Nobody cared that an unmarried couple so brazenly walked the streets, their bodies touching. It was nearing midnight when they arrived, and they made their way to the Hafezieh to listen to Persian music.

The Hafezieh was the tomb of the poet Hafez, and was surrounded by an open-air marble pavilion and lawns. A makeshift stage was set up in front of the tomb for a performance by four musicians, a setar player, a dombak player, a kamancheh player, and a singer, who played the daf drum. People were scattered on the grass quietly conversing, and hushed as soon as the music began. Madjid lay on his side resting his head on his hand looking up at the moon. "There is a full solar eclipse coming next month," he said. "The moon will completely block out the sun." Nasreen brought her face over Madjid's, blocking his view of the sky, and said, "Like this?" They laughed then held still for a moment, to mark the anticipation before a kiss.

The music went on and on. People came and left. Shopkeepers pulled in their wares. Porters folded chairs and swept the stairs. Actors, directors, dancers, and singers dressed for a night out gathered at restaurants and bars. Hotel lobbies hummed with guests. Street sweepers collected garbage and street performers strapped their props to their backs. The show, at last, was over for the night.

And just beyond, just out of sight of the newsstands and hospitality kiosks, the makeshift stages, the concession stands, the restaurants, bars, and nightclubs, the journalists, paparazzi, press conferences, scholars, intellectuals, theater troupes, musicians, dancers, filmmakers, tourists, beyond the floodlights and the streetlights, in the vast darkness that spread across the plains stood a nation on the brink of revolution.

AN OPIUM DREAM

There is nothing more terrifying than poverty, yet nothing more liberating than possessing nothing—not a meter of land, not a single banknote, not the affections of a human being. When all is removed from your possession, you are truly free." So said a wandering dervish, his mouth filled with smoke. Jamsheed was seated next to him in the ruins of Old Naishapur, smoking opium. "Truly?" he said.

"Truly," said the dervish.

"So he who has nothing to lose cannot have anything taken from him."

"He who has nothing is nothing."

"He who has nothing has life. And that can be taken from him."

"He who has nothing and is nothing is truth. And truth cannot be taken away."

"So he does have something!"

"No. It is he. It fixes him to the ground and moves him with the elements."

Jamsheed stared at the dervish, who was now quietly humming to himself. "Who are you?" he said.

"I am a rock. Shaped out of detritus and sediment, unbreakable and impenetrable, formed from centuries of life. Indecipherable, even unto myself. I move with the elements. I dance through time and space. And yet I am ever fixed."

"You are high, my friend. It is the opium talking."

The dervish laughed and took hold of his setar.

Jamsheed asked him, "Will you play a dirge or jubilee?"

"There is no 'or,' only 'and.'"

The dervish broke into a short song in the mode of Shur. Jamsheed leaned into a rock and looked to the bright sky, letting the music wash over him. He had always felt in tune with Persian classical music; the subtleties of the modes, the struggle between emotion and control, held in place until it exploded into full expression. The tension and release comforted him. It was the recognition of what ailed him.

The dervish hopped to his feet, fastening his setar to his back with a tattered lanyard. "A token for the road?"

Jamsheed flicked a coin and the dervish caught it in midair. "Where will you go?"

The dervish looked across the horizon. "Anywhere and everywhere."

"You should take care. Things are getting heated in the streets."

"Things will always be heated in the streets."

"And how will you get by?"

"I will shave my head and shave my beard and act the fool. No one ever suspects the fool."

The dervish laughed and set off through the sand dunes. Jamsheed watched him until he disappeared.

Old Naishapur was a ghost town on the outskirts of the newer city. In the ninth century, it had been the bustling metropolis of Persia, later laid waste by Genghis Khan and his Mongolian army. All that remained was a collection of sand structures that had once been homes, schools, universities, caravansaries, now worn down to prehistoric mounds by time, the elements, and neglect. Under cover of night, thieves had dug out the artifacts of the golden era and sold them on the black market, leaving behind open ditches and holes. Nothing else remained, save an empty Coca-Cola can or candy wrapper here and there. From a distance, in a particular light, one can almost see the city that once stood.

This is where Jamsheed came to smoke his opium and dream his opium dreams.

He was startled awake by a cold breeze that swept into the dunes after sunset. He looked about him. No one was there. His opium pipe had gone out and he could not, for the life of him, remember what day it was, how long he had been asleep, who had been there, or how he fell asleep to begin with. This was how most of his days ended, and began.

The light was sinking fast. A film of dust coated his tongue, but he had no water. A chill ran through his body, not from the cold, but from the sobriety that shook him in tiny fits as he scurried to his motorbike.

The cool air blew into his face, making his nose run. He cut straight down Orchard Road in the dark, the street lit only by the moon that glistened off the melting frost on the trees. His mind went numb. Moving on his motorbike and lying on the ground in an opium haze were the only two states in which he felt himself at ease.

As he neared the town square, he saw a large group gathered near the fountain. He parked his motorbike by one of the entrances. Word had spread through the town that the young man who had killed the merchant's son had turned himself in. People spoke in hushed, secretive tones, describing to one another how he had been accompanied to the police station by the mullah and some followers. The cleric had spoken on his behalf, they said, and explained what had happened. He had not asked the police for leniency on the young man's behalf. He simply asked that he be allowed to wash and pray before his hanging, that he be allowed to wear a white shift, and, most important, that the hanging be public. The young man himself calmly asked that his body be taken to the morgue to be washed and wrapped in linen for a proper Shi'ite burial.

Jamsheed sat on a bench. No one seemed to mention that the young man was so actively participating in the design of his own death. Jamsheed was struck by such faith, a faith so profound that a man was willing to give up his life. Why had he never known such purpose?

That afternoon, the mullah had gathered his most devout followers and escorted the young man to the police station. They all had filed into the police chief's office. The police chief sat at his desk in silence and wrote down the terms and nodded in agreement except for the public hanging. Public execution he would not allow. He asked the young man if he wished to have representation for his court appearance but the young man refused. He had confessed and that was all there was to it. He asked only that his execution be public. The chief looked at the boy for a while before he said, "Why do you wish this?"

"Because I am a martyr."

The police chief sat up straight in his crisp, form-fitting uniform, leaned forward, and said, "You are no martyr. You are a fanatic. And a murderer. And for that you will probably pay with your life. There are no public hangings because we are a civilized society. You will appear in court before a judge who will decide your sentence."

The mullah cleared his throat and asked to speak to the police chief in private. His followers and the young man quietly filed out. He took out his worry beads and leaned into the desk and started flicking them as he said, "It is a busy season for you. I imagine with everything that is transpiring in the capital, it must be a great deal of pressure."

"It is a part of the job. I am certain that things will calm down soon enough."

"Of course. But certainly, you must feel that this is something quite different, no?"

"Haj-Agha, we have been around long enough to have seen it all, uprisings, revolts, usurpations, coups. We are prepared for it all."

"Sometimes a small stone can cripple a giant."

"Not if you have a tank."

The mullah studied the picture of Mohammad Reza Shah Pahlavi that hung above the police chief's head, next to a framed flag—the lion at the center holding a sword, the sun behind it. He looked at the monarch and at the lion for some time, a grin forming as he said, "Let me tell you a story. A true story. It happened sometime before you and I were born, in this very town, not a stone's throw from here."

The Naishapur Zoo had two employees, the zookeeper, a man in his seventies, and his assistant, a man in his eighties. The only animal of note in the zoo was a ten-year-old *Panthera leo persica*. Ousted from his pride by three lionesses that had caught him trying to eat one of their cubs, he had grown up as a starving runt. For several years he attempted to get back into the pride's fold but his own father, the leader, could not forgive such cowardly behavior. The lion became a nomad wandering the sand dunes of Naishapur striking fear into the hearts of the town's inhabitants. At sunset, he often attacked the local livestock, taking a sheep here and there, but was forced back into the dunes by torch-wielding farmers.

One day, the lion walked into the home of a shepherd who had unwittingly left the door open. The lion ate a small block of opium sitting on the kitchen table and passed out on the floor. The shepherd came home that afternoon and saw a lion passed out on his kitchen floor and his opium gone. He looked to the sky and said, "*Allahu Akbar.*"

With the help of his farmhand, the shepherd managed to roll the lion onto a carpet and dragged him to the barn, where he set upon building a cage. Once he was done, his barn became the zoo, the shepherd became the zookeeper, and the farmhand became his faithful assistant.

It was a flush time for the zookeeper. Many of the townspeo-

ple and even some from other towns made the pilgrimage to see
the lion that God had sent to Naishapur—now named Assad'Ullah, or "Lion of God." The spectators sat and watched the beast
pace back and forth, occasionally roaring at them. Children hid
behind their mothers' chadors and men tried to stare him down
through the bars of the cage. The faithful assistant fed him and
cleaned his cage. After a few terrifying and slightly bloody expe-
riences, he learned that a small pinch of opium came in handy
whenever the lion became aggressive.

The fanfare had soon died down. The lion had become old
and decrepit from age, addiction, and confinement. He now spent
most of his days lying in the corner of his cage twitching away
fleas and batting at them with his tail. During feedings, he chewed
listlessly on hunks of ass meat and defecated.

The zookeeper sat next to the cage, leaning his head on a bar.
He looked at the animal and let out a sigh and said, "Ay, Assad'Ullah, how age has dethroned us from our glorious reign."

The faithful assistant sat near him and looked down at the
scars on his hands as he listened to the mournful monologue to
the lion.

"In our days of youth and vigor, how we struck fear into the
hearts of men and life into the loins of women. How with one turning of the head, our bidding was done and our will imposed. Now
we are but a shell of ourselves, a shadow of our desires, shackled to
our carcass. You are the king of kings, they say. You are the master
of your dominion. And yet, there you were that cold cloudy day,
lying in a pool of your own saliva at my feet. *Ay, roozeh gar!*"

This expression of lament and loss was the faithful assistant's
cue to go prepare tea while the zookeeper softly wept and hummed
a tune. For his part, the lion began to audibly snore.

As they drank their tea, the zookeeper looked off to nowhere with squinted eyes. "We need to do something to bring some life back to this place," he said, blowing on his tea.

"Perhaps we can capture some bulbuls and nightingales and sparrows, sir?" said his assistant. "I have seen such colorful birds on the orchard row. They would surely attract a crowd."

"Birds? You want to go from a lion to birds? No. No. No. We need an event. Something exciting that will attract the townspeople again."

"But, sir, remember the last time we had such an event?"

"Ah, yes, the Bee Wars. What a great success that was."

"I was in the hospital for two weeks."

"But a hero for life! Do not fear, my courageous friend. I will think of something even better than a few pesky bees."

"God help me," the assistant muttered under his breath.

Harnessed, mounted, packed, and drafted is how many men spend their lives, as do many animals like the ass. The ass is not admired or worshipped like his cousin the horse. Nor does he proudly gallop into battles. He doesn't run through open meadows and go to sleep at night brushed by groomers. The ass is ridiculed, castrated, and worked day and night. And so he does not spook easily, for he has seen the worst of men already.

In town, there was an old man who owned an equally old ass. The animal was decrepit and had served its purpose. And when the zookeeper offered to buy the animal for a spectacle he called "The War of the Lion and the Ass," the old man agreed. It took an entire day and many sugar cubes to get the ass to walk into the zoo. For a week, the faithful assistant watered and fed him in preparation for the battle. To his surprise, he became quite fond of the animal. He named him Shapur. Naming an animal that close to death was a mistake, he knew. Still, he spent his evenings in the barn speaking to the ass, sharing with him all his tales of wounds and woes.

Each night, he pointed to a scar on his body, and then told Shapur the tale of how the scar came to be. Most of the scars had been inflicted by Assad'Ullah. Shapur seemed unimpressed. "Shapur-jan, for all of my life I have lived in servitude," said the assistant. "And yet I still hope. Is this not the worst of all things?"

He pointed to his hand and continued, "Do you see this one? It was given to me by Assad'Ullah the first time I handed him meat. My friend, we are both burdened with thankless work."

He unbuttoned his shirt and revealed the scars on his chest from the Bee Wars, the last spectacle the zookeeper had organized, once the fervor over the lion had died down. The zookeeper had been convinced that if his faithful assistant split open a beehive with a sword, the bees would be too stunned to notice him grabbing the honeycomb. Such an act would impress the crowd of expectant spectators, each of whom had bought a ticket for three tomans.

He ordered his assistant to don a chain-mail vest and helmet like those of Ta'ziyeh performers.

"This shall be your finest moment, my friend," he said. "I envy you this brave task."

"Then why don't you do it, sir? I hate to rob you of this triumph."

"Oh, no, no, no. I need to set the scene. If it were not so, I should be honored to do it. But, alas, I must defer this great endeavor to you and take the secondary role of the narrator."

The faithful assistant was a whisper of a man. His helmet covered his eyes, and the chain-mail vest dragged him lower and lower, toward the ground. "From the nest of the devil comes the sweetest nectar known to man," the zookeeper said to the crowd. "Today, before your very eyes, this brave man, with the grace of God and Imam Ali's beloved sword, Zolfaghar, will take from the devil that which belongs to man."

The zookeeper picked up his daf drum and began to pound out a rhythm. This was the faithful assistant's cue to run at the hive, whack his sword through the center, and grab the honeycomb.

The faithful assistant took a deep breath, muttered a faint *Bism'Allah*, and with half-closed eyes charged. The hive split in half and the honeycomb crashed to the ground. He bent over to pick it up and that was the last thing he remembered.

Several days later, he awoke in the hospital with a chest so swollen that he could not see his own feet. The zookeeper sat beside him, weeping, and said, "Oh, my dear friend. How I prayed that you would awake. I have never in my life seen such bravery. You are a man among men."

The faithful assistant had no memory of what occurred. But he later heard some whispers around town about how the bees had mistaken the hexagonal shapes of his chain mail for the comb of the beehive and had furiously tried to enter their home, blocked at every turn by his body.

To this day, his chest was covered in scars. "And yet, I still hope," he whispered to Shapur.

News of "The War of the Lion and the Ass" reached as far as Mash'had. At least two hundred were expected. The morning of the performance, the zookeeper ran from one end of the barn to the other, screaming instructions to his faithful assistant, busy outfitting the ass with a lushly woven saddle blanket.

"What are you doing?" said the zookeeper. "I don't think

Assad'Ullah plans on riding your precious animal. Where is your costume? Why haven't you put on your chain-mail vest yet? Where is my drum? Have you seen it? Make sure there are enough pillows in the front row for the children."

As the zookeeper ran around in circles, the faithful assistant slowly set up the barn for the event. He put on his chain-mail vest and removed the saddle blanket, whispering in the ass's ear, "You are in God's hands now, my friend. May he show you more mercy than he has shown me."

The crowds in the square swelled. Whispers floated from group to group. Some believed the ass would be killed instantaneously; others believed that he would put up a fight. A few clandestine bets were placed, the money collected by a young boy who wove through the crowd. A group of old men in the back of the crowd argued the ethics of having such a spectacle, shaking their heads and lamenting the ass's fate.

The zookeeper had hired a few local boys to stand at the entrance and collect fees from the crowd. In exchange they were given free admission. He gathered them in a huddle and warned them, "Be courteous to all of my paying customers."

Then he pulled down the bottom rim of his left eye with his finger, showing the pink underside of his eye to each of them. "I will be watching you," he continued, "and counting heads once everyone is inside, so I will know if a single coin is missing."

The crowd was making its way to the zoo from the square. Families traveled in packs down the road as the young boys weaved through, taking final bets. A jangle of voices, shuffling, and laughter could be heard as they neared the barn.

At the zookeeper's behest, the faithful assistant covered Assad'Ullah's cage with a large blanket, the better to dramatize the showdown of the two animals in the cage once the blanket was removed. In the meantime, he stationed the ass by the cage and pitched him a fresh bale of hay. Shapur stood there staring at him, refusing to eat. The old man's eyes welled up. "Please don't look at me like that," he said. "I am a sensitive man."

As he wiped the tears from his face, he took his place on the other side of the cage and awaited the start of the bloody spectacle.

The townspeople shuffled in and took their places, the children rushing for the front seat cushions, a few dragged into the back of the barn by their mothers. Some of the young men climbed into the hayloft and looked down on the scene with their legs dangling.

Applause erupted as the zookeeper walked out in front of the cage, beating on his daf. He looked at the audience. He stood in total silence. The applause came to a halt and, for a moment, all that could be heard was Assad'Ullah's snoring. A wave of giggles rippled through the audience. The zookeeper looked to the faithful assistant. The assistant happily poked the lion with a rake through the back bars of the cage. The animal growled, hushing the crowd once more. "From the plains of Abadan comes a beast so terrifying that women faint at the sight," announced the zookeeper. "Men shrivel with fear. And children cry at its snarl."

The audience was transfixed by the old man's thunderous voice.

"The king of the jungle. The King of Kings."

The audience let out a collective "ah."

Looking to the ass that stood in front of his untouched bale of hay, the zookeeper continued, "And here is Job. God's beast of burden. Put upon, ridiculed, sacrificed."

The audience let out a collective "oh" and the faithful assistant put his hand over his mouth to muffle his weeping.

The zookeeper ended his monologue with "Ladies and gentlemen, brace yourself for the iron hand of the oppressor as he preys on the weak. It is Nature's law. Only God can reward the weak in the afterlife. In this one, we are all doomed."

He began to pound on his daf and backed away from the cage, nodding to the faithful assistant to lead the ass inside.

The assistant felt his heart pounding through his scarred chest as he walked over to Shapur, took him by the lanyard around his neck, and walked him to the back of the cage, undoing the latch. Just before he took off the lanyard and ushered the animal into Assad'Ullah's den, he caressed the back of his ears, looked into his eyes and smiled, and said, "And yet, I still hope."

Then he closed the latch and yanked the blanket off the cage.

An eerie hush descended over the barn at the sight: a lion stirring awake on one side of the cage, an ass standing motionless and slightly bewildered on the other. The lion began pacing in figure eights, his hackles up, gauging the animal in his territory. A low rumble rose from his diaphragm. He grimaced at the scent of prey. The ass slowly turned his back to the lion and stood motionless. The crowd held its breath.

Without warning the lion lunged at the ass, roaring—just as the ass leaned onto his front haunches and kicked using his back legs with all of his might, sending the lion flying back to his side of the cage. The lion slammed into the bars, rattling the whole structure and landing with a thud. The crowd dropped its mouth collectively. The zookeeper ran to the lion and stuck his hand between the bars of the cage to touch his head. The beast let out a soft purr and then his eyes went blank. His head dropped. He was no longer there.

Someone in the crowd yelled out, "The lion is dead! Long live the ass!"

Outside the barn, the wind had pushed fallen leaves into a whirling frenzy. This was the only sound besides the chants of the crowd. Long live the ass! Long live the ass! *Zendeh-baud Khar!*

The doors of the cage were thrown open. The ass came trotting out with the crowd following behind, cheering and clapping as they marched out of the barn chanting, "Long live the ass! Long live the ass! *Zendeh-baud Khar!*"

The zookeeper sat on the ground beside the cage, holding his head in his hands. There was no one left inside the barn save the faithful assistant who stood behind him with his hand on his shoulder. The solemnity of his voice undercut by the grin on his face, he said, "Perhaps a cup of tea, sir?"

PARIS

III

Shazdehpoor stood behind a news kiosk and watched his friend Trianant across the street at the café. "The War of the Lion and the Ass" had been the first story Shazdehpoor had ever told him, at the exact same table where Trianant now sat. His friend had been so taken with it, he had wanted to know what had happened to the zookeeper and the faithful assistant.

"Well," Shazdehpoor said. "They did get some birds, but the faithful assistant lost his eye in the Hawk Wars a few years later."

Today, Shazdehpoor was more than an hour late for lunch. Trianant had already eaten and was paying his check. As Shazdehpoor watched Trianant leave, he almost waved. He did not like worrying his friend, but what could he say that would excuse his tardiness and appearance. Besides, he was exhausted. He had no words to explain that at all.

Thirty years ago, they had met when Shazdehpoor first arrived in Paris. Trianant had been his waiter. Shazdehpoor's French was still spotty then and he had tried, in vain, to order a well-done hamburger but was given a rare steak frites. Out of propriety, he ate the bloody meat down to the last morsel, controlling his gag reflex as best he could. He had never eaten meat that wasn't thoroughly cooked or cut into tiny portions. He even asked for a wedge of lemon for his sparkling water and used it on the steak, hoping the acid would break down some of the flesh. It did not. It only made it tangy.

Over time, Shazdehpoor took to the romance language—easily adopting the guttural "r" sound. But pronouns proved to be a bit of a challenge, because there were no such gender distinctions as "him" or "her" in the Persian language. He relished telling Trianant just how many words from French had worked their way into the Persian language, such as *merci, toilettes, ascenseur, ananas, chauffage, compote, décolleté,* and *faux col,* and how whole phrases such as "qui est?" were phonetically identical.

Trianant, for his part, liked to talk about unions, strikes, and why mandatory tipping was the only way a Frenchman could serve people. Ever since his retirement, he had invited Shazdehpoor for a weekly lunch, a ritual that Shazdehpoor endured if only to get to the pastries, each delicate hollow center filled with cream or custard, drizzled with chocolate or powdered sugar. *Choux* were a miracle.

His love for his friend also brought him back to the table. It was Trianant who had helped him when he needed it most. Without saying anything, Trianant had noticed how Shazdehpoor's orders had gone from a full meal to just a demitasse. One day, seeing Shazdehpoor doodling in Persian on a napkin, he had suggested Shazdehpoor try selling Persian calligraphy in one of the city squares.

During their weekly lunch, Trianant always ordered for them both, bantering with their waiter, a former apprentice. His order was always the same—two rare steak frites, which Trianant assumed Shazdehpoor adored.

Shazdehpoor could not bear to correct him. He ate the edges of the steak, carving the browned pieces carefully off, but once he got to the bloody flesh of the animal, waves of nausea left him unable to do anything but smile weakly and sip at his water.

He ended each meal by putting his hand to his chest, complaining of heartburn, and offering his plate to Trianant. He watched in horror as the Frenchman cut into the meat, eating it in three consecutive bites, sopping up the juice with mayonnaise and frites.

On one occasion he could not control himself and began to speak about the invention of controlled fire that had begun man's transformation into a civilized being. It was fire that brought us down from the trees. Staring at Trianant's bloody plate, he spoke passionately about fire and cooking. The ease with which one could chew cooked meat, he said, was what reduced the size of human teeth and the time spent digesting. Tribes gathered around fires to cook and tell stories. Clearly, his friend had to understand what he meant.

Busy devouring his frites, Trianant simply smiled and said, "Next week, I'm taking you to a café on Montparnasse for the best steak tartare you've ever had. Then, let us see how you feel about that fire of yours!"

"How delightful," Shazdehpoor said, aware it was his own decorum that caused his suffering. He admired Trianant for the way in which he spoke his mind. If he did not like something, he never hesitated to say so. And if he wanted something, he never hesitated to ask for it.

The first few times, Shazdehpoor had been shocked by his forwardness. Whether it was returning a meal not to his liking or refusing a cup of tea on a visit to Shazdehpoor's apartment.

"Some tea?"

"No, thank you," the Frenchman said.

"I insist."

"No."

"Please, do!"

"I don't want any. But I will take some wine if you have it."

After a while, Shazdehpoor began to envy his friend. Trianant ate what he liked, went where he wanted, leaving if he wished to, and said what was on his mind, even if he was living by his own clock on other people's time. Shazdehpoor was a prisoner of his own propriety. He sat longer than he wished to, held conversations that nearly put him to sleep, and ate meals that made him gag, all in the name of not offending others. It was a cultural chasm that could never be filled. That was not all: he found himself becoming aware of saying things he did not mean at all, things that, if he were to say them where he came from, would be understood clearly.

The first time Trianant came to his home, he fawned over Shazdehpoor's beloved silk hand-woven Persian carpet that lay in the center of the room. Shazdehpoor was so overcome by Trianant's appreciation of the carpet that he graciously offered it to him by saying, "It's nothing. It's yours!"

"Really?"

"Of course! Whatever I have is yours!"

Trianant's eyes lit up as he began to roll the carpet up and thanked his friend for his largesse. Shazdehpoor was so dumb-founded that he did not sleep for several nights. Each time he visited Trianant's home and saw his carpet, he felt a twinge of an-guish rise up in his throat. It lingered there, a black stain on their friendship that only he was aware of. Trianant would always look at the carpet that was now in the study of his home and toast to his friend's generosity.

Their meals at the café always ended with demitasses, after which they languidly sipped while people-watching.

"Did you know that Persians were coffee drinkers before tea drinkers?" Shazdehpoor sometimes mentioned.

"Really? That does come as a surprise."

"Yes. The Russians introduced tea to Iran. They also gave us the samovar. And yet we still call our teahouses 'coffeehouses.'"

"Why abandon coffee for tea?"

"It was popular with the upper classes in the north, especially in the nineteenth century. I suppose more and more people started drinking tea to raise their standing in society."

"But they still drank it in lowly coffeehouses!"

Shazdehpoor, still standing across the street behind the kiosk, watched the afternoon shift change at the café. He was not meet-ing his friend, nor would he be going back for his handcart. He felt heartsick and weary. He had not felt this way in more than three decades. He shook out his legs and began to walk home. He would do his shopping. He would buy his French feta and *barbari* bread. Perhaps some mortadella and a bag of cherries. He would be alone in his room. He would be safe.

BIBI AND AKBAR

Bibi stood in her private bath as the steam from the water filled the tiled room. She looked down at her body, still in fine form for a woman aged fifty-nine, and touched a scar that ran vertically from her navel to the top of her pubis, a thin white sickle that always reminded her of how she had fallen in love with her husband.

At the time, she had been nineteen years old, married already for three years, six months pregnant with her first child. The news about the baby had been a relief. Both families had been anxious about how long it had taken her to conceive a child. She awoke that morning with a cramping in her abdomen. She rubbed her belly and quietly spoke to the baby, as she had been doing from the start. "Settle down. We have some more time to go."

Her husband stirred beside her, and she touched his face. Akbar was a handsome man with honey-green eyes. His composure and position in society kept her in awe of him. Thus far, their marriage had been a formal affair. Even their sex was proper and benign. They had never fought and always addressed each other in proper terms. Each night when they retired to their bedroom, he turned away as she undressed and put on her nightgown, then he lay beside her and asked her permission to be with her.

She looked at him that morning, filled with a respect and compassion that one has for a man of his stature. But not with love.

He started the morning the way he did each day, lying down on the floor to do his exercises. Bibi watched him lunge and push and crunch but said nothing to him of her cramps. When he was finished, he kissed her on the forehead and left the room. Bibi lay back in bed and felt a sudden sharp pain shoot through her abdomen. She stood up. Wetness gushed between her legs. She looked down. She saw blood. She could hear the distant sound of her own voice calling out her husband's name before she lost consciousness and all went black.

She woke up in a strange bed, not knowing what had happened. She put her hand on her belly. It was numb. There was a thick pad between her legs. She sat up to call for her husband, but her cramps were so severe she could only roll up in a ball and whimper. Outside the door, she heard whispers. Her husband's voice. A man. Then footsteps.

As Akbar headed toward her bed, another cramp shot through her body. She began to weep, more from the humiliation and confusion than the pain. He ran to her and sat beside her, putting his hand on her forehead as he said, "I heard you call out this morning and ran back into the room. You were bleeding and unconscious. I brought you here to the hospital and the doctor examined you and said the baby had breached in your womb and must be taken out."

"Is my boy dead?"

"It was a girl," he whispered. He put his lips to her forehead and kept them there as she quietly wept. He was weeping too. She could feel it, but he continued in a calm quiet voice, "The doctor had to take your womb."

A panic rose up in Bibi's chest with such force that it took her breath away. She struggled to breathe and to contain the terror inside her. A barren young wife was a fate worse than the mother of a dead, unborn child. Akbar wrapped his arms around her and held tight. It was of no comfort to her. She could not move, speak, or feel anything.

She healed quickly from the surgery but the fear of her predicament didn't allow her to grieve for her unborn child. She went back to her usual duties of keeping her household running, cooking for her husband and her parents, who still lived in the orchard, and never once discussing what had happened. Her mother did bring up the possibility of her husband taking a second wife who could bear children, which was the only time that Bibi felt her fear rise to the surface. But she took a deep breath and ignored the woman.

One afternoon, not long before his unexpected death, Akbar's father, who was always called by the honorific title of Haj-Agha, paid a visit to the house for tea. Just as he had when he had brought his son to ask for Bibi's hand, he fawned over the expensive décor. Then he lavished praise on Bibi, who could hear his insincere tone all the way from the kitchen. When she walked back into the living room to serve tea, she listened as Haj-Agha spoke about the possibilities for a second wife for his son. He had a few young ladies in mind, from good families who would be appropriate for the role. But of course none of them would ever match Bibi-Khanoom in beauty and grace. He also spoke of how helpful the new wife would be around the house. He was a very practical man.

Bibi felt her hands shaking as she bent down with the tray in front of him. He took a glass of tea and a sugar cube and continued to speak. She served tea to her parents and her husband, not looking any of them in the eye, and went back into the kitchen, pacing in circles to dissipate her anger. She did not come out again until she heard her father-in-law leaving, and then only nodding farewell from a safe distance.

The family sat in silence during dinner that night. When Bibi had finished her work in the kitchen, she turned out the lights and went into her room to get ready for bed. Her husband was already there, waiting up for her. He turned his gaze away as she undressed and slipped beneath the covers, turning her head away and wishing him a good night. After a few moments of silence, he said, "We are not animals to be bred like cattle. I have made a commitment to you and I will honor it. It is not your fault that this has come to pass. And if we are to be childless, then so be it. Let the old man live with that. He drove my mother to an early grave, I will not let him drive my wife to hers."

Bibi broke down and wept in his arms. "My baby is dead," she whispered as he held her. Not until this very moment did Akbar realize that his wife had forbidden herself to feel the full weight of her loss. She had been held hostage by her fear and the society that had caused that fear. Setting her free gave him no solace. What if he had been like his father? What would have become of her?

For four decades, they lived as equals. They traveled throughout the country. They spent hours alone together in the most intimate of silences. They held Shazdehpoor and Saba's wedding in the orchard and let Jamsheed and Madjid run wild through its wilderness. They looked after the young boys after the death of their mother and gave solace to Shazdehpoor as he mourned in solitude. They looked after Nasreen whenever her mother's rages broke down the girl. They took in Mirza and put him in charge of the gardens and trees. They endured the mullah's lectures and made sure he was welcomed to lunch every Friday. And when the midwife told them of a baby being born to a mother who did not want him, Bibi and Akbar brought a child into their home.

Their orchard was filled with broken lives, stunted lives, lost and half-formed lives. But lives nonetheless. Within the four walls of their land, they had made a home that sheltered people without judgment or fear, that allowed for both silence and song.

After Bibi finished her bath, she went into the bedroom and slipped beneath the covers next to her husband. He was reading the day's paper.

"What are you reading?" she asked.

"That young man who killed the merchant's son was hanged this morning," he said.

"God rest their souls," said Bibi.

"There was rioting. My brother organized it."

Bibi felt a twinge of guilt. She had never told her husband about walking to school with Habib when she was a young girl or the hopeful strides he had taken alongside her. "He is playing God with people's lives," she said.

Akbar thought about his brother. His pained childhood, their father's indifference, the fate of their mothers, the daily slights and humiliations—all these moments like a thousand paper cuts that had finally bled his brother's heart dry. "He is a broken man," he said. "And broken men only know their own suffering."

Bibi laid her head on his chest and said, "We have a good life here, Akbar. I thank God for that every day."

"Yes. Within these four walls. But there is a world outside."

"I'm afraid for our family. I don't want our way of life to end."

Akbar put his paper down and rubbed his eyes. He turned off the lights and slipped beneath the covers. In the cover of darkness, he spoke in a half-whisper. "Everything must come to an end, my love."

THE SERMON AND
THE SOLILOQUY

Madjid stared at the picture in the newspaper of the young man who had been hanged. He had met him several years ago at the mosque. His name was Mahmoodreza. Madjid, like many of the young men from his school, used to spend time at the mosque, not only for prayer but also to engage in debates. It was only when the question of politics arose that certain tensions escalated. Mahmoodreza's calls to action for national autonomy inspired Madjid greatly but he found it difficult to square religious fervor with individual freedom.

Madjid fasted for the month of Ramadan but he also enjoyed his wine with Mirza. He planned on marrying the woman he loved, but he also wished to be with her intimately before that day. On Fridays, he sat in on the mullah's sermons, much to his father's disappointment. His father feared that Madjid might become religious, which for him was worse than his son being an addict. But Madjid saw through his father's prejudice and ignored him. Even though he would never say it aloud, he, too, thought of his father as a *fokoli*. He never relied on him for his judgment about serious matters.

On some Fridays, he accompanied the mullah to the family lunch after service. He asked the mullah questions on their walks from the mosque to the orchard. The two had grown close. The mullah's sermons were often about the dignity of man, his service to God, and his compassion for his fellow human beings. Madjid did not particularly believe in God, but he did believe in the ideas that stemmed from this devotion.

There was one particular sermon Madjid found very moving. It was about the Prophet's muezzin, Bilal ibn Rabah, an Ethiopian slave whom the Prophet had freed and had made the voice of his faith by calling his followers to prayer.

On the walk to the orchard that day, Madjid had been very excited to speak about the sermon. "Do you believe that all men are equal?" he asked the mullah.

"The Prophet says that, before God, all men are the same."

"What about women?"

The mullah was taken aback. "What about them?"

"Are they not equal?"

"We have different places in this world. It is our responsibility to protect women."

"Protect them from what?"

"From the evils of this world."

Madjid had fallen silent. The mullah took this as acceptance, and continued to speak: "Women have the capacity to bring life into this world. Without them we would not exist. Our mothers. Our sisters. Our daughters. It is our responsibility to protect them. Even from themselves if need be. So you see, in a way, they are more important than we are."

"Then why is the weight of their word half of ours? Why are their rights half of ours?"

The mullah stopped walking. "What are you getting at, boy?"

"Nothing, Haj-Agha," said Madjid. "I just want to understand why women are not equal to men."

"There is nothing to understand. Women are the weaker sex and it is our duty to protect them."

The mullah's reply was the first time Madjid began to question his authority. After that day, he began to turn to his books for answers and eventually stopped going to Friday prayers altogether.

Madjid stared at the article that accompanied the picture of Mahmoodreza. He read the mullah's words about "martyrdom," "social inequality," and "justice." On the surface, these words sounded noble and righteous but Madjid knew Mahmoodreza. He had watched the other young man, Ardesheer, die in the square. They were not ideas and symbols for a cause but real human lives, ended before they had been lived.

He headed out of the house. The streets were quiet. He walked briskly by the side of the road that led to the mosque. The townsfolk had gathered to mark the third day after Mahmoodreza's hanging. The days of mourning came in increments of three, seven, and forty days. This was the first part of that trinity.

Madjid stepped into the mosque, took off his shoes, and entered the main hall without performing ablutions. It had been a long time since he had been there. The pungent smell of body odor mingled with that of rosewater. He covered his mouth with his sleeve as he walked to the back and took a seat. In all the years he had attended Friday prayers, he had never before noticed this smell.

The main hall was filled with mourners. The men sat on one side and the women on the other, separated by a black sheet. The sounds of talking, weeping, and praying bounced off the mosque's high domed ceiling. Mahmoodreza's mother sat up front, bent over and covered by her chador as she wept. The women beside her held on to her and rocked with her. Every few minutes she would look up and wail "my child, my child, my child" as she beat her head.

The mullah sat with Mahmoodreza's father and male family members. He rhythmically flipped his worry beads and spoke quietly into the ear of the dead young man's father. Then he stood and turned to the congregation. Everyone hushed as he walked up to the platform, climbed the seven steps of the *mambar*, and sat, looking down on the mourners.

Without warning, he began to speak in a quiet, almost private tone, not looking up from his worry beads.

"Three days ago," he said, letting the words ring out in the mosque. "Three days ago I sat inside a prison cell with a young man facing his death. I am a believer as you all are. I know, as you know, that he is in Paradise, where we all hope to one day be. I know this as you know. I rejoice in this as you do. But three days ago, I sat before a conscious man, facing the most difficult task in his short life. You can only truly know what a man is made of when he faces the greatest adversity of his life. Who is he? What does he believe? And does he have the will to give his final breath for that principle?"

He stopped flicking his worry beads and looked up at the congregation, his eyes shining. "Three days ago I sat in a prison cell across from this young man and he answered all of these questions for me. We sat there in the silence of prayer. The guards came to his cell and tapped on the bars. He opened his eyes and looked out his small window and began to speak: 'God has given us a beautiful world,' he said. 'God has given us a sun so that we may see and a moon so that we may contemplate, an earth to stand upon, a sky to look to, fire to keep us warm in the cold, and water to cool us in the heat. God is truly great.' Then he stood up and turned to face me. 'I stand before you a man condemned to death,' he said. 'I have nothing left in this world. There are those here who do not believe; those here who desecrate this gift of life that we are given. Those who force us to abandon our dignity and faith. We struggle against them. We perish in the fight. And yet I say that the greatest struggle of all is the one against myself.' He embraced me and was led by the guards to the courtyard. He stood on a barrel with a noose around his neck and the final words he spoke, before the barrel was kicked from beneath his feet, were '*Allahu Akbar.*'"

The cleric put the tail of his *aba* to his face and began to weep.

A slowly rising tide of "*Allahu Akbar*" began to swell across the mosque. Louder and louder, the chant was repeated, and Madjid felt himself sinking where he sat. The sheer force of the voices, the emotion of solidarity took his breath away. The mullah looked out into the crowd. His tears had dried and his face looked triumphant. Madjid stared at this man he had known all his life and did not recognize him. He stood up and ran for the door, stumbling as he put on his shoes.

Outside, he walked away from the mosque, not looking back. He did not know where he was going, he knew only from where he wanted to escape. He walked without rest until he reached the sand dunes, and in the silence of the wind, he slowed his pace and felt, finally, calmer. Mahmoodreza's final thoughts ran through his brain. The war within. The hardest battle of all.

The distant sound of goat bells blew in the wind. Crows cawed high in the sky. He watched the sun begin to set, bringing with it a slight chill. He missed Nasreen. He needed her, even if he didn't understand why.

He began to run toward her house. Wildly. Almost losing his way.

Still breathing heavily, he snuck into the garden. The light was on in her father's tailor shop and she was sitting by the window, weaving lace. Weaving lace, she told him, was like meditation. As he got closer, he could hear her humming.

He watched her for a while in the dark, his thoughts falling away as he focused on the tension in her delicate fingers, her soft skin the color of raw milk. What else was there but this? What use were lofty ideas in a world run by hypocrites and murderers? The touch of her hand was the truest thing he knew.

Madjid tapped softly on the window, but still he startled her. She jumped from her seat and ran to open the door. "Where have you been?" she said. "Your father was very worried when you didn't show up for lunch. Everyone was very worried."

She crossed her arms. Then let out a sigh. "I was worried."

He stared at her, smiling at her show of concern.

She leaned in and whispered softly, "What is it? Are you all right?"

"Marry me," he said.

She put her fingers on his lips.

"Marry me," he said as he moved her hand and laid it over his heart.

SABA

adjid's mother, Saba, had died four years earlier. Madjid was fourteen at the time and Jamsheed sixteen. Jamsheed disappeared immediately after the burial, leaving Shazdehpoor and Madjid alone.

During the mourning rituals that followed, the father and son walked like ghosts through the house. The shared living spaces began to fall into disarray. Dishes piled up in the sink and unwashed clothes lay about collecting dust. Each retreated—Shazdehpoor to his radio and Madjid to his books. Shazdehpoor could not bear to sleep in the room he had shared with his wife. He took to sleeping in his salon, emerging only to take meals with his son in silence, meals brought in by the women of the town.

After the rituals had ended, Bibi-Khanoom and Ghamar descended upon the Shazdehpoor household like Bolshevik street sweepers with Nasreen and Jafar in tow. They sent the father and son off to the orchard and set upon cleaning.

Bibi-Khanoom took command of the kitchen, emptying the cupboards and refrigerator, wiping down the shelves and rearranging the items. She added pickled eggplants, peach compote, and sour cherry jam to their pantry. Jafar stood near her, motionless, staring at her. She finally gave him a bag of marinated sour cherries and sent him off. Beneath the kitchen sink she saw a plastic basin protruding. She pulled it out. Inside were pieces of moldy hard bread. She emptied the basin and washed it out.

Saba had always kept that basin beneath the sink. She filled it up throughout the week with leftover bread from the family's breakfast. On Fridays at noon, she emptied it into a bag and placed it outside the backyard door with a bottle of milk. Someone whom she never saw, someone in need, took the offering and soaked the dried bread in milk for a hearty meal—always returning the empty washed milk bottle to the door. Saba had died on a Thursday night and the basin, which no one knew about save her, remained untouched, the bread growing thick with mold. Only the stranger who came to the door that Friday and found nothing on the doorstep realized what had happened.

Ghamar tore through the house, sucking her teeth and muttering under her breath. Clothes were strewn everywhere, beds unmade, tea-stained cups and pistachio shells in all the corners. When she finally stopped stomping and stood still, she did a full visual sweep of the living room and said to herself, "Men. One should sooner let a dog into her home."

She rolled up her sleeves and got to work, collecting the garbage in a bag and making a pile of clothes by the washing machine in the hall that led to the backyard. She saw one of Saba's housedresses on the floor. She picked it up and held it over her face as she wept.

Jafar stood in the living room doorway staring at her while he ate his sour cherries, the tartness of which made his left eye twitch. He spat the pits into his hand and put them in his pocket. She stopped for a moment and stared back at him, wiping her tears.

He held out his bag of sour cherries to her and smiled, his fat cheeks dimpling. She took a handful and pinched his cheek.

Nasreen quietly made a beeline for Madjid's room. She had never been inside it before. It was musty and cluttered, littered with newspaper clippings and dirty clothes. She walked around studying his books, the only things in the room with any semblance of order. She did not know any of the titles or covers. She ran her hand over a pile of clothes in the corner of the room, picking up a shirt and holding it to her face as she inhaled. It smelled of soap and sweat. And him. Masculine. Grassy.

To her surprise, she liked it. She smelled it again and held the shirt to her and sat on his bed. Who was Madjid? She had known him all his life, and still he was a mystery to her. On his desk there lay a notebook. She opened it. She did not so much read what he had written as study his handwriting, running her fingers over the letters and words. Some passages were cramped and furiously written. Some bore a carefully flourished, almost calligraphic precision. She did not notice the shift in perspective as the pages progressed. The distant "them" gave way to the collective "we," the lament of "you" to the inner "I."

At the back were drawings. Ballpoint-pen sketches of men exercising in *zoorkhanehs*, lifting heavy *meels* and chains. They were two-dimensional. A novice trying to arrest bodies in motion. Several pages were of the sand dunes, done in pencil and charcoal. These were more assured and seemed in line with the hand that had made them. On one page there were cubist-style drawings of women's breasts in thick black ink. No head or torso, just nippled breasts, of varying shapes and sizes, suspended in white space, cartoonish and grotesque. She laughed out loud and quickly covered her mouth so as not to be heard by her mother. Covering the entire page was another drawing in thick black ink. Her smile disappeared as she stared at it, trying to make out what it was. It was four black curved lines like two sets of parentheses, a black slit in the center and, at the bottom where the curved lines met, a jagged line cut through them, like a tear, red and violent, with short horizontal black lines running through it like stitches on a wound. The brutality of the drawing frightened her. She quickly flipped past the page.

There were fragmented scribbles and random sketches and finally, tucked in the back, was a photograph of Madjid's mother. It had to have been taken when Saba was no more than fifteen. The picture was pearly black and white. Saba's hair was perfectly coiffed, her hands folded demurely. She gazed just beneath the camera's eye, as to avoid being looked at. The likeness of her face to Madjid's startled Nasreen. In all the years that she had known this family, she had never noticed her. Only in death had she truly seen her. Behind the photograph, on the page, she saw that Madjid had written a letter to his mother dated the day after her burial. Nasreen walked over to the door, closed it quietly, and began to read.

Maman-jan,

It is unusually warm today and very sunny for this time of year. I woke before father and made breakfast as best I could. I tried very hard to remember how you prepared it. It will take some getting used to but I am sure it will work itself out.

It is amazing how resourceful men can be when they are hungry.

Your son,

Madjid

She flipped the page and there was another letter, and another and another. Each day the boy had written a letter to his mother. They were all cordial, brief, and matter of fact, describing the days as they had passed. He told his mother of her funeral and the mourning rituals on the third, seventh, and fortieth days. He told her who had attended and gave a list of the food brought to the house and by whom, with a critical review of the dishes. The only signs of emotion in them were the occasional smudges of ink from what might have been the boy's tears. But there was not a word to attest to his sadness. The letters stopped on the fortieth day with a short, polite farewell, signed in his full name, Madjid Shazdehpoor.

Up to this point, she had known Madjid only from a distance. He had struck her as a serious, cold, and fidgety boy. In fact, it had always been in Jamsheed's presence that she blushed. Jamsheed was the charming one who flirted with her, at times making her uncomfortable. At family gatherings, he would always go out of his way to compliment her dress or shoes, coming too close to her arm or body. But not Madjid. He kept to himself and would cast down his eyes when he spoke to her, and then only brought up subjects such as the hierarchy of ants or Khayyam's philosophical theory of mathematical order. She smelled his shirt one more time.

From the hallway, her mother was calling her name. She jumped up and dropped the shirt. "What are you doing?" said

Ghamar, standing in the doorway with her hands on her hips. "Go get the broom from the hallway closet. Start in the living room."

Nasreen marched down the hall.

"While you are sweeping Madjid's room," said her mother, "make sure you leave the door open."

Ghamar threw the shirt back onto the pile of dirty laundry, then made her way to the master bedroom. Bibi-Khanoom was already there, sitting on the floor surrounded by a pile of Saba's clothes and chadors that she had pulled out of her closet. Ghamar could see that she had been crying and sat down next to her. She started to fold the clothes and make piles of shirts, skirts, and chadors. She spoke in a brisk, almost happy tone as she said, "What are we to do with all of these? I can tell you one thing. I have a long list of women that will never get their hands on sweet Saba's silks. Especially Sekeneh. That woman is a beast. I would sooner burn these than let her get those greasy fat fingers on them. She would probably sell them, anyway. Oh, and that ignorant smile of hers. What kind of a woman smiles when she's missing three teeth? I think she's a Gypsy. She says she's from Mash'had but no one from Mash'had would smile with missing teeth, not even children of first cousins."

Ghamar's brash diatribe comforted Bibi-Khanoom. Ghamar always knew how to pull her from the darkest depths, back up to the surface where it was safe.

"And Bibi-jan, that little boy of yours is very strange. Did you know he puts the cherry pits in his pockets?"

"Yes, but it seems to comfort him."

The two women laughed as they continued to put Saba's life away and the Shazdehpoor house in order.

MEN

In the orchard, Madjid crouched by a tree watching an ant colony. He was reading a book on the social structures of animals. He flipped to the chapter about ants, then watched the soldiers march out of the hole in perfect formation. Each carried a tiny bit of dirt in its mandibles, which it deposited next to the entrance, only to turn around without resting and return to the hole to bring up more. He had read this book several times and knew that the queen ant lived inside that hole. She had mated with a male that died as soon as it had inseminated her, detached her wings, and started this entire colony. She was not the head of the colony, just another member of the society. Each insect played its part in the service of all. The egalitarian quality of the ant hierarchy fascinated him. The more Madjid looked at nature, the more excited he was to be in the world. He could hear his father calling his name. He reluctantly closed his book and went to join the men.

Shazdehpoor sat with Akbar-Agha and Mohammad under his tree, taking tea in silence. Knowing Ghamar would be occupied all day with Bibi-Khanoom and the kids at Shazdehpoor's house, Mohammad had closed his shop early, humming, hardly able to contain his glee at this short window of freedom.

Akbar-Agha smiled as he sipped his tea and with a knowing nod to Mohammad said, "So, Shazdehpoor, our wives have thrown you out of your home."

"Yes, sir. We didn't have much choice in the matter."

Mohammad let out a sigh and said, "Are you under the impression that we have ever had one?"

The three men laughed. Madjid paid no mind to them as he buried his head in his book.

Wind blew through the orchard, shaking the trees, along with the scent of pears and plums. Crickets chirred. Bees droned. Finches called and starlings darted from tree to tree, fleeing the threatening cawing of crows. So constant was this melodic drama in the orchard that it faded into the background, unheard.

The three men looked at one another. It was as though they were students in a classroom the teacher had just walked out of. A devilish grin formed on Akbar-Agha's face as he sprang from his seat and went straight to the kitchen, where Mirza was busy washing vegetables. "Mirza-jan," he said. "We need some yogurt and cucumbers."

Mirza's face lit up as he joined in the conspiracy. "Yes, sir!"

Akbar-Agha sifted through the cupboards, taking out a jar of pistachios and inspecting them. They were roasted. He turned to Mirza and said, "Do we have any raw ones?"

"Yes, sir!"

Mirza grabbed a bag of raw pistachios from the cupboard

beneath the sink and dumped them in a bowl. He continued to peel the cucumbers, dicing and adding them to the yogurt, which he then salted, peppered, and covered in dried mint, mixing it all together. With the two bowls in hand, he headed out to the deck.

Akbar-Agha stood at the counter, rolling up his sleeves. He took a bowl of ground lamb out of the refrigerator. He grated a raw onion into the bowl, his eyes reddening, and added turmeric and salt. With his hand, he churned the mixture, then dipped the hand in warm water before taking a handful, rolling it into a ball, and gently slapping it onto a flat skewer as he sculpted it around the metal spear, creating wedges in the meat with his thumb.

When he'd made several dozen skewers, he carried them out to the deck, where Mirza was already fanning the coals in the fire pit with a corrugated piece of cardboard. "Gentlemen," said Akbar-Agha, "follow me."

Madjid, Mohammad, and Shazdehpoor followed Akbar-Agha to his bedroom, where he gave each of them a pair of pantaloons.

The men gathered around a small *sofreh* on the deck, free to move comfortably in the loose cotton pants. Mohammad lay on his side, languidly flicking his worry beads. Shazdehpoor leaned back on his elbows and tilted his head up to the sun. He stretched his spindly legs and relished the freedom of the pantaloons. Madjid sat next to Akbar-Agha and copied his stance—one knee up, his elbow resting on it.

Akbar-Agha noticed and said with a smile, "What were you doing over by the pear tree?"

Madjid blushed. "I was just watching an ant colony. They seem to have a very harmonious existence."

"They engage in warfare, you know?"

"Really?"

"Their tactics are very similar to our own species. I have a book by Maeterlinck on the life of an ant that I will give you."

Madjid's conversations with Akbar-Agha were very different from the ones he had with the mullah. Akbar-Agha always answered his questions with new subjects to explore or study.

Mirza brought over the steaming kebabs laid out on a platter lined with flat bread, surrounded by charred tomatoes and onions. Then he returned with a platter of fresh parsley, tarragon, radishes and scallions, a block of feta cheese, a bowl of sumac, and extra bread.

From the shed in the back of the house, Akbar-Agha returned with a basin and presented it to the group. All the men looked on in awe. Inside the basin was a bottle of vodka, half-submerged in ice. He set the frosted vodka bottle on the *sofreh*. Mirza brought over shot glasses and Akbar-Agha poured, the cold vapor rising off the glasses like smoke.

Each man took a glass and held it up, except Madjid. He looked on with his eyes open wide. His father turned to him. "Go ahead," he said.

Madjid raised his glass and Akbar-Agha toasted to their health, *besalamati*, as each threw back his shot and chased it with a spoonful of the cucumber yogurt. They dug into the meal, Akbar-Agha passing out pieces of the flat bread from underneath the kebab and refilling the shots at rhythmic intervals.

The alcohol began to take hold of them, loosening their minds. Mirza brought out his dombak and leaned on it. Akbar-Agha unfolded an intricately carved wooden bookstand and opened up the Divan of Hafez. He ran his fingers along the book's edge with his eyes closed and opened to a random page, flipping back to the beginning of a poem, and set it down on the bookstand. Then he read, addressing each poem to each man as though he were a seer. Madjid, being so young, was often moved by the music of the language, never fully understanding the subjects of the poems. But today the words spoke directly to him. "Grieve neither at existence nor at nonexistence," Akbar-Agha read to him from Hafez. "Be thy mind, happy. For the end of every perfection that is . . . is non-existence."

Akbar-Agha brought his reading to an end by singing out the first line of a bawdy folk song. On his drum, Mirza added a jubilant rhythm and the men joined in for the chorus, a homage to the beauty of a woman's geography.

After the musical interlude, Mirza brought out the tea service. Akbar-Agha took a sugar cube and dipped it into his tea and watched the liquid infuse the hard white cube. He held the cube between his teeth and sipped his tea through it, lost in thought. "Is there a reason why you dip your cube in the tea?" said Madjid.

"There is a reason for everything, young man."

"What is it?"

"It is a true story. It happened in this very town, just a stone's throw from here. Before you and I were born."

The Imperial Sugar Company of Persia was located on the outskirts of Naishapur. There, three European brothers purchased the land for a pittance from a native farmer who had spent the better part of his life and earnings trying, in vain, to keep his sugar beets in bloom. The brothers took control of the farm with the promise of profit sharing, once the mill was built and operational. The farmer used the money from the sale to buy a modest home in town for his wife and children. But in one year's time he fell destitute when the brothers informed him that there was no profit yet to share.

At last, he came seeking work at the sugar mill that had been erected on the land he used to own, where there was now a flourishing sugar beet farm complete with irrigation.

He was given a job on the production line. His duties consisted of, but were not limited to, standing at the conveyor belt, stamping the boxes of sugar cubes that passed before him in an unending procession with a red-ink mark that read, "Made in Naishapur." He stood there from seven o'clock in the morning until twelve noon, taking thirty minutes for lunch, which he ate outside the factory with the other Persian workers, none of whom were allowed inside the mess hall, at the entrance of which a sign read, "No dogs or Persians allowed."

He returned to the line at twelve thirty, forbidden to take a siesta, and stood on the line exhausted until seven in the evening, at which point he left the mill for home. The walk was long, but the buses in Naishapur were now separated into "Persian" and "European." During the oppressively hot summer, he sometimes waited for more than an hour as several buses for Europeans stopped and continued on, sometimes carrying only one or two people. The Persian buses never appeared. After a few months, he moved into a shanty settlement the three brothers had built within walking distance to the mill, which was simply known as "the sugarhouse."

The brothers hailed from Wallonia, a region in Belgium where the language spoken, Walloon, belonged to the *langues d'oïl*, of which French is the most prominent. Wallonia was at the forefront of the Industrial Revolution and rich in coal mines, blast furnaces, and factories for steel, glass, iron, zinc, wool, and weapons. The brothers owned and operated a textile factory but had to shut down their operations after the Luddite rebellion—which had started in England—broke out in Wallonia. The brothers decided to move to a region that had yet to be industrialized and begin over again. They chose Persia in the hopes that the more mystical-tempered Orientals would be less inclined to fight the machine, and besides, the sugar was already there and the government had invited them to come and cultivate it.

They purchased three orchards for their own families and hired natives to cook, clean, and keep the gardens. They had studied the local flora and fauna and adapted it to their manicured European gardening style. One wife purchased several lambs from a local farmer and had their wool dyed in soft hues of green, pink, and blue, allowing them to roam the grounds during the week of Easter. During her holiday celebrations, as the traditional Persian tea service was passed around by the ghostly gloved hands of the help, the women clapped and tittered with delight as the pastel-colored sheep passed by on the lawns.

The wife that had purchased the sheep was considered the most adventurous of the group, and made many excursions into town. She scoured local shops for trade secrets, always carrying small hard candies to give to the native children who learned to congregate around her. From the shopkeepers, she had discovered that putting cucumber peel on the face cools and calms the skin. Every day during the lunch preparation, she instructed the help to prepare a salad for her face as she lay out on the lawn.

The other wives followed suit, marveling at their friend's ingenuity as she modestly clasped her hands and said with a high honeyed laugh, "When in Rome, ladies. When in Rome."

They often traveled back home with trunks full of local fabrics they had tailored in the latest fashions. Their children were schooled by tutors brought from their home countries until they reached the appropriate age to be sent off to boarding schools in Europe, entrance to the most prestigious of which would be cause for celebration by the parents of said child, and envy and anxiety by the parents of the others.

The sugar that the mill refined, dried, and cubed was unlike any the natives had ever seen. The whiteness of each crystal was so white, it almost shone blue. The cut of the cube was so sharp and precise, it rivaled the blade of a knife. These two improvements were made possible by the machinery that the brothers had shipped from Europe: batch vacuum pans standing thirty feet high and continuous sugar centrifuges that hummed through the mill. There had been a few unfortunate sugar dust explosions that had taken the lives of several native workers, badly burning a few others, but the families of the deceased were compensated generously and the injured ministered to medically.

Because of their beauty, the mill produced the most coveted cubes in Naishapur. Many local families stocked them for the tea service, using them only for special guests due to their high cost. In private, they used the discolored, jagged ones made by local artisans who were all but put out of business by the Europeans.

The exotic, distant origins of the sugar cubes made them a novelty in Europe. High-society families purchased them for entertainment. Usually the lady of the house brought out the box and, after showing it to guests, demonstrated how the Persians drank their tea with their sugar cubes held between their teeth, as the guests gasped in delight and admired their hostess's effortless intercontinental charm.

The three brothers were making profit, hand over fist, with their little factory in the middle of nowhere in the middle of the

East. In gestures of goodwill and grace they honored most of the native holidays. They sent the families of the workers several boxes of complimentary sugar cubes for birthdays, anniversaries, and promotions.

The man who had owned the factory land was informed that, unfortunately, there still was no profit to share since new machinery had to be purchased to keep up with high demand. After a year's worth of good service, he was promoted to the job of overseer of the belt he manned. His duties now consisted of standing at the end of the conveyer belt, staring at the men who stood staring at the boxes they stamped. It was a better-paid position, one that came with a crisp white lab coat to wear. But time seemed to move more slowly. Each day, that hour after lunch when he longed for a siesta—but was forbidden to take one—felt harder to endure. He sucked on sugar cubes to keep his eyes open. His requests to learn how the machinery worked were always met with a stern yet delicate refusal, by the foreman, alluding to his safety and well-being.

Each Friday the factory workers were given their pay and their day off. They gathered in front of the sugarhouse, in their pantaloons and woven shoes with the backs flattened by their heels. Each man carried his worry beads. Collectively they headed to town to attend Friday prayers, smoke *ghelyans* in the town square, and visit with family, occasionally discussing financial obligations that could never seem to be met. The morning's activities were followed by a proper lunch and a proper siesta, the only time their sleep was undisturbed by the mill's constant industrial hum.

After the third sugar dust explosion, several of the workers, including the land's original owner, Ali-Agha, formed a queue at a local government office to file a complaint. After several hours they found themselves standing in front of a clerk's desk. Ali-Agha

represented the group, speaking eloquently about the unsafe practices at the plant, the unsanitary quarters in the shantytown, and
the unlivable wages. Wrapping up his speech, he requested that
the government hold the owners of the mill accountable for their
fiduciary responsibilities to their workers. The clerk wrote out the
demands laid before him, had Ali-Agha sign the document, and
stamped it with the official Imperial insignia.

The following week, Ali-Agha was relieved of his duties at the
mill. Another man on the line was given the crisp white lab coat
and stationed at the head of the belt. Ali-Agha packed his few belongings and walked away from the sugarhouse, the sound of the
industrial hum fading as he entered the sand dunes.

He had sold his land to Europeans for profits that never ma-
terialized. He had filed his grievances with a local government
who answered to a monarchy in business with the Europeans. He
looked at the ground beneath his feet. He watched the wind blow
sand circles around his woven sandals. He had been born on this
land, as his father had and his father's father and so on and so on.
The mill, the sugarhouse, the old city, the bustling square where
his wife and children were waiting for his paycheck were all miles
behind him. On this day in February in the year 1890, also known
as the month of Esfand in the year 1268, Ali-Agha realized that he
had, for all intents and purposes, by powers both East and West,
been exiled from his homeland. There was only one place left for
him to go.

Ali-Agha pushed open the large arched wooden doors of the
mosque and stepped inside, taking off his shoes and socks and
stopping at the ablution fountain to wash before entering the hall.
Shafts of sunlight beamed through the geometric carvings in the
dome. Footsteps echoed behind rows of massive columns. Not a

soul was in sight. He walked into the prayer hall and knelt, taking a deep breath and closing his eyes before placing his forehead on the ground to pray. He mouthed the words by rote, then sat back. He had been inside this mosque on many Fridays but never had he been alone and never had he felt so small beside the symmetrical rows of columns and beneath the grand chandelier.

Ali-Agha looked up at the curved ceiling made up of stalactite tilework, each curved tile intricately painted with the interior of a miniature mosque. He imagined the hundreds of hands that painted the calligraphy and geometric designs over the vast stretches of cobalt blue and turquoise. He yearned for that unity, that brotherhood, that sanctuary. He longed for the dignity of belonging.

"It is a thing of beauty," said a voice behind him.

Ali-Agha turned around and standing before him, admiring the wall, was an old man in an *aba* with a book and worry beads clasped in his hands. It was the cleric of the mosque, whom he had heard speak many times at Friday prayers. This close up, he did not immediately recognize his face or voice. "Yes," he said, "it truly is."

The old man looked at Ali-Agha, who had cast down his head with his eyes closed. "What is weighing so heavily on you?" he said.

"I have lost my land. I have lost my means. And I will lose my family. I left my dignity somewhere. I don't know where. I have nothing. I have nowhere."

The cleric flicked his worry beads and fell into thought. Ali-Agha looked at him, hoping for some words of comfort. "Well," said the old man. "We must find your dignity. Once you have that, all else will be restored."

The following day, Ali-Agha sat upfront for Friday prayers, watching the cleric climb onto the *mambar*. The congregants fell silent. The cleric found Ali-Agha in the crowd and spoke slowly and forcefully, filling the mosque with his resonant voice. "Money?" he said. "Power? Property? Status? Family? What do any of these things profit a man who has lost his dignity?"

He cleared his throat, then continued. "A man can lose his fortune. He can fall from power. His home can be destroyed, his position ruined, his family taken from him. But if he has his dignity, he loses nothing. If he has his dignity, he is in a state of grace. For dignity is given to us by God. Dignity can only be taken from us if we give it of our own free will."

He reached into the pocket of his *ghaba* and held forth a sugar cube. "Each of you take this *ghand* with your tea every day. Each of you make your way to the market and purchase it in boxes that say 'Made in Naishapur.' But who profits from this sale? Foreigners, non-Muslims, who spit on your customs and beliefs. They pilfer our resources and subjugate our people, and force them to work in dangerous conditions. How many families of the dead have I consoled within these walls? These Europeans put us in the company of dogs! They hire our sisters, mothers, and daughters to clean up after their whores! And what do we do? We work for them! We pay them!"

The cleric was shaking with anger, as was the entire congregation. He took a silent moment and regained calm. "There are more than one hundred people who work at the Imperial Sugar Company," he said. "Eighty of those people are our own and twenty of them are foreigners. Not one Persian knows how the machinery works. Not one! Our town is not compensated by the factory's profits. Our elders are not allowed to see their books. And believe me, it is at our expense that they profit. It is at the expense of our dignity that they profit. Sugar is the devil's profit." He crumbled the cube into dust and let it fall onto the floor like sand.

And that is how the cleric began his crusade against the Imperial Sugar Company of Persia and, by proxy, the monarchy. The edict was passed and spread like wildfire through the town. His sermon was the topic of conversation at every home, shop, and street corner. Soon all the coffeehouses had removed their sugar bowls and replaced them with dates and honey. Homes followed suit, wives dumping their Imperial sugar cubes in the garbage, proudly displaying the jagged discolored chunks made by locals.

Every morning the cleric rallied people in the town square and marched to the factory. There he preached in front of the towering double doors, demanding to see the company's books. Every day the crowd grew bigger and bigger. Some people were upset over the moral issues, others were furious at the injustices the workers endured, still others were just curious and needed something to do.

One day a worker looked at the crowd gathered behind the cleric. Instead of entering the factory gates, he walked over and stood with his people. One by one his fellow workers did the same. They stood with the cleric. The factory hired Afghan scabs but even these men soon stood behind the old man with the white beard.

The brothers had workers shipped to the factory from their home country. But the natives pushed back. They set up a blockade in front of the sugarhouse so the Walloon workers could not enter, and began attacking the factory itself. It doesn't take much effort to set fire to sugar dust. Local police refused to attack their own people and even the military battalion sent by the monarchy backed down.

Within a month the Imperial Sugar Company of Persia was on the brink of collapse. The three brothers invited the cleric to a private meeting. He sat in their offices, facing them directly, smiling. A Walloon dragoman, with a pince-nez clipped onto his bulbous nose, sat between them and translated the proceedings.

"We would like to offer a truce," said the oldest brother. "We will split our profits sixty/forty with the town council."

"You will split the profits fifty/fifty with the town, not the council," said the cleric, "and you will give the sugar beet farm back to Ali-Agha and you will buy your sugar beets directly from him. You will hire locals for a fair wage and you will rebuild their accommodations to the specifications that will be sent to you. If you do not do all of these things, you should leave right away. I cannot guarantee the safety of your families."

The three brothers sat with their mouths agape, the eldest rubbing his chin. "And how will you lift the ban on the sugar cubes?" he said.

The cleric had already started to walk to the door as he said, "Leave that to me."

Madjid was mesmerized, almost dumbfounded, and said, "How did he reverse his edict?"

Akbar-Agha took hold of a sugar cube and dipped it in his tea and said, "He simply stood before the congregation with a glass of tea, dipped the cube from the Imperial Sugar Company of Persia in it, and proclaimed it cleansed."

Shazdehpoor shook his head in dismay.

"He was your mother's great-grandfather, Madjid," said Akbar-Agha. "You are the cleric's great-great-grandchild."

Madjid sat up straighter with pride—only then noticing Bi-bi-Khanoom and Ghamar coming down the orchard path. Mirza quickly collected the vodka glasses and bottle and scurried away to the kitchen. Ghamar stood with her hands on her hips and said, "I hope you have not made yourselves too tired."

Mohammad stirred awake. She bent down and brought her face close to his, inhaling. "*Astagfurallah!* Shame on you! Go wash out your mouth."

He lumbered to get to his feet, spinning slightly before getting his bearings.

Nasreen stood behind Akbar-Agha's tree, impervious to her father's humiliation. She watched Madjid, his smile, the glow of his dark eyes, his lanky arms resting on his thighs. Madjid turned to meet her gaze. He did not notice the tilt in her head or the new look in her eyes, nor did he realize that this made him want to be near her. He picked up a sugar cube and walked over to tell her the story, unaware that four years from this very moment, standing on the threshold of her father's tailor shop, with that very same flash of hope in his eyes, he would ask for this girl's hand in marriage.

THE PROPOSAL PARTY

Nasreen sat at her vanity examining her face from every angle. She had spent an hour applying makeup, half of which was spent on the mascara alone. A school friend had given her the precious tube, after pilfering it from her mother. It was Mary Kay, a pricey American import. Nasreen used it only on special occasions. She blinked in the mirror, pleased.

In the distance, her mother was calling. She rolled her eyes and smoothed down her new dress. Her father had made it for her, from iridescent cream-colored silk. The buttons were covered in gold lace and the matching shoes had kitten heels. She was as ready as she would ever be. She opened the bedroom door and stepped out into the living room.

Ghamar, perched on the couch in a navy chador, looked at her awestruck.

Stunned by her silence, Nasreen smiled.

"You look beautiful," said her father.

Her mother nodded. Then without warning, straightened her shoulders and snapped out. "You're wearing too much mascara. It's unseemly."

"The dress fits you very well," her father said.

"It makes your hips look big," said her mother. "And it's tight around the chest."

"The fabric falls gracefully."

"You didn't wear your girdle. Hold yourself in when you bring out the tea."

Her father retreated into the kitchen. Her mother smiled, but Nasreen leaned over and whispered, "If you ruin his proposal for me, I will never forgive you."

Ghamar had never seen this side of Nasreen before. It scared her a little. "I'm only trying to help."

"Don't you dare," said Nasreen heading to the kitchen. The samovar was filled and steaming. Trays of sweets with rosewater and saffron-infused *bamieh*, honey-soaked baklava, and brittle saffron *sohan* lay arranged on the counter. Her father filled the sugar bowl with cubes and arranged tea glasses on a tray. Everything was ready. He smiled and said, "Don't be upset. Your mother is just worried about you. You know how she gets."

There was a knock at the front door. From the kitchen, Nasreen listened intently to her parents as they greeted Madjid and Shazdehpoor. Madjid spoke in short, polite sentences. She could tell he was nervous. He had combed his hair with water, and now it was trickling down his neck and temples. She remembered how he had once told her he loved each and every part of her body, especially her little pouch of stomach fat. She remembered how he once told her he would endure listening to Demis Roussos for her, as long as she danced for him. She began to sway around the kitchen table as she quietly sang "Lovely Lady of Arcadia" in perfectly pitched, flawlessly pronounced English, though she didn't know the meaning of a single word.

Madjid sat on the couch next to his father, his hair stuck to his head as Nasreen had predicted, wet and perspiring. He hunched over his knees, his eyes darting from face to face as the adults discussed the unseasonably warm weather.

There was another knock on the door. Akbar-Agha, Bibi-Khanoom, Jafar, and the midwife all filed into the house and handed Mohammad boxes of intricately wrapped sweets. He ushered them into the living room and went into the kitchen with the sweets, startling Nasreen out of her dance. She caught a glimpse of Madjid on the couch. As their eyes met, the door swung shut, then swayed back and forth, slower and slower until it came to a stop. "Get the tea ready," said her father. "I will come back when the time is right."

Mohammad added the sweets to the appropriate trays and swung the door open again. Madjid was already engaged in conversation with Akbar-Agha, Nasreen saw, just as Jafar slipped into the kitchen. He stood there staring at the rows of *bamieh*, the honey glaze glistening on the perfectly round balls. She took one and handed it to him. He ate it in one bite and went back to staring at the trays, focusing on the baklava. She handed him a piece and he ate that in one bite also, licking the sticky honey and pistachio crumbs off of his fingers. Nasreen gave him a few pieces of the *sohan*, which he pocketed, then he slipped through the kitchen door. She was amazed that one so portly could move with such nimble agility, as though he were not even there.

In the living room, Madjid leaned into Akbar-Agha and spoke softly. "Have you seen today's paper?"

"Yes. Of course."

"A million people gathered in the streets."

"I am not surprised. It was inevitable."

"Do you think this is really it?"

"I'm not sure what 'it' is yet—but yes."

Akbar-Agha remembered August 19, 1953. He was a young man, already a judge, not yet aware of the limits of the law under autocratic rule and overjoyed by the rise in power of the democratically elected prime minister, Dr. Mohammad Mossadegh—even after an attempted coup by foreign forces backing Mohammad Reza Shah Pahlavi.

That day, Akbar-Agha had walked the streets of his hometown and felt the electricity of a people awakened to the force of their own agency. Hundreds marched the streets chanting for the prime minister, "Long live Mossadegh! Long live Mossadegh! Long live Mossadegh!"

A few hours later another crowd angrily tore down those same streets chanting, "Death to Mossadegh! Death to Mossadegh! Death to Mossadegh!"

And just like that, the prime minister was silenced and put under house arrest. The foreign coup that he thought was thwarted had in fact succeeded.

Akbar-Agha looked into Madjid's eyes and said, "Madjid, be careful."

"I am careful. But we are so close to a true people's republic."

"Madjid, do not allow yourself to be swept away. Look with clear eyes. Fate changes on a whim."

Madjid was surprised by Akbar-Agha's cynicism. For him, the

news of the uprising in the capital was a revelation. He wanted to be part of it. He wanted Nasreen to be part of it.

"It is quite an unseasonably warm spring," said the midwife. "It's usually much cooler going into the New Year."

Ghamar agreed. "Last year at this time, it was much cooler. I've had to contend with terrible stomach pains, and that Armenian doctor keeps giving me charcoal pills and charges me a fortune for them. I keep asking him: Why charcoal pills? I have a stomachache from the warm weather. As if I would trust an Armenian."

Everyone looked away, trying to suppress their laughter. Finally the midwife said gently, "Ghamar-jan, charcoal pills are not for a stomachache, they're for flatu—"

"Why don't we get started?" said Bibi-Khanoom. "I could really use a cup of tea."

Mohammad cleared his throat and began by saying, "I would like to welcome you all to our home. We are all family and I think it is best to speak frankly about this union. Nasreen is a very intelligent and kind young woman. She has a great talent with her lace making and a future in tailoring. I plan on leaving my business to her and have no doubt that she will flourish. She is an excellent cook and a pleasure to converse with. She is fair-minded, thoughtful, and sensitive. But she is our only child and her happiness is the most important thing for us. I personally believe she is too young to marry but she insists on it and so I support her decision."

He turned his attention to Shazdehpoor. "I would like to discuss very seriously what your son's plans are in terms of providing Nasreen with a home. The couple is welcome to stay with us as long as they wish, but at some point Madjid will have to provide for his wife. I understand that he will be attending the university in the fall but I wonder how he will be able to handle his studies as well as the responsibilities that come with marriage."

Shazdehpoor now cleared his throat. "First let me say that it is a pleasure to be here and I thank you and Ghamar-Khanoom for your hospitality. Nasreen is like a daughter to me and I would be honored to have her as a daughter-in-law. I, too, feel that perhaps it is too soon for the marriage but Madjid also insists. It is true that he will be going to the university in the fall. I have a modest stipend from the government and a small fund from my wife's dowry left from her too-short life that I have saved for just such an occasion. It is not enough to purchase them a home but it will provide an income while my son finishes his studies and takes on a profession. He and I have discussed his interests, and while he is inclined toward the fine arts, he has also shown quite an affinity for civil engineering, which is a useful and lucrative field."

Bibi-Khanoom took a paper out of her purse and put it on the table. "Akbar-Agha and I would like to deed a small plot of land in our orchard to the bride and groom. They can build a home there. It is our wedding gift."

The sweat on Madjid's forehead turned cold. He unbuttoned the top of his shirt and tried to breathe. He did not recognize himself or Nasreen in anything his family said.

Mohammad walked into the kitchen to cue Nasreen to enter. She stood by the counter holding the tray with glasses and a bowl of sugar cubes, her face like a panicked rabbit, only its nose twitching. Her father reassured her. "It's going quite well," he said. "Bring the tea."

He held the door for her. Slowly, she passed through, the glasses jingling. "He's a very lucky man," her father whispered.

The whole room turned to look at her. Nasreen stopped for

a moment, her eyes landing on Madjid. He looked pale. His forehead was shiny. She walked around the couch and bent down to
offer tea to the midwife first, then to each person. When she got
to Madjid, he looked down her dress, catching a full glimpse of
her bra. As he reached for his tea, he knocked it over, spilling the
rest of the glasses all over her. She let out a yelp. He jumped up,
causing her to drop the tray. Everyone scrambled to clean up the
mess, Mohammad wielding a dishrag.

The midwife leaned into Bibi-Khanoom and whispered, "The
things that a woman's breasts can do to a man."

They giggled under their chadors, until Mohammad said to
Madjid, "I think it's time for you and Nasreen to go to the den and
keep company."

Nasreen was standing at the sink, wiping her dress with a
dishtowel.

"I'm so sorry," he said.

She smiled. "It's all right. I don't mind."

"They want us to get to know each other."

Both of them broke into laughter but managed to nod to everyone as they crossed the living room and into the den. Nasreen
opened the sliding doors, then hesitated. She had always avoided
this room. It was where her parents fought.

Whenever that happened, she tried to hide in her father's tailor
shop. The counters were covered in rolls of colorful fabric, half-
sewn garments, pattern paper, needle pillows, thread spools, and
sewing machines. It was the happiest and sunniest room in the
house, with its own entrance at the back of the house. Her mother
avoided it, except when her husband had to take out her dresses.

Year after year, Nasreen had watched her mother stand on the fitting stool while her father bent over with his pinking sheers and measuring tape.

Ghamar loathed him for his low station in life. But she loathed him even more for his passiveness. Neither of which he seemed to notice. "These cotton fabrics are a mystery," he said over and over. "You wash them a few times and they shrink."

The kinder he was to her about her waistline, the more she seethed until she literally and metaphorically burst at the seams, letting out a screed of vitriol. "My aunt married a judge. My sisters married doctors and engineers that whisked them off to the capital, and I am left here pinned to a seamstress."

"I know you're upset about the dress," he said, showing no reaction. "I'll fix it right away."

This only made her angrier. "The dress did not shrink, you fool. I am fat and getting fatter and it's all your fault. Always stuffing me like a floor pillow." She stomped out of the shop and into the den, her husband following her.

Through the walls of the house, Nasreen could hear her mother screaming and beating on her father. She sat on the floor, rocking back and forth, frightened and waiting for her mother to finally burst into tears and slap him across the face. Only then did she fall into his arms, remorseful. Mohammad never hit back. He only held Ghamar until she calmed down and lay in his arms breathing heavily. After a fight was the only time they were affectionate.

Was it possible that her marriage would turn out the same? Nasreen stood in the doorway of the den. Two chairs had been arranged in the center of the room. Madjid closed the sliding doors behind him. He came over. He put his arms around her, his chin on her head. They stood there in silence for some time before she said, "Promise me that we will always speak openly to each other about our problems. Promise me that and I will endure any hardship with you."

"I promise," he whispered.

She let out a sigh of relief. "You look so pale," she said and sat in her chair.

"I feel sick. This whole thing is just awful."

"It's tradition."

"It's barbaric."

Madjid leaned forward and furrowed his brows like Mohammad, saying in a deep voice, "Our daughter is an excellent cook and fine conversationalist. She also has supple breasts, child-bearing hips, a full set of teeth, and comes with livestock."

Nasreen started laughing. "He did not say supple breasts!"

"I added that."

"And a full set of teeth?"

"You have very good teeth."

"So you're marrying me for my teeth?"

"Oh no. I'm marrying you for the breasts."

"You are so wicked."

"San Francisco."

"Stop it!"

"Did you know that you're going to become a lace maker and take over your father's shop? And I am going to be a civil engineer. Also, we will be building a house in the orchard."

"What?"

"It's like we're invisible to them."

"I'm used to that," said Nasreen. A tear formed in the corner of her eye.

Madjid reached over and held her hand. "Things are changing. I can feel it. Everything that's happening in the capital will happen to us, too. A million people in the streets, Nasreen. A real revolution. This is our time."

The family languished in the living room waiting for the suitor and his bride-to-be. Mohammad filled a plate with sweets and put them in front of Ghamar. She sucked her teeth and turned away. Shazdehpoor nibbled on a piece of baklava. "I knew there was something between them after that first spring lunch a few weeks ago."

Mohammad turned to him in amazement. "They told you?"

"No. I could sense it."

Mohammad shook his head. "I worry that they're too young."

"We were their age when we married," said Ghamar.

"Exactly," said Mohammad, only then realizing the cruelty of that word.

He waited for one of his wife's brazen comebacks but she said nothing. She simply hung her head. Her husband's countless infidelities, of which only she was aware, had finally exhausted her.

DROWNING

Jamsheed woke up disoriented, his vision blurred. He was sitting on the ground. His head felt wrong. He ran his fingers through his hair, feeling that a long strip had been shaved off from back to front. He was lying in the courtyard of the jail, not far from the town square.

A man was squatting in front of him with his arms crossed on his knees. He was an unkempt old man with a white beard—a vagrant, not an addict. He still had his hair, but his stench was so powerful that it woke Jamsheed up completely. "You're in trouble, brother," said the vagrant. His accent was Afghani.

A boy no more than sixteen years of age, with a Kalashnikov rifle, walked by and with no warning hit the vagrant on the back of the head with his rifle butt. Down the vagrant went in the dust, blood streaming down his ear and into his beard. He lay there, laughing wildly as the boy stepped over him and moved on to the next group of prisoners.

Only then did Jamsheed help the vagrant up. He handed him a napkin from his pocket. The man held it to his head. "I saw them bringing you in last night. You were very high. They dropped you like a sack of rice. One of them said they had found you by the side of the road. You had fallen off your motorbike."

Jamsheed shook his head in disbelief. He had no recollection of how he got there.

"You're in big trouble, brother," said the vagrant. "They found a block of opium on you. And the chief of police is clamping down. He thinks it'll save his head with the religious types."

The boy with the gun looked over in their direction. He spat on the ground and gestured for Jamsheed to stand. Jamsheed kept his head down as he got to his feet. The boy poked him in the back with his gun. Jamsheed stumbled. The boy poked him again. This time Jamsheed swung around and tried to grab the muzzle of the gun, but his hands were trembling and slick with sweat. He was sick already.

The boy laughed at him. Then held up his gun and placed the muzzle on Jamsheed's forehead. Jamsheed shut his eyes. He heard voices and footsteps in the distance. And the click of the safety switched to off.

There was a hand on Jamsheed's shoulder.

"Follow me," said a voice. It was a voice he knew, but not until they were inside the building did he dare look up. It was the mullah who had saved him. Tears welled up in his eyes and his body now began to shake so violently that his knees buckled. He landed at his great-uncle's feet and tried to make the shaking stop but it wouldn't. He lay there, his arms wrapped around himself.

The next day, Jamsheed woke up with the sun shining on his face through lace curtains. He recognized neither the bedroom nor the window by his bed. His clothes were wet, as if he'd urinated on himself, but the smell was wrong and his hair was also wet. It was sweat all over his body, sweat burning in his eyes. When he sat up, sharp pains shot through his body, down to his bones. Then came the shivers and more sweating. He was frightened and could not tell what was causing what and how to stop it. He began to cry and called out for anyone, someone to help him.

The cleric slowly opened the door and walked over to him with a small tray of tea and sugar cubes. He said nothing to the young man, but sat on the side of the bed, placing the tray on the nightstand. He filled the glass of tea almost to the top with sugar cubes and stirred until they melted and turned the tea the consistency of syrup. Jamsheed lay there, trying to limit the involuntary fits of his body. The mullah brought the tea glass close to his face and nodded to encourage the young man to drink.

The sugar and heat moved down Jamsheed's throat and coated his stomach, warming his body. His great-uncle refilled the glass from the teapot on the tray and added more cubes. He held it once again to Jamsheed's lips. As the young man drank, the mullah began to speak in a quiet, uninflected tone. "You must be aware that the pain will continue for some days. Your heart will beat rapidly and the sweating will get worse. You will have trouble while sleeping and trouble when awake. This is the price you must pay for the indignities you have subjected your body and spirit to. But know this, it will pass. It will pass."

Jamsheed drank his tea and listened to his great-uncle and felt tears running down his cheeks. He kept repeating to himself, "It will pass, it will pass." The cleric stood to leave, but Jamsheed grabbed his hand. "Please don't leave me," he said.

"I will be right back."

The mullah left the door wide open and came back with his

worry beads and Koran. He sat on the floor pillows by the bed, opening the Koran on the bookstand. He began to rock back and forth, holding his beads in his left hand and turning pages with his right. He read in an almost inaudible whisper. Jamsheed felt his eyelids grow heavy and flutter closed.

He sat up suddenly with a gasp. The room was pitch black. His heart pounced in his chest and he was drenched in sweat. "Are you there?" he said, his voice raw and afraid.

"Yes," said the cleric, as calmly as before.

"How long have I been asleep?"

"Not long, a few hours."

Jamsheed's eyes began to acclimate themselves. He made out the shape of his great-uncle leaning against the wall with one knee propped up, worry beads dangling from his hand. He was still reading the Koran but now from memory.

"I dreamt," Jamsheed said. "I never dream."

"One always dreams. It is just that one does not always remember."

"I don't know where I was. It was sunny, almost unbearably so. There were trees and rocks everywhere and I was thirsty. So thirsty. My tongue felt as if it was covered in sand and I could hear a waterfall, very close by. I started to walk toward the sound. It got louder and louder but I couldn't find it. I pushed through the foliage, the sound of water rushing nearer and nearer, but at the end of the path I tried, there were only trees. My throat was on fire from the thirst. I kept going, but the waterfall was never there. The ground started to shake, and I could still hear the water but now it was rumbling and rushing toward me, breaking the trees and swallowing me. That is when I awoke—catching my breath as I drowned."

TWO MOTHERS

Dusk was setting on the quiet, narrow street where Akbar-Agha stopped to rap on a door. He could hear the clanking of silverware and dishes inside the neighboring houses: the clear then suddenly muted voices of women going in and out of kitchens carrying platters of food, the squeals of children leaping from their seats and running around the *sofrehs*, being chastised by mothers and ordered to sit down again. He heard laughter from one home, arguing from another, silent feasting from yet another.

His brother opened the door, still wearing his *aba* and holding his worry beads. They nodded to each other. Akbar-Agha took off his shoes on the doormat and leaned down slightly to kiss his brother on both cheeks. The physical difference between them was startling. If one did not know they were brothers, one would have never guessed. They did not have the same mother. Akbar's mother had been his father's second wife, whom his father had married when Habib was two years old.

Their father, known to them only by the honorific title Haj-Agha, had been an ambitious young man of little means who worked his way into a fortune by taking Habib's mother as his first wife. She was the oldest and dowdiest daughter of a patrician family who gladly gave her up, despite Haj-Agha's lowly station. To his surprise, she was an excellent cook and housekeeper. Because of this, Haj-Agha endured her presence for the first three years of their marriage, even after she produced a son and daughter who glaringly resembled her. On the fourth year, after complaining that she could not produce more children, which was true due to the lack of physical contact between them, he demanded a new wife. Her family was scandal-shy and he was able to force her to sign a legally binding letter of consent.

The second wife was a younger woman from a modest village family. She was an exceptionally tall, slender woman with bright green eyes and light brown hair. Haj-Agha was taken by her beauty, and with the means from his first wife's family was able to procure the second wife without much wrangling. Akbar's mother came into the home and the first wife, initially devastated by the event, could not help but be dazzled by her rival. It was an envy so strong that, over time, it metamorphosed into adoration.

Delicate and graceful, the second wife had no domestic skills to speak of and the first wife, known within the family as Haj-Khanoom, took it upon herself to shoulder all the responsibilities of the house, especially since the second wife, known as Simin-Khanoom, was already with child in the first month of marriage.

Akbar's birth was difficult and permanently injured Simin-Khanoom's back. Despite her stature as the first wife,

Haj-Khanoom upended the household order and waited on her day and night. Washing sheets, tending to the garden, and scrubbing floors left her hands wrinkled. Folds of skin puckered across her knuckles. Crow's feet formed on her eyes. Her legs grew thick and muscular from repeated squatting to lift children and basins. She soon resembled a charwoman.

In response, Haj-Agha doted on Simin and her young son, Akbar, practically ignoring Haj-Khanoom and her children, Habib and Zahra. Even nursing exhausted Simin-Khanoom. When her monthly feminine bleeding returned, it wouldn't stop and the doctors in town were unable to find the cause or cure. She became anemic and bedridden and more frail than before. Her hip bones jutted out from beneath the piles of blankets on the bed and her skin paled to an almost bluish translucence, which for Haj-Agha only added to her allure. He sat each evening by her side, entranced by her matted blond hair and glistening green eyes.

Though Haj-Khanoom ran the household and reared the three children, her own offspring were not allowed in Simin-Khanoom's room when Haj-Agha appeared. Each morning, Haj-Khanoom made a special wildflower-infused tea that she held up to Simin's lips and urged her to drink. She wiped her face with a washcloth doused in cucumber water. She changed the menstrual cloth in Simin's undergarments, each time easing the tension and embarrassment of her sister-wife, saying, "Shhhh. It's all right. Don't be ashamed. It's natural."

Still Simin's pain in her womb began to get worse. The bleeding increased and she moaned constantly. Haj-Khanoom gave her more tea to calm her.

One afternoon, Haj-Agha came home early from his gold souk in the town square and found his first wife in the kitchen, steeping her wildflower concoction. He looked at it suspiciously. "What are you doing?" he asked.

"Making tea for Simin-Khanoom."

"What is in it?"

"Dried starflowers. It calms her."

He grabbed the tea, smelled it, then quickly scooped out the wilted flower petals and inspected them. "No more of this," he said. "Regular tea is fine."

Later, Haj-Agha carried his little son Akbar into his mother's room and sat him down on her bed. She stared at him with her wide pain-filled eyes, their color shifting from green to blue to a strange, cool gold. Akbar was frightened. He called out to Haj-Khanoom.

On the doctor's next visit, Haj-Agha showed him the canister of dried starflower petals. The doctor was shocked and said, "Do not, under any circumstances, give this to her. This flower is a blood thinner."

Haj-Agha went into a rage. He accused Haj-Khanoom of trying to kill Simin and forbade her to go into Simin's room alone. He recruited her own son, Habib, to spy on her, which Habib gladly did in order to impress a father who otherwise ignored him.

Simin-Khanoom slowly bled to death and died one year later. Akbar was not yet two years old. From that day forth, Haj-Agha turned to stone, showing any human affection only when in Akbar's presence or when recalling Simin's unearthly beauty and kindness. Every day he found some way to compare her graces to his first wife's clumsy, unsightly failures, and within a few years Haj-Khanoom was more than happy to leave this earth herself, leaving behind her eight-year-old son, Habib, her seven-year-old daughter, Zahra, and her six-year-old stepson, Akbar, who loved her as the only mother he had ever known. She whispered her final words into Akbar's ear: "I didn't know about the starflowers."

Haj-Agha clung to Akbar, focusing all of his attention on the boy, lavishing him with gifts and luxurious clothes. He funded his education and moved him into the brightest room in the house, replete with books and fine furnishings. Over and over he lectured the boy on the importance of money and station. But secretly, Akbar remained unconvinced. Watching his father turn his sister into the new housemaid and his brother into an invisible squatter, he felt nothing but guilt. His countless attempts to share with his siblings failed. Both accused him of pity.

Standing in his childhood living room—where he had played and studied—Akbar felt overwhelmed by the past. The house was no longer his or his father's. It was Habib's home. He noticed a plate of bread, cheese, and herbs on a small *sofreh* on the floor. "I have interrupted your dinner."

"Not at all," said Habib, then served tea in silence.

Akbar cooled his tea by pouring it into the saucer. "Many lifetimes have passed through these doors," he said. "So many mistakes. So many regrets."

Habib just stared at his brother and continued flicking his worry beads, the sound resonating through the silence.

"It was kind of you to take Jamsheed in and see him through this illness. Shazdehpoor gave up on him a long time ago. It isn't right. We're all family."

"I would walk any man toward the right path."

Akbar felt himself smarting. "And those who do not wish to follow this path?"

"Are lost."

They fell silent again.

There was a knock at the door and the cleric stood up to answer it. Akbar could hear the sounds of male voices greeting his brother. When Habib returned, three young clerics followed behind him. "This is my younger brother, Akbar-Agha," he said. "He used to be a judge."

The three young men, in their crisp seminarian uniforms and white turbans, nodded their respects to the former judge and did not move. The cleric stared at his brother, devoid of any expression. Akbar realized that he had interrupted a meeting. The tea and food had been for the young clerics. He suddenly felt foolish and out of place. He immediately stood and walked toward the door. He stopped to give a general farewell but no one was looking at him. He walked to the foyer and put on his shoes. No one came to see him off. He stood there for a minute and could hear his brother offering tea and sustenance to the men, holding court as he spoke of the day's events and of events in the days to come.

Akbar stood on the narrow street looking at the houses, their lights still burning. He could hear the sounds of televisions, radios, and murmurs as the families settled in for the night. It was like any other night on this street, the street where he was born. In the window of his old home, the curtains were drawn and he could see the shadows of the three young clerics sitting and listening intently to their elder. He saw Jamsheed's shadow come into the living room and join their circle. There was nothing more to be done.

He started homeward on foot, along the narrow alleyways leading into the town square, past the roasted-beet vendors handing their newspaper-wrapped cones of steaming treats to their customers, past the storytellers holding court for their rapt listeners.

When he reached the orchard, he slammed the door shut be-hind him and hurried up the path to the house. His wife had left the living room lights on for him.

He took off his shoes in the vestibule and went straight into the kitchen to get a glass of water. He had to get ahold of himself. It is one thing to know that everything ends. It is another to ex-perience that ending. The ring of the telephone startled him. He ran to pick up the receiver and before he could even say a word, he heard the frightened, shaking voice of Shazdehpoor say, "My boy is lost."

PARIS | IV

Shazdehpoor stood on his street corner, holding his bags of groceries, watching a young Parisian mother kneel before her child. She was wiping chocolate off his face with a tissue, reprimanding him in a playful tone. Shazdehpoor had no recollection of his own mother. She had died giving birth to him and there were no pictures of her. He knew only that she was his uncle Habib's full sister and his uncle Akbar's half sister. Shazdehpoor had spent his youth in his father's house in Mash'had. Once his father remarried and started a new family, he was sent away to boarding school. Only Akbar ever spoke to him about his mother and how difficult life had been for her growing up in their household. "Your mother walked me to school every day," he said. "She fed me and bathed me and made sure I knew my lessons. If anyone at school bothered me, she jumped in to protect me. My life was better because of her, and I know she would have done the same for you. Never think for one moment that she wanted to leave you. And never think that you were the cause of her death."

Shazdehpoor opened the door to his apartment. He placed his walking stick in the umbrella stand. He took his groceries to the kitchenette and put them away, folding the plastic bags and shoving them into another plastic bag under the counter. He lit the burner under his samovar.

It was early afternoon and light still poured into the studio from the French doors. He took off his seersucker jacket and trousers, laid them on his bed, and wiped off the residue from his outing with a lint brush. He hung the suit carefully on its hanger, pulled the plastic cover over it, and put it back into the closet. For the first time in thirty years, he took out his Persian pantaloons and put them on with his buttoned-down shirttail hanging out.

It was siesta time, even though it had been years since he had taken an afternoon nap. He placed his tea service at the ready on a small table. He poured himself a glass and watched the steam rise as music from the radio wafted through the air. He did not know which piece but he knew Mozart when he heard it—light and airy, joyous, and realized with such depth.

The announcer's soothing voice identified it as the Sonata no. 16 in C major. The news followed: The incumbent, Nicolas Sarkozy, and candidate François Hollande were neck to neck in the presidential polls. A wave of terrorist attacks across Iraq had killed 50 people and injured 240. A 7.4-magnitude earthquake had struck the Mexican states of Guerrero and Oaxaca. And, of course, the eclipse was due to take place in a few hours. Do not look at the sun, the radio advised. Even if you don't feel it, you'll damage your retinas. Shazdehpoor winced and turned off the radio.

The club chair in which he sat was a knockoff he had purchased years before at the *puces*. Unlike his real club chair back home, the wine-red fabric had not aged with character. The imitation red leather was worn and tattered in spots. He watched the steam rise from his tea. Then gave up.

A bottle of cognac stood on the small desk in the entranceway with a snifter next to it. He popped off the stopper and laid the snifter on its side, pouring himself a proper measure to the brim. Only then did he open the drawer and take out a floral carved wooden box.

Everything in his stark apartment was not his and not to his liking—only what he could afford. The small bed was really nothing more than a glorified cot. The faux club chair. The banker's lamp with a plastic shade on a nightstand piled with unfinished translations of classical Persian texts that could never truly be translated and for which he was never commissioned, and unpublished articles he had written: "Iran's Post-Revolutionary Cinema: Renaissance or Repression?" and "Aviary Aspirations: The Significance of Bird Flight in Persian Mythology." Now that his rug was with Trianant, the wooden box on his lap contained his only real possession. He opened its hinged top.

Inside there were no photographs. All of them had been lost or destroyed by the authorities. All that was left were the letters, aged and delicate, the last thing he wanted to remember. But this was the painful truth about memory, you didn't get to choose what you got to forget. Most of the letters were on paper from loose-leaf school notebooks, the edges frayed, the ink slightly smudged in parts. The handwriting ranged from furious and jagged to fluid and measured. He ran his fingers over the first letter in the pile.

Dear Father,

I am in the capital. I apologize for having frightened you by leaving without notice but I knew if I were to tell you, you would not let me go. Please do not worry. I am safe and among friends. I do not know where to begin to tell you what I have seen in the past several days. It's unlike anything that I have ever dared imagine. My first night here, I arrived by train and it was late and I was so tired. A taxi driver took me to the central square, refusing my money—which is for the best, since I have so little to spare. Stepping out of the car, I was shocked. The streets were a war zone. Fires burning everywhere. Papers, filing cabinets, and other debris littered the streets and sidewalks—all of it hurled from windows. Thousands upon thousands of people milled about. I walked for what seemed like hours. From north to south, east to west. The electricity that ran through the city came from the people. I stopped to speak to as many as I could. Each told me a piece of the story that I had missed. About the people killed. About the flight of Mohammad Reza Shah Pahlavi and the arrival of Ayatollah Ruhollah Khomeini. As I walk the streets of the capital I can only describe it thus: It is as though all of the people here are one. From the farthest regions of the country to the middle of the city they have gathered in brotherhood. We look at and acknowledge one another as we pass.

We are aware of the same thing. And in each and every face that I have seen, I saw the spark of possibility. I have been offered meals, refreshment, and a roof under which to sleep. I have been given sweets, embraces, and salutations along all of the streets I walk, by young and old, man and woman, from north and south, in chadors and blue jeans.

Father, it took my breath away. I had never imagined such a thing was possible. I had begun to believe that one had to go somewhere else and build a new life, that a country with thousands of years of history could not change, that we could not see past our differences, could not forgive our past aggressions, could not let go of our prejudices, that we were incapable of change. But I am watching that change and I know my place is here with my people, my brothers and sisters.

Please know that I am safe. I've been staying at the dorms in the university. There is much activity here and some of the students that I met on the street have shown me such immense hospitality. Sleep is impossible! Night and day, we stay awake discussing all that needs to be done in this beautiful new Iran. Just last night I sat at dinner with several students—one was a Communist, another was a seminary student. Still another had just returned from Paris. There were many differences of opinion but we all agreed on one thing, that our fate is in our own hands.

Last night, we started making posters and

flyers. We've made plans for student unions and are in the process of starting a paper to spread news and information throughout the country. I have personally interviewed a young cleric who has been sitting in on our student meetings. He's a fine fellow and is as excited for the future as we are. We visited with his congregation and spoke openly about the concerns that affect us all. There are some who worry about outside intervention, which is to be expected, but I think with all of us banding together that would be impossible—never again. The past is the past. We are ready to determine our own future.

This fall, I want to enroll in university. Nasreen and I can live here in a small apartment during the school year and come home for holidays and longer breaks. It would be wise, I think, for her to attend university as well. Once I finish my studies I want to work in Naishapur with the local engineering corps. There is a sand dunes project I have in mind. It's something I've been thinking about for years, and I think that with my education under my belt and the new possibilities before us I will be able to realize it. But I'm getting ahead of myself. You must forgive me. I'm just so terribly excited! Please give my regards to everyone, especially Nasreen. Do not be worried—I am among family here as well.

Your son,

Madjid

Dear Father,

I hope this letter finds you and the family well. I am sitting here in the dorm room, writing to you by candlelight. Everyone is asleep and it's unusually quiet. It's the first chance I have had to sit alone and think after the whirlwind of the last few days. Today was not a very good day. In the morning's paper there were photographs of the high military officials who had been executed, their bodies laid out in a row in the prison yard. I was shocked by the severity. I had expected proper public trials to address the grievances of the people, and to examine how these injustices were allowed to continue. It is not possible to build a house on a gutted foundation. There have been some officials who have resigned in protest or who have been dismissed. People whose work and reputation I am aware of. It was a great loss to my brothers and sisters. And to myself. But I take refuge in the fact that while change can sometimes be messy, setbacks can't derail it completely. Others agree. I spent most of today at our table outside the university, speaking to passersby who stop to read our pamphlets. There have been some reports of violence toward people across the capital but they have been sporadic. A girl here at the dorms was badly hurt by a group claiming to be defenders of morality. They threw acid in her face, and her parents came and took her back home.

Violence is a potent enemy, Father. If you let it fill you with fear then all will be lost. But we are standing firm. We know that the majority is on our side and we will press on. Please do not worry. I am among family here.

Your son,

Madjid

Dear Father,

I am sorry it took so long to write again. There have been several student raids at the dorms. Not to worry. I am doing fine. But they have taken many away. We've been spending most of our time inquiring of their whereabouts at the prison and hospitals but to no avail. It's frustrating. I am worried for my friends. It's been uneasy at the dorms. Some of the students are beginning to suspect that there are informants among us, but informants for whom? I don't fully understand what is happening. But please do not worry. I am among family here.

Your son,

Madjid

Dear Father,

I stood in line for several hours today to vote. It was the first time I have ever cast a ballot. When I reached the building and stepped inside, my heart raced in excitement. But Father, when I got the ballot, it said: Islamic Republic of

Iran, yes or no. I don't fully understand what is happening.

Your son,

Madjid

Dear Father,

The carpet I came to the capital for is not what I had expected. The central motifs do not correspond to the ones in the expanding circle. One of the central shapes overpowers the rest and is causing an imbalance in the entire design. In fact, upon closer inspection, I realized that it has overwhelmed what was otherwise a very promising design. It is unfortunate that such a beautiful design has been so grossly realized but what can one do? Not all grand ideas imagined can come to fruition. As we discussed before, I left to come here for the sole purpose of purchasing this carpet and since it is not the one I was looking for, I will be returning home on the next train. Perhaps I will be able to find a more appropriate one in our own town.

Your son

Shazdehpoor folded the letters and held them in his lap. The room was silent. He labored to catch his breath. He had forgotten how much it upset him to open his wooden box. He started to pace around the room but it only made his breathing more rapid. And the loneliness more acute. He needed to see other people. He couldn't stay in this room for another moment.

He took off his pantaloons and changed back into his seersucker suit, slipping his feet into loafers.

He headed toward the foyer, stopping at the door. He buttoned his jacket. He closed his eyes and took a deep breath, touching the cold sweat on his brow. All would be well once he was around other people. Even strangers.

THE UNIVERSITY

W ho are you?" the man said as he stood over Madjid, leaning in close to his face. Madjid, blindfolded, hands and feet bound, sat on a chair in a windowless room. He could feel the man's breath on his face, and it made him shake. But he managed to answer, "I am a student."

The man stood straight and turned with his hands clasped behind his back. He took several paces and suddenly turned back, lunged at Madjid, and slapped him across the face, hurling him from the chair. Madjid's full weight landed on his shoulder and dislocated it with a muted snap. He screamed. The man leaned over and lifted him off the ground by his shirt collar. Madjid's arm muscles began to spasm and a film of sweat covered his face. He tried to swallow his saliva but drooled.

The man paced the room leisurely with his hands clasped behind his back. His shoes had taps on the soles like those of a 1930s movie star. He walked to the door and knocked several times. Two men entered. They walked over to Madjid and lifted him off the chair by his elbows. He whimpered in pain, his shoulder throbbing. "We will continue this conversation very soon," said the man.

Nausea heaving in his chest, Madjid stumbled at the foot of a stairwell. He blindly climbed the steps, trying to keep up with the men at his elbows. Suddenly there was a wall. Then blood oozing from his forehead as the two men laughed. "Watch where you're going," one of them taunted as they turned the corner. He felt dizzy, confused, and shuffled his feet trying to keep up.

Keys jangled and unlocked a door. The rope that bound his hands was violently untied, leaving nail scratches on his wrists. Then the blindfold was removed. In the dim light, his vision was blurry. He was shoved into a cell, the door slammed behind him. He stood there as his vision became acclimated, making out several men sitting crouched on the floor.

They all stared at him. "You have dislocated your shoulder," said one of the men. "Come, I'll fix it for you."

Madjid stood there shaking from the spasms in his arm.

Another man said, "Let him fix it. He's a doctor."

Try as he might, Madjid could not move. Blood oozed down his forehead, rolling down his cheeks like black tears.

The doctor slowly walked over to him, reaching for his shoulder, but Madjid pulled away. The doctor spoke again, his voice calm and gentle. "It's all right. I won't hurt you."

Madjid relaxed his stance as best he could, his eye fluttering from the blood. The man unbuttoned Madjid's shirt and gently slipped it off his shoulders and motioned to two others to help. He turned to Madjid and said, "I need you to lie down flat."

The two men helped Madjid to the corner. The doctor took a bed sheet and looped it under Madjid's armpit. He nodded to the other men. One took his dislocated arm while the other sat on his legs, holding his other arm to the ground. The doctor held on to the sheet and leaned over Madjid and said, "The pain will be excruciating but it will pass quickly."

On the count of three he leaned back, pulling the sheet toward himself as the other man pulled his arm from his body and the third man held down Madjid. With a crack, his bone slipped back into place. The doctor let go of the sheet and the man sitting on him got up. A shiver ran down Madjid's body, and he turned to the wall and vomited.

The doctor leaned over him. "Is the pain gone?"

Madjid nodded yes.

The two men helped him sit up and covered his vomit with a rag. He joined their circle and counted four altogether, including the man who hadn't moved to help him. His face was hidden by the shadows and his propped-up leg. In his hand, his worry beads clicked, invisible in the dark.

The cell was damp and frigid but large, as if meant to hold more captives. The four men had attempted to create dignified living quarters. Their blankets were laid out like beds. A sheet cordoned off the pail they used as a toilet. Their cups and plates were laid out on another sheet they had improvised as a *sofreh* and their few books were stacked against the wall, along with a few pens and pencils.

The doctor pressed a damp cloth on Madjid's forehead to soak up the blood. He held up his index finger and moved it, instructing him to follow it with his eyes. "Do you feel dizzy?" he said.

"No," said Madjid.

"It's best to stay awake for a while just to be sure. The bump on your head is quite significant."

"I feel all right."

The doctor sat back and, smiling at his patient, said, "Welcome to the university."

They all laughed, and Madjid smiled, confused. "What do you mean?" he said.

The man who had been sitting in the far corner in the dark moved closer. "We call our cell the university because he is a doctor." He pointed to the next man. "He is a writer." And the next. "He is a historian." Then he pointed to himself. "I am a defrocked cleric."

He swept his hand across the cell. "And this is a place of higher learning."

"Who are you, my boy?" said the doctor.

"A student."

"Then you have come to the right place."

They all laughed and Madjid felt a little like himself again. He asked the cleric, "Do you know what time it is?"

"No. That is one thing you can never be certain of here."

"What do they want from us?"

"Nothing."

"Then why are we here?"

"To be broken. They know as well as we do that we are a threat to their power. They once survived this same university."

"Who are they?"

"They are us."

Hours passed as the men told Madjid about the rotation of guards, the nightly roundups, and the dreaded Section 209, where screams of agony could be heard throughout the nights that bled into days and the days that bled back into nights, time a constant stagnant state of darkness, anticipation and dread, captivity and subordination. Madjid suspected Section 209 was where he had been held. Had they heard him?

He moved closer to the cleric, intrigued by his presence in the prison. "Haj-Agha," he asked. "Why are you here?"

The cleric seemed amused. "You think because I am a cleric that I am one of them?"

"Well, I assumed—"

"There are two schools of thought among the clergy: those who believe that they will create a state based on the principles of their faith; and those who do not believe that this is possible and that we should not be involved in matters of state. The latter have ended up assassinated, exiled . . . and imprisoned."

Madjid fell into thought for a few moments then wished the cleric a good night. He walked over to the corner of the cell where the historian had laid him out a blanket. He lay awake and stared at the darkness until he slipped into a waking dream in which he was standing over a colony of ants, a line of uniform black shapes without distinction, moving in unison, his foot suspended over them.

"Who are you?" the man said as he stood over Madjid, leaning in close to his face. Madjid sat on the same chair, in the same room, bound and blindfolded. He did not speak but tensed his body and prepared himself for a blow to the temple that never arrived. He could hear the man's tapping footsteps going to the door, opening and closing it. He sat there alone for what might have been an hour, he could not be sure. His cellmates had shared with him what they had suffered during interrogations. The cigarette burns on the naked thighs, the switches on the soles of the feet, the punches to the face, the leather straps rubbed on the scrotum that resulted in a pain so excruciating that one of them had passed out. The ice-cold water dumped on the head to wake one up, only to be subjected to more. And the most unbearable part of it all was not being able to see or know when the blow or punch or slap would come, and the silence of not being asked a single question whose answer might end the torment.

The door opened again. Madjid's heart began to palpitate. He sat there in the dark, his lungs pushing against his chest as he labored to catch his breath, tears running down his cheeks. The men started to laugh as they taunted him. One of them said, "Awww, don't cry. Are you afraid? What are you afraid of?"

Madjid's fear gave way to rage. He breathed heavily, trying to yank his hands and feet out of their bounds.

"Oooh, he's getting angry," said a new man. "That's good. That's very good."

Madjid was boiling over and almost wished one of them would strike him. He screamed, "Go ahead! Do whatever you want. I don't care. You can kill me if you want. I don't care!"

Madjid started to flail on the chair and fell over. There he lay, on the cement, on his side, still tied to his chair. Silence flooded the room. Madjid felt the interrogator's breath on his ear. "They will not kill you," he said. "They will not cut you or break a single bone in your body. No. They won't even strike you."

He grabbed Madjid by the collar, lifting him with the chair back to his sitting position, and once more brought his face close to Madjid's. "They will do something to you that is far worse and you will wish that I had killed you."

He heard the interrogator's footsteps heading to the door. He heard him whisper to his henchmen and then the door slamming behind him. A few seconds of silence followed and then he heard the unclasping of belt buckles and he knew the interrogator was right.

He woke up in a four-by-six cell in the fetal position, alone. It was pitch black except for a shaft of light that streamed in from a high window, and for a brief moment he felt triumphant that he could distinguish day from night. There was nothing in the cell save a bucket for his waste and a wiry, damp blanket next to his head. He moved to sit up and felt a sharp pain shooting through his bowels. He lay back down again. He touched his rectum and felt the blood and raised his hand to the shaft of light to make sure that it was blood, which it was. He began to weep softly and gently rocked on the concrete floor until his mind gave way to unconsciousness.

He woke with a start, raising himself by his arms. There was a metal cup and plate inside his cell. He leaned over and sniffed at the cup. It was water. The cold, mucus-like sop on the plate smelled of oats. Looking up to the window, he wondered how long he had been asleep. Only then did he realize the light was unnatural, unchanging. He hung his head in quiet defeat.

He could not tell if hours or days passed. The only thing that broke the silence and sameness were the guards bringing him his meals. After sleeping through the first of these, he set his mind on separating the days from nights by the food that was shoved into his cell. But every meal was breakfast. The first was the porridge, then some stale bread and moldy cheese, then some milk with dried bread, then porridge again. His frustration grew. He decided to address the guard upon his next visit.

As he heard the hall door open, he scampered up to the bars and waited. The plate came rattling in and he called out to the guard but the guard was already gone. He looked at the plate. It was porridge. He threw it against the wall and yelled out.

He used his blood-caked pinkie to clean his other nails, then used some of his drinking water to wash his face. He unrolled his blanket and hung it over the horizontal bar in the middle of his door to dry it out. The air was damp and the blanket remained so as well. Slowly, he paced about the cell and began to recite poems, mathematical equations, and school assignments from memory. He sang songs. He even danced. He told himself jokes and laughed at their punch lines. He sat in the corner, out of the spotlight, and touched himself as he tried to recall every single part of Nasreen's face and body, but he could not get erect and so he tried to remember her taste, how she felt to his touch, her movements, and even imagined her bent over naked—but to no avail. He began to feel sick to his stomach and gave up. He recited entire conversations he had had with people throughout his life. Some he re-edited to his liking. He stopped and changed words or inflections, then, once satisfied, moved on to the next scene.

Finally a cockroach arrived in his cell, and with elation he greeted it, cornering it on the wall. He cupped it in his hands and brought it over to his nook, buttressing the hapless vermin with his blanket. He scraped a bit of old porridge off the wall and left it at the insect's feet. "Go ahead," he said. "It's all yours."

The bug simply wavered its antennae. Then it climbed the lump of porridge and began to feed. Madjid was elated. He jumped up, his eyes filled with tears, and said, "Yes, my friend! Feast to your heart's content!"

He named the bug Abdi, laughing each time he said the name

out loud. Abdi was the name of a school friend with whom he had spent hours discussing various types of engineering, from environmental and structural to the mysterious, as yet unstudied female.

Every day and night, for hours, he spoke to Abdi the cockroach about his ordeal inside the university: how he missed his new friends and wished he was in their cell, how he missed his life back home. He described, in great detail, the beauty and warmth of his wife-to-be. He told Abdi some of the jokes at which he had laughed alone and asked it rhetorical questions such as "I wonder if bugs have ears?" and "I wonder if you see me as I am or am I a prism?" knowing all the time that it was a cockroach he was talking to, ending each monologue with the phrase "I may be desperate, Abdi, but I am not mad."

Madjid woke with a start. Abdi was gone. He scoured every inch of the cell but eventually it was clear: he was alone again. He began to weep for the loss of his only friend. He recalled their time together, remembering each conversation with Abdi, re-editing it in his head more to his liking. He chastised himself for not saying things he now realized he should have said, but each thought was one he'd already had and he began to panic that his thinking was over, he had no new thoughts and would never have any more again, and went back to the beginning and felt like a fool for re-thinking used thoughts and somehow ended up back on his last final thought and finally surrendered to a kind of frantic blackout he knew was madness.

Again, he woke with a start. Two guards lifted him by his arms and dragged him out of the cell and down the hall. Doors flew open and sunlight burned across his face. He squinted to try to adjust his eyes. He was in a courtyard, a vast concrete enclosure without a roof. He clocked the cardinal direction by the sun. From the shadows it cast he knew that it was close to noon. He was elated. He knew the time.

The guards dragged him to the far side of the courtyard and held him up against the wall next to a wooden post.

A few moments later the doors opened again and several more guards came out, dragging a man, his head slumped, his legs dragging. They dropped the almost lifeless body beside Madjid. The man had been beaten and badly scarred. He lifted up his head and Madjid saw it was the doctor. He smiled at the young man and asked, "How is your shoulder?"

Madjid was taken aback. "Are you all right?" he said.

"I've seen better days," the doctor said. And laughed.

The guards lifted the doctor, held him up against the post, and tied his hands behind it.

The door opened again and the interrogator walked leisurely toward the scene, his taps echoing across the concrete of the courtyard. He was shorter than Madjid had imagined him. Taps had given him heft. Perhaps that was why he wore them. He put his arm on Madjid's shoulder, the one he had dislocated, and walked him around the perimeter. Madjid's eye twitched at every tap of his shoe.

"Tell me something, young man," the interrogator began, "how old are you?"

"Eighteen."

"Aaah, I remember that age. All I could think about was girls! It's a good age. Do you have a girl?"

"No."

"Come, now. There must be at least one girl, no?"

"No," Madjid said. He was terrified that the man could read

his thoughts and tried to erase Nasreen from them. "No. No one. I swear."

"It's okay, it's okay. You can relax. You'll be all right. Nothing will happen to you or your girl. You have my word. Nothing will happen to you and your girl. I promise. On my honor, I do." He spoke emphatically with one hand on his heart and then immediately asked, "Would you like to go home to her?"

Before Madjid could think, he said, "Yes."

"Aaah, so you do have a girl! I knew it. What's her name?"

Madjid was now panicking and on the verge of tears as he said, "Please, sir."

"Come, now. Tell me her name."

He squeezed Madjid's shoulder. Madjid closed his eyes in despair and said, "Nasreen."

"Aaah, beautiful Nasreen. She is beautiful, I assume? Yes, yes, of course she is. Nasreen, the wild rose. Beautiful name. Beautiful Nasreen."

They had walked the whole perimeter of the courtyard and were now back where they started. The doctor looked haggard, almost as though he was about to collapse. The interrogator nodded to one of the guards, who took his gun out of the holster, turning away to inspect it, then walked over to Madjid and held it out to him. The young man looked at him in disbelief as the interrogator leaned into him and said, "I want you to take that gun and shoot that man."

Madjid looked at the doctor in shock and said, "No, no. I will do no such thing."

The interrogator turned Madjid to face him and said, "You will take that gun and you will shoot that man. And if you don't, I will shoot you then I will pay a visit to your beautiful Nasreen."

"No, please. If you want to kill him or me, you do it. Please, I can't."

"It's him or your girl. You choose."

Madjid stared at the doctor, who smiled at him and said, "It's okay. Do it. I am dead already. It's okay."

Madjid was shaking as he said, "I can't."

"Don't be a fool," the doctor continued, "they are going to kill me anyway. Don't sacrifice your life and a young woman's. Please don't put that on my head. I beg you."

The interrogator took the gun from the guard and put it in Madjid's hand. He had never held a gun before. It was heavier than he had imagined. He stared at it. The interrogator cocked the hammer for him and held up his arm, aiming at the doctor. Madjid felt tears running down his face as he stared at the doctor and said, "I'm so sorry. Please forgive me."

The doctor smiled and said, 'It's okay, young man. It's okay."

Madjid shook his head and said, "I can't. I can't"

"Do it!" the interrogator screamed. Madjid looked into the doctor's eyes, smiled, and turned the gun on himself, pushing its muzzle under his own chin and looking up to the cloudless sky above. He let out a breath and pulled the trigger.

Nothing.

It was a blank. Everyone started to laugh except Madjid and the doctor. The interrogator laughed the loudest, the taps of his shoes echoing through the courtyard. He slapped Madjid on the back, then said, "You can't even manage to kill yourself!"

The guard then grabbed the gun from Madjid's hand and re-loaded it with bullets from his pocket. The interrogator grabbed his collar, the laughter on his face vanishing as if it had been turned off with a switch. "Listen to me, boy," he said. "I have been doing this long enough to know what men are made of. Your godless ideas are nothing more than woman talk. When it comes down to the bone, you break. They all break."

He looked to the guards and nodded. They dragged Madjid toward the door. The guard who had reloaded his gun held it up to the doctor's head. There was the sound of a shot, darkness, then nothing.

WOMEN

Shazdehpoor sat with Akbar-Agha in his room. Akbar-Agha looked up from a letter in his hand. "When did you receive this last one?" he said.

"Three days ago," Shazdehpoor said. "I have been to the train station every day and asked the attendants if they had seen him and no one has."

"Was the last letter about the carpet tampered with?"

"I did notice the envelope had been taped. None of the others were that way. I'm not sure what the carpet business is about."

"He's speaking in code. He knew he was being watched and the letter was read before it reached you. They have probably arrested him."

Shazdehpoor put his head in his hands and wept. Akbar-Agha touched his shoulder. "Do not worry," he said. "I will make some calls and get him home. Though you must, please, say nothing of it. As far as anyone knows, he's in the capital staying with friends at the university."

The family lunch was quiet and tense. Shazdehpoor and Akbar-Agha repeatedly reassured everyone that Madjid was safe, but they all felt something was amiss. Bibi-Khanoom stood silently at the kitchen counter with Nasreen. The girl burst into tears. "Don't worry," Bibi-Khanoom said. "He is fine. He will be home soon."

She was reassuring herself as much as the girl. Nasreen pulled herself together and dished the food onto platters, while Bibi-Khanoom made a plate for the midwife and covered it with a linen cloth. Today's main stew was *khoreshteh bamieh*, a stew made of lamb with okra and a tomato base. She had made a *tahdig* with yogurt and saffron, the bottom burned evenly almost brownish red, from the saffron caked to it. She called out to Jafar, who was already in the doorway, smelling what was to come. He was holding his chicken, Mina. "Please take this plate to the midwife," said Bibi-Khanoom. "Do not eat her food. There is plenty here for you. And leave that chicken in the coop where it belongs."

He returned Mina to her coop with a sour look on his face. Bibi-Khanoom handed him the plate and shoved a *loghmeh* in his mouth. He stood there chewing, his face brightening from the flavors. Only then did he walk the orchard path to the entrance, setting down the plate to open the doors slightly, carefully picking it back up and slipping through to the dirt road. He walked along the adobe walls, the rich scent of the food wafting toward his face. Past the orchard, on the open road, the wind kicked in, helping him resist the temptation to peel back a corner of the cloth and break off a piece of *tahdig*.

Jafar liked food very much. He enjoyed anticipating what was to be served, consuming it, and even memories of it. The rice pudding his mother made just for him, drizzled with grape syrup. The *khoreshteh fesenjoon* she made in the dead of winter. The scent of pomegranate syrup and walnuts spreading through the house and making his mouth water.

Past the sand dunes, there was a row of rough shacks. He climbed the three steps to the midwife's door. Holding the plate, he knocked and waited. There was no answer. After a minute, he put his head to the door to listen, but there was no sound of movement. He knocked a little louder. The midwife did not answer. He walked over to the window and looked in. The lace curtains were drawn but he could see that she was lying in bed. He stared at her, knocking on the window. She did not stir. He walked back to the door and tried the knob. The door opened and he stood on the threshold with the plate. He did not know whether to enter. He had been told to never enter a room without permission.

He looked to see if anyone was on the street. There was no one. He stood for a while longer staring into the house. It was a small room with a *tanoor* oven. Stacks of freshly baked *taftoon* lay on the counter. He closed his eyes and inhaled the cardamom-and-saffron scent of the buttery bread. There was not much to see inside but what was there was meticulously placed. A table in the center was covered with hand-knitted doilies and a small bowl bearing fruit. A single chair faced the one, small window. He did not know what gave him the courage to move his legs but he headed straight for the chair and sat on it, holding the plate in his lap and looking out the window, not once looking in the midwife's direction. Across the street was a one-story mud house like the midwife's, with a woman tidying up inside. Behind it lay the wind-rippled sand, and beyond them, the old city, staid and golden under the sun, and beyond that the open desert plains that framed the whole city. The sky looked huge to him, vast and impossible, most of his life having been enclosed by the four orchard walls.

He turned and looked at the midwife. She had been lying there the whole time watching him. When their eyes met, she smiled. He brought the plate over to her. She waved it away and he placed it on the table, looking at it longingly. She motioned for him to sit beside her. He plopped down, his legs dangling from the chair, T-shirt stretched tightly around his belly. He couldn't help but look at the stacks of bread. The midwife watched him, her smile never waning. She had brought him into this world and watched him grow for ten years. In all of that time, she had never heard him speak nor seen him waver from the simple pleasures of life: his love of food, his adoration for chickens, and his ability to drift away from those around him—happy but distant. She had thought, many times, to tell him who his mother was, but always, in the end, decided against it for fear of leaving him with that burden. What good would come of it? Over and over, she convinced herself that she had done the right thing but never felt better. She motioned to the bread. "Take a piece. It's still warm."

He bounced out of the chair and returned gnawing on a soft, steaming loaf. His cheeks dimpled as he chewed. "You love to eat," she said.

He nodded yes and took another bite.

"I have never cared for food. I always ate it because I had to." The midwife turned her head slightly away and looked through her window. "It's quite a view, no?" Jafar nodded as the midwife continued, "The things that are closest to you are the things that you cannot see." She lifted herself up and said, "Will you help me? I would like to sit by my window."

With great effort, she lifted the covers from her legs and put her feet on the floor, slipping into her house shoes as she struggled to breathe. The boy supported her as she stumbled forward, her arms around his neck. He grabbed her chair with his free hand and held her while she slowly sank into it. He took a knitted afghan from her bed and laid it on her lap. She reached up and touched his face and smiled. "Perhaps you should go and get your mother," she said. "And please take the food and a loaf of bread to the lady in the house across the way. Just leave it by the door. Don't let her speak to you. Then take the rest of the bread to your mother."

With the plate and stack of bread, Jafar crossed the street to the shack and peeked through the window. The lady was still there. She was gaunt but wrapped in a colorful chador. He watched her quick, fidgety movements for a few moments, then placed the plate with a loaf by the door, knocked, and walked away. As he ran off, he could hear her opening the door and picking up the plate.

The midwife watched the prostitute set the plate on her table and use her scissors on the bread, cutting small squares and wrapping them in cloth. She kept a few pieces, saving the others to eat when there was no other food.

Ever since the day she had delivered Jafar, the midwife had shared all her meals with the prostitute, but had never engaged her in conversation. She left loaves at her door. She made sure the prostitute was unharmed after a man had visited. She even taught the prostitute how to bake bread in the *tanoor* and instructed her to take over the oven after her death so that she could sell the bread in the town square and make an honest living. Moved, the prostitute had tried, on many occasions, to thank her or discuss the weather or the windstorms, but the midwife would cut her short, returning to whatever necessary business was at hand. They had fallen into a rhythm together, two women alone, existing in close proximity in the middle of nowhere, worlds apart.

Jafar stood in the kitchen doorway, watching Bibi-Khanoom spoon pickled vegetables into a bowl for the family lunch. She felt eyes on her. "What is it?" she said.

He handed her the loaves.

She set them on the counter, then asked, "How is she doing?"

He shook his head and she immediately wiped her hands, wrapped her chador over her head, and went out of the kitchen.

Her family was gathered around the *sofreh* waiting to eat. "Ghamar," said Bibi-Khanoom. "Let's go. Akbar-Agha, please start lunch. We might not even be back for dinner. Mirza, please come with us. Bring your doctor's bag."

Ghamar pushed herself up and followed, calling out to Nasreen, who came scurrying out from behind a row of trees, wiping her face. "Where are we going?" she said.

"The midwife," said Bibi-Khanoom.

Ghamar looked at her daughter. "Have you been crying?"

Nasreen said, "I just went for a walk."

Jafar followed, trying to keep up with the women's brisk pace. Mirza grabbed his satchel from his shack and caught up by the time they hit the dirt road toward the dunes.

As they came upon the midwife's shack, they heard a thud from inside. Bibi-Khanoom started to run to the door. Entering the house she saw that the midwife had fallen a few paces from the chair, presumably trying to make it back to her bed. Seeing Bibi-Khanoom, her eyes filled with tears of pity and shame.

Mirza carried the old woman to her bed, the women quick to cover her up. Nasreen brought over the chair, and he sat down, opened his satchel, and laid out his instruments. He gently placed the bell of his stethoscope over her heart and looked away as he listened. He then wrapped a cuff around her upper arm, pumped it up, and listened again with the stethoscope.

"Are you in any pain?"

She shook her head.

He put his hand on her abdomen and pressed down on the left and said, "Now?"

She shook her head.

He moved his hand to the right and pressed down and said, "Now?"

She shook her head.

"Do you have an appetite?"

Again, no.

He lifted the bottom of the covers and looked at her feet, noticing that they had begun to swell. The women stood around the bed, speaking to the midwife, asking her what she needed. Mirza took Bibi-Khanoom aside. "She is dying," he said. "Her blood pressure is very low and her heartbeat is irregular. Her systems are failing. She might not make it through the night. I have some pain medicine if it is needed. Other than that, there is nothing to be done."

"Thank you, Mirza-jan," Bibi-Khanoom said. "We can take it from here. You should go home and let the men know we will stay tonight. And please, take Jafar with you."

The sun was setting on the midwife's shack as the women settled in. Nasreen lit kerosene lamps, putting one on the table, one by the bedside, and one by the window. She noticed the prostitute standing by her window looking at the midwife's house. "Who is that woman across the road?" she said.

Ghamar whipped around. "Get away from the window. That woman is a disgrace."

Bibi-Khanoom was sitting by the midwife with a washcloth doused in hot water and scented oil. "Ghamar! That's enough!"

"What, Auntie? She's a prostitute. That's not disgraceful?"

"She's also a human being. Where is your compassion?"

Nasreen was now glued to the window. She wondered how many men the woman had been with. She wanted to see inside the house. To see her bed. Her makeup. To know if she loved any of the men. Or if she was afraid of them. Were they cruel to her? Did they even see her? She hadn't noticed that the prostitute was now staring at her.

"I said get away from the window!" Ghamar said.

Nasreen jumped at her mother's voice. Bibi-Khanoom shushed Ghamar and went back to wiping down the dying woman's limbs. She gently cleaned her face, combed her hair, and adjusted her covers, kissing her on the forehead and holding her hand. The midwife, whose given name was Fatemeh, watched Bibi-Khanoom the whole time through half-closed eyes. "Will you please see that she takes over the *tanoor*? She deserves to make a decent living."

Bibi-Khanoom cast a disappointed look at Ghamar. She then turned to the midwife with a smile and said, "Many years from now, when the time comes and you leave this earth, I promise, if I have not left before you, I will."

The midwife squeezed her hand as hard as she could. "Bibi-jan, I am dying."

"Fatemeh-jan, we all are."

"My friend, we have no time for doublespeak."

Bibi-Khanoom stared into her friend's face, remembering

the countless afternoons they had spent smoking the *ghelyan* and sharing secrets and confidences in its blinding smoke. She remembered the first days after Jafar's arrival at the orchard, when the midwife stayed with her, showing her how to care for the delicate infant. She remembered the old woman's undying love of all things girlish, be they bejeweled bobby pins or flower-print chadors. "You are dying and I don't want you to die," she said. "You are a piece of my life." She looked away from the midwife, casting her head down as she continued, "I am ashamed at my selfishness."

"Don't be," the midwife said. "It is a relief to hear the truth."

The midwife closed her eyes. Bibi-Khanoom watched her breathing for signs of change. Ghamar brought over a platter of bread, cheese, and greens and placed it on the table. She spread a *sofreh* on the floor, setting it up for three. Nasreen and Ghamar sat together, while Bibi-Khanoom went off to the corner of the shack with the midwife's prayer rug and prayer stone. That night, she did not engage in the usual rites and ablutions but simply knelt down and turned her hands up to God, praying for a peaceful end for her dying friend, for the health of her husband, for the safe return of Madjid, for a happy union for Nasreen and Madjid, for a resolution to the war of Ghamar and Mohammad, for Ghamar to make room in her heart for compassion, for her son to finally speak, for Mirza's broken heart to heal, for Shazdehpoor to love Jamsheed as he was, for the prostitute to be treated with kindness, and even for Habib, that he may finally accept the love of his family. Last, she asked God's forgiveness for asking so much.

Throughout the night, the midwife breathed on rhythmically. Nasreen sat on the floor, making lace with a few bobbins she had found, while her mother played solitaire at the table with a deck of cards. Bibi-Khanoom held firmly on to her friend's hand.

Shadows from the kerosene lamps wavered over the walls. Wind howled through the sand dunes, along with the lonely songs of the few crickets that braved the arid landscape.

Bibi-Khanoom turned to Nasreen. "I can't tell you how excited I am for your wedding," she said in a sudden burst of happiness. "The veil you made is the most beautiful lacework I've ever seen. Ghamar, isn't her lacework wonderful?"

The two women were confused about the shift in mood but Bibi-Khanoom continued, "We have so much to do. The guest list, the food preparation, your dress."

Nasreen smiled. "I've been talking to Baba about the dress. White satin."

Ghamar put down her cards. "Then you will have to wear a girdle. Satin is very unforgiving."

"I hate girdles," Nasreen said. "They are so uncomfortable."

"And so are lumps!" said Ghamar.

"She does not have lumps, Ghamar!" Bibi-Khanoom said.

The three women began to bicker, sucking their teeth and pouting about the festive occasion to come, occasionally laughing and interrupting one another. The sound of their voices lit up the room and Bibi-Khanoom felt the dying woman's hand squeeze hers.

It was time for sleep but the midwife's condition remained the same. Ghamar found some blankets from the linen cabinet. She laid them out on the floor and took her spot at the end and said, "I'm going to shut my eyes for a little. But I'm a very light sleeper, so if anything happens just whisper and I'll wake up."

She turned her back to them and immediately started snoring.

Bibi-Khanoom and Nasreen looked at each other and laughed. Then stopped together.

"This must be difficult for you," said Bibi-Khanoom.

"I don't know what to do," Nasreen said.

"No one ever does."

Nasreen studied the flickering shadows of Bibi-Khanoom and the midwife. She thought of her Madjid. "I feel guilty. We are here and I can't help but think of him."

"He will be home soon. I promise."

"How can you be sure? Everything is in chaos."

"I am sure."

Nasreen looked at Bibi-Khanoom and felt better. Bibi-Khanoom smiled and stroked her hair. "What was the first thing you loved about him?"

"His eyes," Nasreen said. "The brown in them has a reddish quality."

"Like Saba."

"When I'm talking to him he looks at me." Nasreen cast her eyes to the floor. "I mean really looks at me. It's almost unnerving. It's the closest I have ever come to the certainty that I exist."

Bibi-Khanoom kissed her on the forehead. Nasreen laid down on her blanket and watched the shadows on the wall as she prayed to God for Madjid's safe return. Bibi-Khanoom could not yet fall asleep. She held the midwife's hand to let her know she was there. The lamp by the bed dimly lit her friend's face and the night grew silent, save for the sound of the wind.

Bibi-Khanoom awoke from a deep sleep, her friend thrashing the covers off. The midwife was burning up and moaning. Nasreen and Ghamar stirred, not fully aware of what was happening. Bibi-Khanoom ran to the sink for a washcloth. She wiped the midwife's face and laid it on her chest, calming her. The heat emanating from her skin was shocking. The midwife opened her eyes and looked at Bibi-Khanoom, clear and wide-eyed, a slow smile turning on her lips. Then she closed her eyes. Her breathing resumed and over the next two hours became more and more labored, her entire being focused on the act of breathing until it stopped, taking her life and the truth of Jafar's birth with it. Bibi-Khanoom never moved from her spot on the bed, never let go of her hand, never once took her eyes off her dearest friend.

The prostitute stood at her window and watched the scene unfold at the midwife's shack. Two men carried the linen-wrapped body of the midwife and loaded it onto a platform attached to two mules by chains. They slapped the mules on their haunches and walked beside them. The three women from the night before stood in the doorway, in broad daylight, watching the cart pull away. The oldest one held her chador over her face and did not take her eyes off the cart. The burly one stood with her hands on her hips, inaudibly arguing with the youngest one. It was the youngest one who had been watching her from the window the night before. When the cart was out of view, they all turned and went back inside and shut the door.

The prostitute sat at her table and let the tears roll down her face. It was a face ravaged by circumstance and the elements. She had lost the only two people in this world who cared for her. First Saba and now the midwife. The prospect of taking over the *tanoor* so that she could stop selling her body meant nothing to her in the face of such loss. A hundred *tanoors* could not replace the concern and kindness these two women had shown her.

Bibi-Khanoom sat on the midwife's unmade bed and watched Ghamar and Nasreen go through the linen and clothes closets.

They made piles of the midwife's things on the floor, arguing as they went along. Ghamar sucked her teeth at her daughter and said, "Don't put that chador there. It was her favorite."

"Then where should I put it?"

"Make a pile of things that won't be given away."

"Fine. But how will I know what goes where?"

"I will tell you as I am doing now!"

"Don't yell at me. I'm trying to help."

"Then do as you're told!"

"Enough!" said Bibi-Khanoom in a deep guttural voice, terrifying the two women. Neither had ever heard Bibi-Khanoom yell.

Bibi-Khanoom began to weep. Nasreen and Ghamar dropped the clothes and rushed over to her. Nasreen grabbed her leg and began to cry too. Ghamar comforted her the only way she knew how to. "Don't you worry, Bibi-jan. I will make sure that everything is done right to honor our beloved Fatemeh. I won't let that Sekeneh anywhere near the midwife's things. I bet everything I own that she will come to the funeral. She always has a way of showing up in times of calamity. Vultures have more decency than her. They wait a few days."

Against all odds, Ghamar managed, once again, to lift Bibi-Khanoom's spirits a little. Bibi-Khanoom shook her head and said, "For God's sake, Ghamar. What is it about Sekeneh that gets you going so?"

"She's a rotten woman. It's probably why her teeth fall out."

Ghamar went back to putting things in piles. Bibi-Khanoom noticed the midwife's favorite chador. It was the one with the flower print she had worn to the first spring lunch a few weeks earlier. She unfolded the bundle, and there inside was the bra that held her most precious belongings: a ring, cotton pads, pins, the bejeweled bobby pin, and her *amjid*. Bibi-Khanoom stared at the items. What surprised her was how these things no longer had any meaning for her, as if the soul of them had left too. She looked out the window and saw the prostitute standing at her window watching them. When their eyes met, the prostitute stepped away from the window. Bibi-Khanoom picked up the *amjid* and headed for the door. "Where are you going?" said Ghamar.

Bibi-Khanoom turned around and shot Ghamar a stare. "Stay here and mind your own business."

After a few moments of knocking, the prostitute's door slowly opened. She was fully covered in her chador. Bibi-Khanoom smiled and said, "I am Bibi-Khanoom. As I'm sure you know, the midwife passed away last night. We are putting her things away and I thought you might like to have this." She held out the *amjid*. The prostitute looked at it and said, "I don't have a *ghelyan*. And even if I did, I don't much care for smoking."

"You can take it and come to my home whenever you wish and sit with me."

The prostitute let go of her grip on her chador, exposing her face. "Do you know what I am?"

Bibi-Khanoom was taken aback by the prostitute's candor. She did know what she was. Everyone knew what she was. But no one, not even Saba or the midwife, knew who she was.

The prostitute had been the daughter of a prominent cleric in Mash'had who had all but ignored her, turning his focus and attention to his two elder sons and his congregation. As far as he was concerned, his daughter was nothing more than a receptacle for breeding and cleaning. She sat silently in doorways, following the lessons for reading and mathematics that her father lavished on her brothers, quietly mouthing words and rounding numbers under her breath, bewitched by the communion of the men in her family. She never spoke, fearing the low register of her voice would draw unwanted attention, and so the family thought her mute and dumb.

It was in the fifteenth year of her life that she finally received the attention of a man, twenty years her senior. He was a traveling salesman from the south passing through Mash'had on his way to Naishapur. He smiled at her as she stood behind her father and brothers, who had stopped to look at his wares. As he pulled his horse-drawn cart away from the crowds, she ran to his side and whisper-yelled, "Take me with you." And he did. And when he had had her and was done with her, he loaded his cart and left Naishapur for home, where his wife and children waited for him, leaving her and some trinkets behind. She had been in Naishapur ever since, living by selling the only thing she had. No one from Mash'had ever came to look for her. When the midwife told her that a family in Mash'had had taken the son she had given up, she liked to imagine that it was her family. That her father lavished the love and attention on her son that he had never given to her.

She asked Bibi-Khanoom again, "Do you know what I am?"

"Yes," Bibi-Khanoom answered, "but I don't know your name."

"Mehry."

"Mehry. Take the *amjid*. And I have left everything in the *tanoor* as the midwife instructed. It is yours now to do with as you please. In fact, I would like to order some bread to be brought to the orchard on a weekly basis. Twenty loaves to start."

She reached into her dress pocket beneath her chador and took out some paper money, handing it to her as she said, "For the bread."

Though still a bit leery, Mehry took the *amjid* and money.

"We will be leaving soon to go to the burial site," Bibi-Khanoom said to her. "Then everyone is coming to my orchard for lunch. You are welcome to join us."

Mehry was almost offended by the naïveté of Bibi-Khanoom's offer. She said "no" and "thank you" as she shut the door.

Bibi-Khanoom stood there for a moment, the image of Mehry's face still in her mind's eye. A face so weathered for one so young. She returned to the midwife's shack to the sound of Ghamar complaining. It was oddly comforting. She said, "Ghamar-jan, we need to go. I want to be there when they wash her."

At the cemetery, Bibi-Khanoom stared, unmoved, through a glass window at two *mordehshoors* washing her friend's lifeless body. The two burly women's lives were dedicated to washing the dead, an act that had hardened their resolve and roughened their hands. Bibi-Khanoom kept her eyes on her friend; the aged, ashen hanging skin, the wiry white hair with shocking orange traces of henna, the mouth hanging open, while thick, strong, indifferent strangers' hands flipped over her body, the water bouncing off, not one drop absorbed by her corpse. This all played out against the stark white marble stage of the washroom and ended with the midwife's body wrapped in linen and placed on a slab.

It was in that moment that Bibi-Khanoom panicked at the thought of never seeing her friend again. Bibi-Khanoom racked her brain trying to remember if she had any pictures of her. The personal effects that only hours earlier seemed insignificant to her were now everything. She almost regretted giving Mehry the *amjid*. She told herself that she would go back to the shack and take the things that the midwife kept close to her heart.

The whole family had come to the small cemetery, where they had buried everyone they knew. It sat atop a hill that looked out to the sand dunes on one side and Old Naishapur on the other.

The sun mercilessly beat down on the headstones and the black-chadored mourners visiting the dead.

The mullah stood over the hole in the ground, looking down at the body wrapped in linen. Jamsheed stood behind him. Akbar-Agha and Mohammad stood together on the other side of the hole. Burying decomposing corpses in the ground seemed horrific to Akbar-Agha. He thought about the ancient Zoroastrian practice of excarnation. If Madjid had been there, they would have engaged in a long discussion about Zoroastrian burial rites and the ossuary where the bodies of the dead are left exposed to the elements and scavenging birds. In that moment he missed Madjid terribly. He looked at Mohammad and said, "God rest her soul."

Shazdehpoor had quietly slipped off to his wife's grave. The flowers that he had laid on the horizontal black marble tombstone on his last visit had wilted and dried. He picked up the bouquet and used it to sweep away the dust and dirt that had gathered on the stone. He looked around him to make sure that no one was looking, then sat next to the stone and touched it. It was scalding from the midday sun. A professional mourner walking by saw how he was nursing his burned hand. She had a bowl of cold water for cooling a grave that she was due to weep over. She bent down and poured it on Saba's grave instead. Shazdehpoor thanked her but she didn't move. He realized why and reached into his pocket for some coins and handed them to her. She smiled and walked away. "Barbarism," he muttered under his breath, turning his attention back to the wet stone. In his mind, he asked his wife to look after Madjid and bring him home. Then, in a rush, he asked her to forgive him for his indifference to Jamsheed.

Bibi-Khanoom and Ghamar stood together with Nasreen wedged between them. Nasreen had tears streaming down her face. She was grateful for the opportunity to weep for Madjid's disappearance under the guise of a funeral. Ghamar put her arm around her daughter and consoled her with tenderness, surprising everyone. "I know. I know," cooed Ghamar. "She was like a mother to you. She was there for your birth and watched you grow. It's very hard to lose someone you love."

Nasreen wept anew and threw her arms around her mother's neck—not for the midwife or even now for Madjid—but for this rare moment of affection.

The gravediggers came and started shoveling the soil as the family watched in silence. Shazdehpoor noticed Jamsheed standing beside the mullah. His son wore a shirt buttoned to the top and he had worry beads in his hands. He was dumbfounded by the radical transformation. Jamsheed timidly inched over. "Hello, Father," he said.

"Hello, Jamsheed."

They stood together in awkward silence for a few moments before Jamsheed continued, "I think the last time we spoke was at—"

"Your mother's funeral."

"Yes, Mother's funeral."

They fell silent again. Shazdehpoor was ashamed of the disgust that he had felt toward his own son and even more ashamed that he had always felt this way about him. The opium addiction was simply an excuse he had used to abandon him. Even now, Jamsheed's religious piety was as humiliating to him as his drug-fueled lethargy. But it never once entered Shazdehpoor's mind that it was this very disdain that might have driven his son to such extremes. That would have been too great a burden for him to bear.

The quiet was suddenly broken by a shapely woman in a black

chador tumbling toward the graveside, arms flailing about. Recognizing the professional mourner, Ghamar squinted and hissed, "Sekeneh."

Sekeneh hurled herself inside the half-filled grave, followed by two young black-chadored women who kept yelling out, "No, Mother, no, please, don't!" She landed at the bottom with a thud. Everyone ran over to see if she was all right. Sekeneh lay prone to the ground, grabbing mounds of soil, hitting herself over the head, wailing. The cleric motioned to the gravediggers to lift her up as he chastised her, "Woman! Get ahold of yourself!"

She fought the diggers as they grabbed her arms. Jamsheed helped them calm her. They sat her by the grave as her daughters tried to console her, to no avail. She continued to weep and whimper, hitting herself. One of her daughters looked up at the cleric and said, "Please forgive her, Haj-Agha. She loved the midwife very much."

Ghamar leaned into Bibi-Khanoom and whispered, "That bitch did not once come to see the old woman. The only time they ever met was for the birth of those two retarded daughters, who have not had a single suitor. Do you know one of them is pushing thirty and the other one talks to herself in public? What do you expect with a mother like that?" Ghamar stared at the convulsing woman and continued, "I swear if that toothless hyena tries to take any of our gentle midwife's things, I will pull the rest of her rotten teeth out myself. You are not letting her come to the orchard for lunch, are you? She will eat everything!"

Bibi-Khanoom started laughing under her chador, muffling the sounds as she said, "My God, Ghamar, you are a mean woman."

Ghamar was taken aback and said, "I am not mean, Aunt Bibi! I am honest!"

Bibi-Khanoom straightened her face and leaned into her niece and said, "They are coming to lunch and you will be nice to them. Now, let's go. I need to get back and help Mirza set up."

Mirza had spent a harrowing morning in the kitchen preparing lunch alone. He had made *gheimeh polo*, the traditional funeral stew, from lamb, yellow split peas, and dried limes. But he had made too much rice. He decided to also use it for a *zereshk polo ba morgh*. Bibi-Khanoom loved *zereshk polo ba morgh*. He lifted the lid of the giant pot and smelled the saffron, the pistachios, the barberries. It was perfection. The rice was fluffy, the scent of butter from the *tahdig* was unburned, and the chicken was roasted and juicy.

Mirza was beside himself.

That morning, he had gone into the chicken coop to grab two birds for the impromptu dish. When he did not see any red ribbons, he thought perhaps Jafar had taken Mina out somewhere. It was only after he had beheaded and defeathered the birds that he realized that one of them had nail varnish on its claws. He panicked and ran into the coop and found Mina's red ribbon on the straw of an empty brooding patch. He had killed Mina. He was sure of it. Guilt-stricken, he tied the red ribbon around another fluffy white hen and placed it back in the coop.

Through the open window, he heard Bibi-Khanoom and Ghamar-Khan—he always dropped the feminine "oom" when thinking of her—approaching the house. His lower lip quivered as soon as the women entered the kitchen. Bibi-Khanoom saw the pained look on his face and ran over to him and said, "Mirza-jan, what is it? What happened?"

"I killed Mina."

Bibi-Khanoom looked confused.

"Jafar's chicken," said Mirza, gently.

She shook her head, claiming it was all right, today was a hard day for everyone. Neither of them noticed Jafar standing in the doorway, his face stained with tears. When they saw him, he turned and ran off. "Jafar-jan! I'm so sorry! Please! We'll get you another one!" Mirza and Bibi-Khanoom called after him.

Mirza and the women set up the platform for lunch as the family arrived. Akbar-Agha walked ahead with his hands clasped behind his back, followed by Sekeneh, who was held up by her two daughters, stopping every few steps to whimper. Shazdeh-poor was last, walking shoulder to shoulder with Mohammad, who kept throwing uncomfortable glances at Sekeneh.

Bibi-Khanoom noticed that the mullah and Jamsheed were not with them. "Where is Habib-Agha and Jamsheed?" she asked her husband.

"They had a prior engagement."

"I see."

There was a silence in which both thought the same thing. Habib had stopped coming to the Friday lunches for some time now. It was the final break from his former life. He was now solely a cleric in all of his relations. Bibi-Khanoom turned to her husband and said, "Well, Mirza made a lovely *zereshk polo ba morgh* out of Jafar's pet chicken."

Akbar-Agha started laughing and Bibi-Khanoom playfully slapped him on the arm and said, "Akbar! Stop it. Jafar is devastated. He's hiding in the coop."

Sekeneh and her daughters sat on one side of the *sofreh* for the lunch in honor of the midwife. Shazdehpoor and Mohammad sat on the other, next to Bibi-Khanoom and Ghamar. Akbar-Agha had made a plate with just the barberry rice and yogurt. He excused himself from the *sofreh* and headed into the chicken coop. Sekeneh buried herself inside her giant black chador. Bibi-Khanoom looked at her and said, "Sekeneh-jan, eat something. You need your strength."

"I can't," Sekeneh whimpered, "I'm too upset."

Ghamar sucked her teeth. Bibi-Khanoom pinched her leg and continued to address Sekeneh, "Please, Sekeneh-jan, for me. I insist."

Sekeneh broke into a quiet sob and dug into the platters of stew, yogurt, herbs, and pickled vegetables, even managing to scoop up a good portion of the *tahdig* as she cried. "For you, Bibi-Khanoom! For the midwife, God rest her soul!" she said, through a mouthful of food.

Ghamar's nostrils flared. She wanted so desperately to say something scorching to Sekeneh, but her aunt's relentless pinching held her back.

Akbar-Agha opened the door to the chicken coop. He saw his son hunched over Mina's brooding patch. He had taken the ribbon off the impostor chicken and shooed her away. Akbar-Agha set the plate down next to Jafar. He pointed to the plate and said, "I brought you some rice and yogurt. Will you eat?"

Jafar shook his head no.

Akbar-Agha bent down and said, "May I sit here with you?"

Jafar nodded yes.

Akbar-Agha sat back and took his worry beads out of his pocket and held them out to his son. Jafar looked up at his father wide-eyed. Akbar-Agha nodded at the boy and Jafar took them in his hands. He had never held the worry beads before but had seen his father flick them every day from the time he could remember. He started to flick the beads slowly at first, then picked up his pace, falling into a rhythm. Mirza opened the door of the coop, startling them both, and said, "Akbar-Agha, it's the telephone."

Akbar-Agha knew exactly what the call was about and jumped up. He followed Mirza back to the house. Shazdehpoor followed his uncle with his eyes as Akbar-Agha went into the house. He watched him through the window talking and nodding on the telephone. Akbar-Agha hung up the receiver and came out on the deck. He looked straight at Shazdehpoor, who was now standing, and said, "They have released him. He's on the train heading home."

PARIS | V

This late in the afternoon, hordes of Belleville residents spilled out of the metro onto the streets. Shazdehpoor stiffly moved through them on Boulevard de Menilmontant, shooing the more aggressive passersby with his lion's-head walking stick. Believing the old man was blind, most of them apologized. Near the entrance to Père Lachaise, the crowds changed from determined locals to meandering tourists. The famed gate was supported by two pillars with Latin inscriptions. As was his custom, Shazdehpoor stopped to read the one on the left. *Spes illorum immortalitate plena est.* "Their hope is full of immortality."

Shazdehpoor entered the gates and walked along the tree-lined main path of the cemetery, comforted by the murmur of birds and hushed human voices.

He had visited here more times than he could remember. It was the one place in this city where he felt at home. In 1979, not too long after he had arrived, he had first come to the cemetery to visit the grave of Sadegh Hedayat, one of his own countrymen.

The tombstone of Sadegh Hedayat, made of polished onyx, was almost identical to Saba's. The first time Shazdehpoor saw it, he was overcome with the memory of his dead wife. Now he studied Hedayat's name engraved in Persian calligraphy. The two dots over the last letter were encircled by a line in the shape of an abstract owl in homage to his most famous book. On April 9, 1951, Hedayat had plugged all the doors and windows in his apartment on Rue Championnet in the Eighteenth Arrondissement. Then he turned on the gas. It would have been a brisk spring day, not unlike today. Shazdehpoor had seen the photograph of Hedayat's corpse lying on the bed in his suit pants and a fine cotton shirt and sweater vest, his wire-rimmed glasses placed on the nightstand. Before he had fallen asleep, Hedayat had left one hundred thousand francs on the kitchen table to cover the cost of his burial, so as not to impose on others after he was gone.

The propriety of this final act moved Shazdehpoor. He recalled the first sentence in Hedayat's *The Blind Owl*, "In life there are certain sores, which, like a kind of canker, slowly erode the soul in solitude."

He looked around, suddenly self-conscious, and busied himself clearing the fallen leaves and dead flowers left behind by other mourners. It embarrassed him to see a gentleman's grave in such disarray.

Not far from here was the grave of Frédéric Chopin, another stranger from a strange land in a strange place. Inside the tomb was Chopin's body but not his heart. On his deathbed he had asked that it be taken back to Poland, his home.

Shazdehpoor closed his eyes. He breathed in the cool spring

air and finally looked up into the canopy of trees, the sun cutting through the leaves in shards of light. He listened to the crying of blackbirds and starlings, the choruses of the moths and crickets, and in that moment he was in the orchard. He could smell the saffron and butter. He could hear the women's voices from inside the kitchen, Ghamar's being the loudest. He could see Madjid sitting with Akbar-Agha under the black walnut tree, his son in rapt attention as Akbar-Agha read from Attar's *The Conference of the Birds*. Shazdehpoor knew the last stanza by heart and recited it in a whisper, "Come, you lost atoms, to your centre draw, / And be the eternal mirror that you saw: / Rays that have wander'd into darkness wide return, / And back into your sun subside."

He looked down at his watch. It was nearing five. The lion's head of his walking stick fell as he lifted it. He had had to glue it on many times before. He let the walking stick fall as well. He headed up Rue de la Roquette, at first fighting the swelling crowds heading to the river with no walking stick to protect him, no handcart to anchor him. Finally he let the movement of the people take him to the water, as if he had been headed there all along.

THE SON RISES

Madjid had not spoken to a soul since his release from prison. When the train pulled into the station, he descended the stairs and stood on the platform holding the plastic bag that the prison guards had given him. Through the crowd, he spotted Akbar-Agha standing alone by the station door. Their eyes met and he felt such relief. He walked over quickly, almost running. As soon as they kissed each other on both cheeks, he started apologizing. "Sir, I'm so sorry for all of the trouble I've caused."

"What trouble?" Akbar-Agha said, "We're all glad that you are all right."

Madjid furrowed his brows.

"Are you? All right?"

Madjid nodded feebly, then looked away.

"The midwife is dead," said Akbar-Agha. "We buried her today."

"How is Bibi-Khanoom?"

"She's very sad," said Akbar-Agha, who led him toward the street. "And so is Mirza. By accident, he killed Jafar's chicken."

"He loved that chicken," said Madjid. "He wrote her name on the wall next to her brooding patch with some nail polish he stole from Nasreen."

"Mina," said Akbar-Agha as he looked down at the bag in Madjid's hand.

"The prison guards gave it to me," said Madjid. "It's a bag of pistachios and a box of *sohan*."

"They gave you souvenirs?"

They looked at each other and burst out laughing. Madjid laughed so hard that it convulsed his body. He laughed until the strain of his laughter turned into sobs. Akbar-Agha stopped walking and took the boy into his arms and held him as he wept.

They walked homeward together along the main road. In the distance, the sun was setting and cast a golden glow on Old Naishapur. The adobe ruins were once universities, mosques, homes, and caravansaries. "Old Naishapur must have been a beautiful city," said Madjid. "But now it's just a few mounds of sand."

"Buildings crumble. It's what happened inside them that matters. Did I ever tell you the legend of the apothecary?"

"I wish you would."

"It's a true story. It happened right where those ruins are now."

It was the year A.D. 1221 and the old city on the border of the eastern plateau was a kind of desert port for all who passed on their way west and beyond. Local and foreign travelers mixed on its narrow streets, jostling toward the universities, shops, mosques, and market squares. In the distance, the turquoise mountains glistened as the sun cast its glow on this city in the midst of its golden era.

It was here that an apothecary lived and worked. He had a small shop on the main street, which he inherited from his father, who had inherited it from his father. He spent every morning inside, the doors closed and shades pulled while he hunched over the counter measuring, in the smallest weight units, medicines for the townspeople. Once he had finished this quotidian task, he opened his doors for business. Patients came from every quarter of the city to pick up their elixirs. Newcomers lined up by the dozens to describe their ailments and order tonics, salves, and medication. The apothecary sat behind his counter and listened to their stories. One woman could not sleep at night, sometimes staying awake until she could not tell whether she was asleep or awake. One man complained about indigestion after eating any sort of dairy but could not eliminate the foods due to his love of yogurt. One young man nervously cleared his throat as he relayed a problem in his bedchamber with his new bride. Sweat beads formed on his forehead as he spoke about the horror and humiliation he faced each evening, wondering if he would be able to perform his duties. A young woman, looking nervously at the door, spoke in hurried tones about the pain in her womb each month and how she dreaded its arrival.

The apothecary had become quite adept at ministering to the sick. He knew exactly what to ask and what to give his patients. After speaking to the woman with insomnia, he asked her to describe a time in her long, varied life when she felt safe. She told him about sitting in her father's garden, splitting open sweet lemons. And so he advised her to split one open whenever she could not sleep. The man with indigestion he told to savor one bite of yo-gurt followed with lemonade to break it down. He gave the young man with bedchamber troubles a ginger-laced ointment to rub on his upper lip—a scent so vigorous it quickened his blood. To the girl with aches in her womb, he gave a salve with herb vapors to rub on her belly, which relaxed her muscles and released the pain. Though he knew a cure for every human ailment, what remained a mystery to him was the suffering of the human spirit.

One day he closed his shop and went on a journey. He trav-eled east and west, north and south, meeting people from the ends of the earth, and listening to their stories as he crossed seven val-leys over seven years. Upon his return, he opened his shop again as though it were any other day, ministering to the suffering resi-dents of the town. In the evenings, he closed the doors and pulled the shades and by candlelight wrote, mostly in rhyme, the stories he had gathered over the years describing their daily struggles and yearnings, their unforeseen disappointments and unbearable losses. Some had perished under the weight of their misfortunes, some had sought the comfort of prayer and worship, some had tried to fill the void within them by crushing others, and some had destroyed the very thing they loved by small, repeated measure. But above all, he told the story of those who had the grace and courage to seek truth.

From then on, he continued to listen to the patients who came and filled their prescriptions, but with each dose of medicine, he also gave them a poem. He grew in reputation and status. His shop was always filled with people. You could hear his work read aloud on the streets, performed by storytellers in the coffee shops, sung by dervishes on the roadside. And yet he never left his shop.

One day an army from the Far East swept into the old city at twilight. By dawn the whole town had been decimated. The general of this army broke down the apothecary's door and took him hostage. The general kept him locked up in a local caravansary, staring at him as his dragoman translated, "You are worth a great deal to this town. This is why I have not killed you like all the others. Who are you?"

The apothecary looked up at the towering general and said, "I am an apothecary."

"That is all?"

"Nothing more."

"Then why has a local merchant offered one thousand silver pieces for your life?"

The apothecary thought it over for a bit, then finally said, "My worth is not measured in silver."

The general conferred with his henchmen and came to the conclusion that the apothecary must be worth far more. He sent the merchant with his silver away. "Now," he turned to the apothecary, "we will wait for the gold."

A local shepherd stood at the entrance of the tent asking to see the general. He was given admission and entered holding a bushel of wheat. He bowed before the apothecary and the general and said, "Sir, I have come to trade this man's life for all that I have."

He placed the bushel of wheat at the general's feet. The general's face burned red with rage as he kicked it away and shouted, "Is this some kind of mockery?"

"No, sir. It is all I have left. You have burned down my home and fields. You have killed all of my livestock and every member of my family. All I have left is this bushel of wheat and I want to give it to you for this man's life."

The apothecary looked at the general and said, "This is the measure of my worth."

The general flew into a rage and kicked the shepherd and his bushel of wheat out of the tent. He turned to the apothecary, lifting him by his collar out of his seat, bringing his face so close that his breath moved the man's lashes as he said, "You mock me? I have killed thousands for less. And now I will certainly kill you."

The apothecary calmly said, "You can rampage across this land, kill every man, woman, and child, tear down every man-made structure and scorch the ground within its borders, but you will never kill me. You can hack my body into a thousand pieces, burn my remains, and bury the ashes deep beneath the earth— but I will live on."

"Who are you?" the general asked again.

"I am a story. You cannot destroy what you cannot grasp."

Madjid and Akbar-Agha had reached the Shazdehpoor house. Madjid was so moved by the apothecary's story that for a moment he forgot all that happened to him. He turned to Akbar-Agha with the same old enthusiasm he always had for his great-uncle's tales and asked, "And what happened to the apothecary?"

"The general stepped back, drew his sword from the scabbard, and cut off his head."

Madjid looked at the ground. "But the general was still the one who lost."

"Yes."

"The apothecary was Attar."

"He was."

"Come, you lost atoms, to your centre draw," said Madjid, reciting the final stanza of *The Conference of the Birds*. Akbar-Agha joined in and together they finished the last lines, "And be the eternal mirror that you saw: / Rays that have wander'd into darkness wide return, / And back into your sun subside."

Akbar-Agha watched the changed expression of the young man. It pained him to break up this moment but he had no choice. "Madjid," he said. "I think it is best if you leave."

"For good?" said Madjid.

"For now."

"Where would I go?"

"I will help you get across the border to Turkey. From there you will apply for political asylum in France. I have a colleague there who will help you. I can give you enough money to get you started but you will have to find work and get yourself into school on your own. If things change, you can come back."

"And if they don't?"

"You make a life for yourself."

"Not without Nasreen."

"Let us worry first about getting you out."

Madjid nodded in silence, his eyes full of tears. "You were right. You tried to warn me."

"I was wrong, Madjid. This is your time. And people like my brother and I have stolen it from you."

"You didn't do anything, Akbar-Agha."

"Exactly. I did nothing. And that is just as bad."

Madjid kept his head down and took in Akbar-Agha's words. He motioned to the house and said, "Akbar-Agha, please come in for tea."

"No, no. You go see your father and get some rest."

"Thank you for getting me home."

Akbar-Agha embraced the young man and said, "Whatever they did to you diminished them. Not you."

All the lights were off in the Shazdehpoor house except for those in his father's study. He walked through the door and saw his father slumped in his club chair. Shazdehpoor winced at the sight of his boy's face—now gaunt and aged, with the faint remnant of a scar on his forehead. He walked over to his son and put his head on his chest and wept. "Don't worry, Father," said Madjid. "I'm all right."

Madjid helped his father back into his club chair, then sat on the divan to face him. On the radio, the BBC commentator announced that a full solar eclipse would take place the next day and described where its path of totality would be visible. His father said, "Every thirty-three years the solar and lunar calendars overlap."

"Yes, Father."

"This will be the first time in your life that you will see the moon eclipse the sun."

Madjid knew what his father meant. His town had been overrun by morality police like the ones who had dragged him off to prison in the capital.

He stood up from the divan and said, "I'm tired, Father. I think I'll go to bed."

"Do you need anything? Food? Tea?"

"No, Father. Just sleep."

It felt odd to be in his room. Each night that Madjid had lain on the cold floor of the prison, he had dreamt of nothing else but to be back in his room again. Yet now that he was back, all he felt was the claustrophobia of confinement. He slipped out the window and walked onto the open road and let the warm spring evening wash over him.

Tomorrow was Ashura, the holiest day for Shi'ite Muslims, the day that marked the death of Imam Hussein and his family. But because of the overlap of the solar and lunar calendars tomorrow was also Chaharshambeh Suri, a fire-jumping ritual of Zoroastrian origin that had become a part of the Iranian culture, which always took place on the last Wednesday before the New Year. One ritual was a religious lamentation, the other a cultural celebration.

Madjid remembered the last time he jumped the fire during Chaharshambeh Suri. His mother was still alive, though she already showed signs of the illness that would take her life. She sat and watched him jump over the fire again and again, chanting the purification rite, "My yellow is yours, your red is mine." That particular year Madjid had prayed to the fire, lit every year to keep the sun alive, to take the sickly pallor from his mother's face.

Madjid also remembered the last time he attended an Ashura ritual. It was after his mother's death. He sat among the men in the crowd watching the Ta'ziyeh play. He wept for his loss. He joined the procession of self-flagellating men and whipped himself with borrowed chains, until his back was bloody, his mind exhausted and free of grief.

Now he headed to Nasreen's house. He walked quietly through the garden and stood behind the willow tree in front of the tailor shop, staring at his beloved sitting at her table by the window, weaving—an act that now seemed frivolous to him. He could see that she had pinned her hair up and stained her lips red, expectantly looking up into the darkness outside, waiting. But he felt so far from her now. She seemed almost like a painting or a photograph.

For one brief moment he almost stepped out from behind the willow tree, but the thought of speaking to her about what he had been through seemed impossible. He turned and walked out of the garden. He needed to be alone. Past the city wall, the moon-light reflected off the sand dunes like a shadow of the sun to come. The emptiness of the land, the vastness, was at once both peaceful and painful. He sat on a mound and listened to his breath against the wind.

A life with Nasreen, full of small fleeting pleasures but con-fined inside the walls of the orchard, now seemed absurd. The last words of the interrogator rang in his head: "I will watch every sin-gle move you make, and if you step, if you even think of stepping out of line, I will destroy you." A life with Nasreen somewhere out in the world, in a foreign land, free but lost now seemed pitiable.

The next morning, classical music blasted from his father's radio. The first fight Madjid had ever had with his father was over music. It was during their sequester in the house, after his moth-er's death. Madjid had sat in the salon listening with his father to string quartet after string quartet. He turned to his father and asked, "Why don't you ever listen to Persian music?"

"I like the complex melodies and thoughtful compositions of Bach and Beethoven and the other Germans," said his father. "Persian music has too much improvisation."

"But those complexities and compositions exist in Persian music as well."

"It's a matter of taste, I suppose."

Madjid had looked at his father for some time and studied his face, his dress, his salon, before he said, "You don't like where you come from."

"That's not true at all."

"You hate to sit on the ground. You hate our food, our music, our décor, our traditions. You are like an exile in your own country."

Shazdehpoor had stormed out of the salon. They'd never spoken about it again.

Madjid now understood something he did not then. He understood why his father surrounded himself with the finery of a foreign country. It was light and capricious, weightless and inconsequential. It was everything this place was not.

Madjid opened the door to his room and, to his surprise, found Nasreen. She was draped in a black chador, holding one of his shirts. She did not look at him nor did she move. "Four years ago, I was sitting on this bed, holding one of your shirts. I didn't know who you were at the time. I was young and impulsive. I must confess something," she said. "I looked through your notebook." Only then did Nasreen look up, her face visibly shocked by the changes in his own. He leaned on his desk with his arms crossed. She moved her mouth a few times as if to speak before words arrived, then said, "I wanted to know you."

She turned her gaze to the window, the light hitting her face. She had been crying. Her eyes were red and swollen. "I saw you standing by my willow tree last night, looking at me. Why didn't you come to me?"

"I didn't know what to say."

"You didn't have to say anything."

She stood, the shirt still in her hands, and walked over to him, the chador falling to the floor. She kissed the faint scar over his eye. He kept his arms crossed but pressed his lips against her forehead. In the three weeks that he had been gone, Nasreen had watched the world around her change as people took sides. Friends she had

had for years suddenly stopped speaking to her. She had seen a group of militant boys throw acid in the face of a girl who had dared to walk the streets uncovered. She had watched as a group of militant girls held down their friend and wiped the lipstick off her mouth with a napkin that had a razor hidden inside, the blood turning the girl's pink lips red. "I'm so afraid," she said. She looked up at him. "Jamsheed is one of them now." She shook her head. "There's nothing you can do to change it. They are killing people like animals. Please. Let's get away. We can start a new life together. I'll go anywhere with you. Anywhere. Please."

She buried her head in his neck and softly wept. He put his arms around her and tried to console her, his mind racing. "We will," he said. "I promise."

He walked Nasreen to the front door and kissed her on the lips. She stepped outside then turned to face him. Not that long ago, they had walked arm in arm through the streets of Shiraz during the festival, her hair falling on her shoulders, her laugher matching his. Now she was dressed in a chador, separate from him. As she walked away, the black fabric rippled behind her. The wind carried the jasmine scent of her perfume.

Madjid looked around his room at the clutter of books and papers. One by one, he removed the photographs from the mirror above his desk, crumpling them up and throwing them in the wastepaper basket until there was nothing left in the frame but his own reflection. His notebook was buried beneath a stack of old magazines on the top shelf of his bookcase. He had not looked at it since writing its last page. He leafed through its pages, skimming the letters to his mother, anguish rising in his chest as he looked at her photograph. A few entries later, he smiled at his doodles and drawings, his lofty and heartfelt proclamations, quiet details of a life he had lived, thus far, as consciously as he could manage, realizing as he read that there was still so much beyond his comprehension. And then he came upon the jagged image that took up an entire page. He stopped to look at the thick black parentheses, the red gash and thin black stitching. He remembered drawing it, and, even more, the day he had seen it.

That day, Madjid was still too small to see over his brother. He had stood on his toes behind Jamsheed's shoulder, peeking into his father's salon. "Stop breathing on me!" said Jamsheed, who then nudged him, almost knocking him off his feet.

"Well?" said Jamsheed. "Go in."

"No, no way," Madjid said. "You go."

"It's time for you to do it," Jamsheed said as he stepped aside.

Madjid just stood there, on the threshold. A bowl full of loose change sat on a rococo carved table beside his father's club chair. The tomans were all round nickels engraved on one side with the lion at the center holding a sword, the sun behind it, and on the other, with the profile of Mohammad Reza Shah Pahlavi.

His older brother was against the arched door frame, arms crossed, his right leg kicked over his left. At fifteen, Jamsheed still towered over his younger brother in more ways than one.

"He'll know," Madjid said. "It's not right. We'll get into a lot of trouble."

"He won't know. I've watched him throw his change in that bowl from his pockets and he never counts it." Jamsheed leaned forward, holding his cocky position. "Now, if you're afraid to do it, I'd be happy to."

"I'm not afraid! It's just . . . it's just not right."

"Fine, I'll do it," Jamsheed said as he stepped inside.

But Madjid grabbed his arm.

"No. I will," he said, walking slowly toward the bowl. He turned back. "How much do we need?"

Jamsheed smiled and held up four fingers. Madjid carefully removed the coins, trying not to move or disturb those around them. "Let's go," he said, with a newfound swagger in his step.

Jamsheed saluted him. "Whatever you say, sir!"

The two brothers took the dirt road past the sand dunes. Madjid walked at a brisk pace, jangling the coins in his pocket. He wanted to feel good about what they were doing. He had been thinking of nothing else for weeks, ever since the night his brother had suggested the plan. Stealing money from his father to do something that he could never tell a soul about made him feel vile but he had been determined to do it anyway. Besides, there was no way out now, he assured himself.

They reached the edge of the dunes where a few boys still milled about. For a brief moment Madjid thought of running home, but Jamsheed took the lead, walking straight to the group. He greeted the boys with a nod, then ushered Madjid ahead. "You first."

Madjid looked at him for a few moments, saying nothing, the only sound that of the coins in his pocket.

"Give me two tomans," said Jamsheed. "You only need two for yourself."

Madjid handed half the money to his brother, then slowly walked into the cool, dark cave. The sound of the boys' whistles and cajoling soon faded. His eyes became acclimated to the lack of light, only a faint kerosene lamp. Behind it the shadow of a woman lay splayed against the wall like an ancient cave painting. He stood motionless, staring at the shadow, afraid to look at the actual person. She was small, marginally plump. She stood with her back against the wall and her legs slightly open. She wore a dusty black chador that brushed against her shins. "Come closer," she said. "You can't see from there."

The guttural depth of her voice surprised him. He inched his way closer but could not make out her face. Her head was against the wall, out of sight. She pointed to a woven basket a few feet away from her and commanded him, "Put the money there."

He obliged.

"Come, boy," she said, "I don't have all day."

She pointed to a spot on the ground directly in front of her legs. He walked over and sat, cross-legged. But he looked down at the ground.

"Up, boy," she said. "Look up." She opened her chador. She was naked beneath it. He stared at her breasts. They were engorged, terribly large, as though about to burst from her skin. His eyes moved down. Her belly was round and slightly swollen. She spread her legs wide open. He leaned in a little. The shape was an abstraction to him, four parentheses surrounding a dark opening. At the bottom, where the parentheses met, were fresh stitches, with dried, glistening blood surrounding the wound. He looked at her, trying to make out the face behind the veil, and asked, "Are you hurt?"

"Okay, that's enough," she said abruptly. She closed her legs and pulled her chador around her. Wet spots darkened the fabric around her breasts, and he caught a glimpse of her face as she leaned forward to adjust her veil. Her eyes were black and shone fiercely. Her mouth was an upward wisp, her lips defensive and thin. She seemed young, perhaps twenty, but he could not tell.

Her face was as weathered as a desert rock, almost cracking from what must have been constant exposure to the elements. "Go on," she said. "Go out that way."

A passage lay to the other side of the dune. Madjid walked into the blistering sunlight and waited for his brother. After a few silent minutes in the wind and desert, his brother came out of the cave laughing and clapping his hands, throwing his arm over Madjid's shoulder as he led him to the road.

"She's something, no?" Jamsheed said. "It's been a year since I've seen her. She's put on some weight. But at least it's done her breasts a world of good. Hooo!"

Madjid walked silently under his brother's arm and mustered a faint "yeah," then drowned out his brother's detailed description of the prostitute's body and its flaws.

It was the first time Madjid had seen a naked woman with such intent. He was, much to his own discomfort, not aroused in the way he thought he should have been. He could not shake the image of her engorged breasts, swollen belly, and the barely visible stitching along her woman part. He did not know that the stitches repaired a perineal tear and that it was the body of a woman who had just given birth. He did not know that he would meet the infant who had torn through her only days before. He had only felt the power that emanated from every inch of her body, and this had thrilled him. And confused him. And inspired him.

As soon as they reached the house, Madjid headed straight for his room, ignoring his brother's inquiries about his need to touch himself. He sat staring out the window at the manicured trees, and the sand dunes beyond the yard, and the horizon beyond everything. The image of the woman and the smell of her sex lingered in his mind. He had innately understood that beneath her soft skin and delicate frame, a feral, fundamental life force simmered—more powerful and more mysterious than anything he dared imagine. He opened his notebook and took out two markers, one black and one red, and drew what he had seen, branding the image in his mind forever.

A BED OF FLOWERS

Madjid stopped at the entrance of the orchard. The perfume of blossoming pears filled the air. The fruit pickers were due to arrive in two months, and Madjid had never missed a harvest. He loved the fruit pickers. They were all from one family, the head of which was a five-foot-tall matriarch who acted as the foreman over her six towering sons. They came from a small village called Fadisheh that was forty-five kilometers southwest of Naishapur. In the beginning of summer, they came to pick cherries, sour cherries, plums, apricots, and pears. They worked every day from light to dark, harvesting all of the orchards in Naishapur. For the remainder of the year, they traveled to nearby towns, threshing and winnowing grain fields.

They arrived at the orchard before daybreak in their pickup truck loaded with stepladders, baskets, hedge shears, wheelbarrows, and mesh plastic bags. They divided the trees into three groups, two brothers working a single tree. One climbed the stepladder, picked the fruit, and threw it in the basket. The other bagged the fruit, then filled the wheelbarrow, then carted it out to the truck, while the last brother sheared the branches and moved his ladder to the next tree. Among the six of them, they went through three trees at a time, while their mother paced back and forth, keeping time with a switch that she smacked against her leg. She worked her boys until noon, when she allowed them to break for a quick lunch. Mirza called her "the colonel." Sometimes, in the afternoon, when the heat became unbearable and the boredom of the repetition set in, the colonel would break into a call-and-answer song that kept her sons going at a productive clip.

Today, the house seemed mysteriously empty. Madjid peeked through the windows on the deck, then circled the house and barn. Only the animals milled about, none of them ruffled by his presence. He sat under Akbar-Agha's tree, leaning against the smooth trunk, one leg straight, the other bent at the knee with his arm resting on it, tilting his head upward as he closed his eyes. He would take a siesta. Just a short one.

"My friend," a soft voice called out.

He opened his eyes and saw Mirza standing there holding a tray with tea service. He had not seen Mirza since his return from prison. Mirza was shocked by his transformation and it showed on his face. Madjid smiled. "It looks a lot worse than it is. I ran into a wall. That's all."

Mirza set down the tray. "Where I come from it's called 'falling down the stairs.'"

He poured the tea. Madjid dipped his sugar cube before taking a sip. "I was just thinking about the colonel and her sons."

"They'll be coming a little earlier this year. It's been unseasonably warm."

"Where is everyone?"

"It's Ashura. They're at the square to see the Ta'ziyehs."

"Why didn't you go?"

Mirza blew his tea cool and without looking up said, "Stories of warring men, long dead. Families broken and dislocated. Lovers torn apart before they ever love. Nations turned upside down, almost unrecognizable. And all of it set to beautiful melodies and poetic words? No. Not for me."

He waved the notion away as he sipped his tea and continued, "Besides, I have already lived the past. I would rather take tea with you, here and now."

Mirza drained his glass, slammed it down on the tray, and hopped to his feet. "Come with me."

Madjid followed him to the beds along the side of the house, listening as he pointed out the rosebushes, the ice flower patch, and the horned poppy clusters, thinking of the difference between those flowers that germinated, flowered, and died in one brief stroke— and the breathtaking flashes of vigor and scent that resulted—and those that must be coaxed to bloom only to wither under the harsh gaze of a summer sun. His favorites were the perennials, those that live and die every season, over and over again, deeply rooted, self-contained and constant, fading out without ostentation.

They circled back to where they started and walked up the path together. Madjid smiled and said, "I heard about Mina."

Mirza put his face in his hands and said, "Oh God, I still feel terrible. He won't even look at me."

"I don't think he'll ever eat chicken again."

They laughed and walked the rest of the path in silence, the sound of pebbles under their feet. Madjid looked up at the canopy of trees that hung over the path and squinted his eyes at the sunlight that cut through them. "Say what you want, I can't imagine this place not ever being here."

Mirza laid a hand on his shoulder, the look on his face the same grief-stricken one from that day, so many years ago, when he held the lifeless body of the fainting goat in his arms. Mirza said to him, "My friend, there are things beyond our control."

"I understand."

"I speak from experience. I lost one life. So I found another." Mirza searched the young man's eyes. "Land is land, Madjid. Everything you are is with you."

"I know."

"Then do as Akbar-Agha bids you. Go to Paris. Start a new life."

"I will be by tomorrow afternoon for a game of backgammon."

"You like to lose?"

"Only to you."

He stepped through the massive doors and watched as Mirza closed them. Their weight echoed in his ears. He stood on the road that led to the town square in one direction and homeward in the other. He knew he should head to the house to avoid the Ashura processions and crowds, but he needed to see his brother and he knew exactly where he would find him. He turned left, the wind kicking up the dust and the sun ablaze above.

The mullah paced back and forth, flicking his worry beads. Before him, the entire *heyat*—all of them devoted young men—sat crosslegged in rows. Jamsheed sat front and center. He had gathered them all in here after breakfast. Now all the men had five o'clock shadows. Their dress shirts had sweat marks. Sitting next to Jamsheed was Amin, a staunch traditionalist and loyal follower of the cleric. He rocked while flicking his worry beads as the cleric said, "This is a solemn day for us, a day of mourning and remembrance for Imam Hussein. What he suffered and sacrificed in the name of human dignity. But it is also a day of reckoning." He stopped pacing and faced the boys and continued, "Many will gather to mark Chaharshambeh Suri. A pagan ritual on the day of Ashura. But we are Muslims first. They are the very same people who were responsible for Mahmoodreza's death—the privileged sons who would have us desecrate this holy day. They would have us forget Mahmoodreza and the sacrifice he made with his own life. They would have us forget his sister who was violated and hanged herself from a tree with her child still in her womb. But we will not forget. We know who we are and we know what we must do."

He paused. Then added, "Stay in your groups and be vigilant. This is only the beginning."

The young men stood as the mullah left the room. Amin flipped off the light switch. He stood before the congregants and slowly began to beat his chest with the open palms of both hands until everyone joined him. Their beating grew louder, more powerful. Amin then began his chant, a lamentation to the beat about Imam Hussein and his death. Each phrase was sung to the rhythm of the men's hands. Each brought Hussein back to life, from his lush black beard to his defiant noble stance. The last few lines of the chant captured, in great agonizing detail, the bloody massacre of Imam Hussein's killing, right down to the severing of his head. Tears rolled down Amin's face as he sang, and the young men fell deeper into the trance, beating themselves on the chest, harder and harder, some letting out guttural sounds, some weeping, some whimpering, all together, completely rapt.

Jamsheed closed his eyes. His brow was slick with sweat from the swaying and beating. He felt himself at peace, a feeling that had always eluded him except on a motorbike or in an opium haze. He wept not in lamentation, not in despair, but in relief.

He opened his eyes, the worship now ending. "Most of the fires will be set along the road toward the old city," said Amin. "They'll be lighting the fires during the eclipse. We need one group to patrol the shoulders and round them up. We need another group on the side streets of the square to keep the Ashura crowds in line." He pulled Jamsheed to the side and whispered, "Keep your brother out of my sight. For his own good."

The young men headed out of the *heyat* room. In twos and threes, they mounted the motorbikes lined up against the curb. The bikes were covered in religious slogans with painted pictures of the Twelve Imams wedged across the handlebars. Each passenger carried a weapon; bats, brass knuckles, chains, even knives. As each motorbike hit the road, the men called out, *"Allahu Akbar."*

Jamsheed stood alone inside, a sudden feeling of unease coming over him. He quickly put on his shoes and left by foot. The mid-afternoon sun was blinding. As his eyes adjusted to the burning light, he saw his brother across the street, staring right at him. His eyes were sharp and deliberate, his face gaunt, scarred somehow, now older than Jamsheed's own.

Jamsheed walked to his brother, grabbed his arm, and dragged him homeward without a word. Madjid flailed and managed to free one arm. But Jamsheed spun around and forced him back onto the sidewalk. "You stupid little boy," he said. "This isn't a game. Go home!"

Madjid was startled by his brother's fury. "What are you doing, Jamsheed?" he said. "This is madness. These people are fanatics."

"These people you call fanatics are the very same ones that you championed as a student. They *are* the revolution."

"They are thugs."

Jamsheed softened his voice, then said, "You should go home. All hell will break loose in a few hours. Please, go home."

Madjid did not take his eyes off his brother. "Jamsheed," he said, "you are a part of something that will destroy you. I know what Habib-Agha did for you. I know that he cares for you. But he can only lead you down toward his own darkness. You can't see it because you're desperate. Please, don't do this."

"Do what?"

"You forget that I ran into a few of your so-called brothers in prison. Don't do it, Jamsheed. The violence you commit will ruin you."

"Did no one tell you that if it wasn't for Habib-Agha you would still be rotting in that prison? Who do you think got you out? Akbar? Akbar is nothing now. Nothing. He went to his brother begging him to make the call to release you. One call from Habib-Agha and you were free."

Jamsheed stepped even closer to his brother, their faces almost touching. "We are the revolution."

Then he turned and began to walk away, stopping only once to say, "Do not come to the square. Everyone knows where you've been and where you stand. I am warning you for your own good."

Madjid was dumbstruck. Jamsheed's skepticism, his humor, his carefree spirit had been replaced with clarity of purpose—and blind allegiance. It occurred to him that in all the years of their lives together, he had never fully understood the depth of his brother's despair. Like everyone else, he had simply accepted Jamsheed's masks because it was easier than confronting his pain.

The watchmen from the *heyat* room parked their motorbikes near the arches of the town square. They spread across the crowd of townspeople waiting for the final processions and the performance of Ta'ziyeh, which ended the day of mourning.

A Ta'ziyeh performer walked to a partitioned corner of what had been the dress shop earlier that day but was now a dressing room. He slipped behind the curtain. His horse stood reined to a nail in the wall. She nickered at his approach. He took down the bridle and laid his hand over her muzzle, holding it as he eased the bit into her mouth and smoothing the straps into place. He then flung an embroidered saddle pad over her flank and placed a leather saddle over it, cinching the wide, worn leather strap, tugging at the stirrups, and gauging her reaction to see that she was comfortable. She kicked her head up and whinnied. He ran his hand over her mane and slipped a small apple into her mouth.

The performer, who owned the dress shop, looked at himself in a shard of mirror nailed into the wall. He adjusted his headgear, a metal helmet with chain mail draped over the back of his neck, ear-to-ear, down to his shoulders. With his sword in its scabbard, his green tunic and black riding boots, he was a visage from thirteen hundred years ago. A holy warrior.

He turned to the other performers—several men his age dressed in the same fashion as himself and several leaner, more compact others dressed as women with black veils covering their heads and beards. Three small boys, his own sons, were dressed in bright colors, illuminating their young, plump faces. As soon as they finished the final adjustments to their costumes, gear, and horses, he gave a single small nod of approval to his troupe.

A procession of men from several *heyats*, flagellating themselves with chains attached to wooden handles to the rhythm of a man's voice belting over a loudspeaker, formed a circle in the center of the square and began to take their seats. The townspeople perched in clusters behind them, some of the younger ones climbing onto the rooftops of the shops where they could better see the play about to take place. Whispers filled the air about the bad omen of the approaching eclipse and many cast frightened glances at the watchmen stoically planted among them. The watchmen scanned the crowd, on the lookout for forbidden smiles and laughter. A group of women dressed head to toe in black, only their eyes peering out, filed in beside them. Almost instantly, they spotted a girl in a loose headscarf, descended upon her, and dragged her away. Their male counterparts did the same with a young man in a short-sleeved shirt.

Akbar-Agha slowly paced outside the circle, keeping watch over his family on the farthest edge of the audience. He had spent the morning trying to talk his wife out of going to the performance, but Bibi-Khanoom was not about to break tradition. Seeing his wife arguing over something with Ghamar, he smiled. Then he waved to Nasreen and Jafar.

"Ghamar," Bibi-Khanoom said, "stop looking at Sekeneh."

"I can't believe she's weeping already."

"Ghamar, everybody cries at the Ta'ziyeh."

"Yes, when it's actually started. Not before."

Nasreen put her head under her chador. She had not understood—or appreciated—the privacy that chadors allowed in public spaces. In a barely audible whisper, she chanted her private name for Madjid, like an incantation: "Madjiddy, Madjiddy, Madjiddy." Then punctuated it with ownership, "Madjidam."

Mohammad sat with the men adjacent to the women's section, flicking his worry beads. He noticed his wife arguing with Bibi-Khanoom. He turned his gaze to Sekeneh, who was staring right at him. She winked when she caught his eye then went back to her convulsive weeping. He panicked, then looked back at his wife, who was now staring right at him, her face devoid of any expression save the tears that rolled down her cheeks. In that moment, he knew that she had always known of his affair with Sekeneh.

He cast down his head and covered his eyes in shame.

Akbar-Agha stood next to an old man, a member of the *ghelyan* shop clique and its most outspoken political speaker. Surveying the crowd, the old man said, "This had always been a day of solace for us."

"And now?' said Akbar-Agha.

The old man dusted off his coat, preparing to step into the center of the circle. "My old friend," he said. "Look at the aggression around you. There is no comfort in it."

Akbar-Agha looked at the groups of young men and women who policed the crowd and understood, finally, that the old man was right. He thought about his brother and everything that Habib had overcome in his life. But what difference had overcoming adversity made? The moment his brother gained power, he became the very thing he had fought against.

The band of percussionists began a drumbeat. The horn players blew a melody. Slowly, the crowd hushed as the old man walked into the center of the square, his eyes half closed at the sight of a town shifted beyond his recognition. In a soft-spoken voice he began to recite:

> Twilight falls on terra and time
> As we recall another place and clime.
> The sun and moon about to collide,
> No place is left for our time to hide.
> It cannot leave nor will it stay,
> It must be left exactly as it lay.
> And as the years lay layers upon its back
> A fossil will form in the recess of our head.
> Sunset, nightfall, crepuscule, gloam,
> As we, for the moment, lose our way home.

The old man's eyes searched the crowd for just one person who understood what he was saying, finding only Akbar-Agha. He nodded to the judge, then finally launched into the prologue of the Ta'ziyeh of Ghasem. Slowly, in a voice building with power, he told the story of Imam Hussein's daughter Roghayeh betrothed to Imam Hussein's nephew Ghasem. In the midst of the Battle of Karbala, their wedding is celebrated right before Ghasem is killed in battle.

Already the crowd began to weep and sway. The watchmen and women were moved by the tragedy about to unfold before them. The less devout moved by their own private losses and the sudden freedom of being able to grieve both so openly and so secretly, in the midst of so many others.

With a single clap of his hands, the old man was finished. He exited the circle, passing the performers and their horses in the dressing area.

The dress shop owner stood behind his eldest son, who was

cast as the warrior groom, Ghasem. Behind him was his middle boy in a veil as Roghayeh, the bride-to-be. The bandleader kicked off a military march of drums and horns, and the troupe filed out, walking inside the circle of spectators before coming to a stop in a semicircle facing the three boys. The call and answer between the men and boys began, recounting in melody the tragic love story.

THE MOON ASCENDING

Akbar-Agha stood listening to the dirge of Ghasem. His heart was broken and he had never, in all of these many years, felt so alone. He walked through the byways of town, listening to the clanging of pots, the hiss of voices, the howl of dogs. He looked up to the sky and saw the moon beside the sun.

At the mosque, he stopped. Light broke through the crack of the door as he pushed it open and stepped inside. There was nothing but silence, the room empty.

The first time he had ever come here, it was to do his ablutions at the fountain and pray alongside his father. The exhilaration of belonging had filled him with a sense of comfort.

When had he realized that the sermons his father so admired never addressed his doubts? When had he begun to see the men and women, prostrate before their scriptures and icons, as schools of fish swimming in circles?

In the main hall, he found his brother sitting on the *mambar*, alone. Pots clanged in the distance, crowds chanted. The performance was over in the square, the processioners flagellating themselves as they left.

The mullah glanced up from his worry beads.

"Something has been bothering me for quite some time now," said Akbar. "Perhaps you can help. You knew the young man who was hanged, I believe."

"The martyr, you mean."

"How did he figure out the identity of the man who impregnated his sister? No one in her family knew she was pregnant until after she killed herself."

"She went to see her brother the night before. Perhaps she told him then."

"I don't think so."

"Perhaps the boy that ruined her boasted about it."

"Not by name."

They locked eyes. A slight twitch fluttered through the mullah's expression and Akbar moved in. "How did you know who it was?"

"I didn't."

"Then why did you tell him you did?"

"I didn't."

"You are lying."

"I am not."

"You are lying!"

"No. I am not! I did not tell him who it was, because I did not know. I simply guessed it and one of my students informed him. And I was right."

The mullah stood up and glowered at his brother as he continued, "Doubt is like a cancer, Akbar. The more you feed it, the faster it spreads. And the young man died with his dignity intact."

"False pride is not dignity."

"You cannot understand."

"Then explain it to me."

"They must pay for the abuses we have suffered."

"Who are this 'they'?"

"You know very well, Akbar. The pagans and infidels. The aristocracy who have whored our nation to their Western masters. You of all people should know the value of justice. What could possibly be more important?"

Akbar stared at his brother. "I am sorry, Habib."

"For what?"

"For what he did to you. And to our sister and our mother. I am sorry that I didn't know how to make it stop."

"This is not about us."

"This has always been about us."

"Think what you want. What is done is done."

Akbar looked into his brother's face, a stranger's face, and said, "Chaos reigns outside these doors, your chaos. And soon, when the dust settles, you will be in charge of it all. Tell me, how does it feel?"

The mullah looked up at his brother and, without a trace of irony or contempt, said, "I feel nothing."

Mehry hid among the women in her chador watching the Ta'ziyeh, her eyes welling up as Ghasem sang a song for his beloved while he dressed for battle. She melted into the crowd of black cloth where she could let herself feel a belonging that eluded her on any other day. She swayed with the womenfolk, basking in the warmth of shared communion as she touched shoulders with the very women who would otherwise shun her and swat her away like a fly.

She smiled at a cluster of children fidgeting and giggling in the front row. But Ghasem was exiting the stage on his horse. The spell that held the audience captive had broken. Mehry felt seen and abruptly stood and made her way past the huddles of women to one of the arched entrances of the square. She walked homeward, her chador wrapped tightly around her, only her clenched hand and half of her face exposed. She held her head down as she hurried through the dark narrow byways of the town. The sound of the Ta'ziyeh became fainter and fainter.

The sky turned a slate color. The moon began to eclipse the sun. All along the road leading to the old city, young men were jumping over the fires built in the brush. Some men burned the legs of their pants. Others shot past with flushed cheeks and singed holes in their shirts, chanting even louder, "My yellow is yours, your red is mine."

The Zoroastrian ritual was ancient—far more ancient than Ashura. Up and down the orchard road, logs snapped and popped. And more men gathered, defying the clerics. A pickup sped along the road, coming to a jerky halt. Jamsheed sat tensely in the passenger seat beside Amin, the driver. Kicking the door open, he jumped out of the truck followed by several of his henchmen.

Brandishing his club, he led the way to the nearest fire. The jumpers stood still, staring. Jamsheed looked at a young boy, no more than fourteen. Then he looked to the truck. Amin was sitting behind the wheel, watching him. He faced the boy and swung his club at his head. The boy hit the ground and Jamsheed dragged him by one foot to the back of the truck, lifted him by his shirt, and threw him in.

One by one, all the young men were beaten and dragged to the back of the truck, kicked once more by the henchmen if they tried to escape. His job finished, Jamsheed took his seat up front. Amin nodded his approval, then slammed his foot on the gas to make a sudden U-turn as he sped to the next fire. A few boys ran into the forest, too far off to chase down.

By the time they reached the fire closest to town, it was abandoned. Word had spread. Jamsheed stood over the smoldering flames, the light flickering over the blood on his club. A few drops rolled down the length of the wood and fell, like burned rain, with a hissing sound.

In the back of the truck, the captives cowered together, looking at him with frightened eyes that didn't mask their contempt. He liked this contempt. He was stronger. He was in control. He was righteous. "Amin," he shouted, "go ahead and take them to the holding area. I will walk to the square and wait for you."

Madjid walked briskly, twigs snapping under his feet. His cheeks were flushed from the pyre he had jumped over, his mind horrified by what he had just seen: his brother beating his friends while he hid in the trees, his brother dragging a boy into the back of a pickup truck then standing over a fire with his club, his face almost serene.

Madjid cut through the forest, following the ascending moon. Pots clanged sporadically in the distance as townspeople prepared for the eclipse. Harsh sounds helped ward off evil spirits. He could also hear the Ta'ziyeh. Ghasem's song for his bride. Madjid pictured the scene: young Ghasem preparing for battle, sweetly describing her beauty. He pulled his chain-mail vest over his head as he sang about the delicate curve of her eyebrow. He fastened his belt with his sword and scabbard around his waist as he admired the cupid's bow of her mouth. He put on a white shroud in preparation for martyrdom as he praised the curl of her raven-black hair. And then he stopped singing, erased her image from his mind, and rode out on his horse to meet his fate.

The moon continued to inch over the sun. The sky became darker. Madjid walked through the trees, following the fading light. He saw the road and ran toward it.

On the shoulder, he found Mehry looking up at the eclipse. She squinted.

"Don't stare at it," he said. "It will burn your eyes."

She gripped the chador tightly around her face.

"I know you," he said.

"Lots of men know me."

Madjid averted his gaze. "No. I mean, I know you. Years ago, in the cave, I saw you."

"What do you want?"

"That day in the cave," he said. "What happened to you? Who had done that to you?"

"Done what?"

"Your woman part. It was stitched and bloody."

"Oh. Yes. I remember you now. Who are you?"

"Madjid."

Her face softened. "My God. You look exactly like your mother. The same exact eyes."

"You knew my mother?"

"No. But she was kind to me. I was sorry when she died."

"I miss her still." The expression on his face was pained, and so young.

"I had a son once too," Mehry said. "The midwife, God rest her soul, took him to a good family in Mash'had. Ten years and three months ago, exactly. The day he was born."

Madjid looked at her in disbelief. It was impossible—and yet all too possible she was Jafar's mother. "Please," he said. "Let me see you home."

"I'll be fine."

"For me. It will make me feel better. Please."

High-beamed headlights cut by suddenly. Madjid grabbed Mehry's arm and pulled her into the thick of the foliage. They crouched among the trees as the truck sped past, the bed now empty. Madjid felt the bones in her arms, the frailty of her body. He breathed, and when he did, Mehry could feel his breath on her neck. It was unlike that of the men she had known, over and over. She closed her eyes and inhaled him, the scent of green almonds, the scent of youth and its ignorance of desperation.

As the truck disappeared around the bend, they stepped onto the roadside and began to walk, him in front, her behind. Twigs and rocks snapped beneath their synchronized gait. He could feel her slight frame behind him, and felt a sense of purpose, of usefulness that he had not felt since prison. Mehry stopped dead in her tracks and stood looking up at the sky. The moon had totally eclipsed the sun now—a night in the middle of the day. Thousands of brilliant stars scattered across the sky. She closed her eyes and Madjid felt as if this was the phenomena he should observe, the hard, broken face of a woman who no one had ever stood up for, a woman who had survived far more than he ever had, every day of her whole life.

"Madjid," said a voice.

It was his brother. With his club. "What are you doing? I told you to stay home."

Mehry pulled her chador over her face.

"Don't bother, sister," said Jamsheed. "We all know who you are."

Madjid held his arm out to the side as though this could protect her. "I'm just seeing her home. I promise."

Jamsheed held up his club and pushed his brother with the blunt bloody tip. "I warned you to stay away and now I find you on the side of the road with a whore. She is going where she belongs and never coming back."

Madjid shook his head. "You will have to go through me to get to her."

Amin's pickup truck came speeding down the road, the high beams blinding them all. In the flood of dust, it came to a stop, "Madjid," Jamsheed whispered. "Run."

But Madjid did not move. The men jumped out from the bed, following Amin. He was visibly angry. "Jamsheed," he said. "I warned you to keep that traitor out of my sight." Then he looked at Mehry. "I know you. You're a whore."

Mehry stared back at him. "I know you, too. And your father."

The accusation sent a rumble through the men. They moved toward Mehry. Madjid tried to block their way. "Please, leave her alone. She's done nothing wrong. We've done nothing wrong. I'm only seeing her home."

Several of them grabbed his arms. The others went for Mehry, pushing her to the ground, raising their clubs. She screamed. There was the dull thud of wood. Screams.

Madjid howled in anguish and fought against the men. He kicked. He flailed. Amin slapped him across the face, hard enough for him to taste blood. He kicked Amin in the stomach, sending him to his knees.

Everything, all at once, went silent. Even Mehry's screaming. The men who had beaten her lifeless began walking back to the truck. One picked up her chador and covered her. Madjid looked up at Amin. He said in a quiet voice, "You are nothing more than murderers."

"You defend a whore?"

"It's you who is the whore."

Amin's face flushed red. He stepped behind Madjid, grabbed his hair, and pulled his head back. Jamsheed lunged to help his brother, but the men held him back. Pots clanged and far, far away the women continued their shrill cries at the moon that covered the sun, leaving the world in total darkness save for the high beams and the glint of the knife in Amin's hand.

Madjid's knees buckled and he fell to the ground, gasping for air. The blood was terrible and dark. He couldn't breathe. When the sun burst through, red at first, he stared straight into the light and saw himself in the orchard. He could hear birds and insects sing in the dense green leaves, the milky skin of Nasreen's face. He felt the touch of her hand and the softness of her hair. His eyes went black, his mind crowded with the cacophony of voices from the town square, the hagglers, merchants, families, laughing, arguing, shouting, almost singing. He heard the protesters in the capital chanting and celebrating. He felt their bodies press against his and they moved together like a single wave, growing and flooding and rising until his body went numb. He gasped for breath, and all of it—the orchard, Nasreen, the square, the crowds, the sweat and heat and sun—were gone. All that remained was the fading beat of his heart.

PARIS | VI

The crowd of onlookers on the riverbank pressed against Shazdehpoor. It was no comfort to him. He started to feel as though he were being crushed. He felt a tap on his arm. A young refugee girl stood at his side, holding out a pair of paper glasses.

It was not the same girl as in the Place du Tertre, of course. She was older. Wearing a headscarf. She cast down her head to avert his gaze, as if she were new to this way of life. Shazdehpoor felt her shame and dug through his pockets for a few euros. She slid through the bodies in search of the next customer. For a moment, he thought to follow her. But she, too, was gone. He slid his glasses over his eyes.

The moon had already started its diagonal slide over the sun, a slow and steady movement almost imperceptible to the eye except for the darkness that spread from its progression. He focused on the outline of the moon. As the eclipse reached its totality, the sky turned the cool dark of caves, the air tasted leaden. The pigeons and the vendors and the clapping went silent.

In that moment of utter darkness and silence, he felt so alone. He could not bear it anymore.

Savagely, he pushed through the crowd, stumbling on the stairs at the riverbank, almost stepping on a young man. He paid no mind to the curses and shoving. He reached the street-level landing and trudged through a patch of loose gravel, tripping as his foot dug in. Falling to his knees, he began to laugh. At first he laughed for his hatred of pebbles and the lifetime he had spent fighting them. The laughter convulsed through his body and shifted to agony. He was wailing, blinded by his own tears. Several passersby gathered around him, and one young man stepped forward but Shazdehpoor waved him away. "I'm fine," he said, creaking to his feet. He kept his eyes on the ground and managed to escape. Such a loss of control had terrified him. He walked as quickly as he could, to the place he should have gone hours before.

In the three decades of friendship Shazdehpoor had shared with Trianant, he never once told him the story of his family. He had skirted all questions that arose and launched into fabulist tales of sugar factories and wars between lions and asses. At times, the beauty of his tales was so entrancing, so seductive, he understood the myths of Imam Hussein and the apothecary and the pleasures of opium and the books of Madjid—the joy of escaping until you forget yourself. None of it had ever been calculated. It was simply that, after all these years, he no longer knew what was true. Except that he had lost one son to a revolution and another to the war that followed. His family scattered and passed, the orchard—where these lives had unfolded—sold off piece by piece.

But today they all stood before him, as real in his mind as they had been in life. He softly rapped on Trianant's door. His friend opened it. "My God!" he said. "Where have you been? Are you all right?"

"I am sorry to disturb you," Shazdehpoor said. "May I come in?"

Trianant led his friend into his study, switching on the desk lamp. Shazdehpoor sank onto his sofa. Trianant poured the cognac. He handed Shazdehpoor a glass and placed his on the table between them. Then he crumpled some newspaper and shoved it under the logs in the fireplace. The small twigs caught quickly and spread to the thicker logs. The fire began to rise, flooding the room with a warm orange glow, crackling and snapping.

"Tell me what happened," said Trianant. "I waited for you for hours. I went to your apartment."

"I'm so sorry," said Shazdehpoor. He turned his face to the fire, his feet planted on his son's carpet. Every morning, he thought to himself, when I begin to shave, there is a moment when I look down at my hand and feel it as if it's not my hand, and when I open my mouth, I speak in a voice that I know is not my voice—

But still he said nothing.

"What's going on with you, my friend? What has happened?"

Shazdehpoor abruptly stood and walked over to the radio and, without asking Trianant's permission, slid the dial through the stations. Until, at last, he heard the first three notes on the violin. Beethoven, the Adagio ma non troppo e molto espressivo. On the twelfth note, just as the second violin began to weave through and echo the notes, he closed his eyes and backed away from the radio, standing on the medallion of his son's carpet, softly conducting the strings in the air, now joined by a viola and cello as the four instruments wrapped their notes around him.

The music, only in that moment, was a perfect expression of what couldn't be expressed by the sound of words. His melancholy, his regrets and reticence, his bitterness, his alienation—his loss. If he could exist solely in its notation, nothing in this world would ever be unbearable.

And then, as it had to, the Adagio ended and went straight into the Allegro. Shazdehpoor shut off the radio. The only sound was the crackling of the fire. His friend was staring at him, bewildered.

"Shazdehpoor?" said Trianant.

Shazdehpoor sat on the sofa and took a swig of his cognac. "I want to tell you a story," he said. "It begins in an orchard, just before the first Friday lunch in spring."

Acknowledgments

I would like to extend my gratitude to Cecile Barendsma for her unwavering dedication to the book and to Leigh Newman for her transformative edits. And to the Catapult family for their care and enthusiasm in shepherding this book out into the world. I would also like to extend my gratitude to both readers and friends along the way who have enriched my life and work: William O. Beeman (Amoo Bill), Frank Farris, Zohreh Shayesteh, Shirin Neshat, Shoja Azari, Phong Bui, Nazzy Beglari, Peter Scarlet, Salar Abdoh, Houra Yavari, Irakli Gioshvili, Angela Levin, Esther Crow, Cara Gorman, Sophie-Alexia de Lotbinière, Nariman Hamed, and Sherry Haddock. And in memorium, Hassan Tehranchian and Assurbanipal Babilla. And finally, my deepest gratitude to my mother, Soraya Shayesteh, my father, Mohammad Ghaffari, and my family, both in New York and Iran, for always giving me a home in the world.

RABEAH GHAFFARI was born in Iran and lives in New York City. She is a filmmaker and writer, whose collaborative fiction with artist Shirin Neshat was featured in *Reflections on Islamic Art,* and her documentary, *The Troupe,* featured Tony Kushner. *To Keep the Sun Alive* is her first novel.